LAST HOPE
THE BROTHER'S CREED BOOK 5
JOSHUA C. CHADD

BLADE OF TRUTH PUBLISHING COMPANY

Apocalypse Road Trip Playlist

This playlist was spawned as I listened to music while writing *Outbreak*. Before long, some of the songs found their way into the book itself. As the story continued, music took on a bigger role, even inspiring not one but two titles and some key themes woven throughout the series. The playlist has since grown as I continue to add more and is my go-to when writing apocalyptic stories. Music is powerful and has a way to inspire and motivate when other things fall short. As Connor says in *Last Hope*:

"Some thought it odd how much they loved music, but what they didn't understand was that these songs were more than just melodies; they were expressions of emotions when they couldn't express any themselves. Music had helped them through some hard times, even before the apocalypse. It wasn't just about the tunes or even the lyrics, but rather what they represented. It was a celebration of what made them human."

Scan the QR code or visit the URL to be taken to the official ***Apoc-alypse Road Trip Playlist*** and listen along with the group as they embark on a road trip through the apocalypse!

https://spoti.fi/2SB9jKM

This series started off as a single book, as most do, but the thing is, it was never meant to be more than just that. But after all the encouragement, I began to plan out the series that would become the Brother's Creed. *Knowing that you guys were reading these and enjoying them so much was what kept me going through the tough times in writing and when things didn't go as planned. Through your support and suggestions this series has become more than I ever planned for it to be.*
That is thanks to my awesome fans and readers. And why this book is dedicated to you. I cannot thank you enough for everything and I hope you enjoy the last installment in this epic adventure.

This one's for you guys & gals.
It's been one helluva ride!

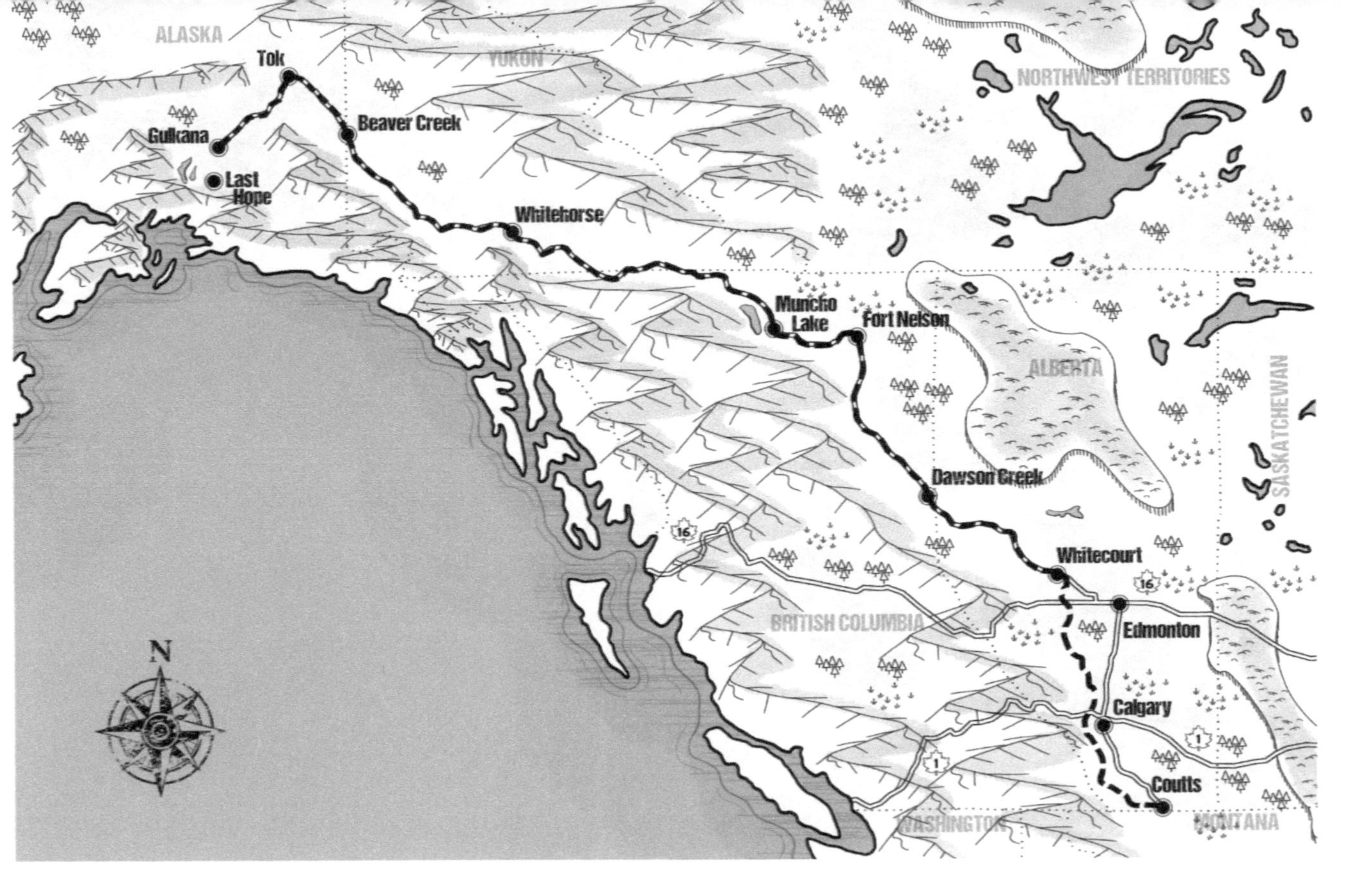

ALASKA
YUKON
NORTHWEST TERRITORIES
SASKATCHEWAN
ALBERTA
BRITISH COLUMBIA
WASHINGTON
MONTANA
Tok
Gulkana
Last Hope
Beaver Creek
Whitehorse
Muncho Lake
Fort Nelson
Dawson Creek
Whitecourt
Edmonton
Calgary
Coutts
16
1
N

PROLOGUE

Ana sped down the highway in her black Ford Raptor. She'd let the Reclaimers get too much of a lead and lost them, not that it mattered much. She knew which direction they were headed and would catch up with them soon enough. Still, she wasn't sure what she'd do once she found them. Should she stage an ambush and end them all? But that didn't seem right anymore. She couldn't put her finger on it, but something was holding her back from indiscriminately slaughtering them. Jezz was going to die as soon as Ana laid eyes on the woman, but the rest didn't have to. They could be useful.

"*Udalite etu mysl'*," Ana said out loud, more out of habit than anything else. "Remove that thought."

Her mind slowly—much too slowly—came back under control. It'd been a rough couple of weeks on her own as the contents of boxes she'd kept shut all her adult life were beginning to ooze into her mind, and the largest box—the one that kept *that* part of herself locked away—was missing. Now, every waking moment was a struggle to keep her sanity. She wasn't even sure if that part of her was separate anymore. This realization should've shocked her to her core, yet she found herself unable to care. It *was* frightening that she was changing and unable to control her mind, but she was tired—exhausted from fighting her own thoughts.

"Control," Ana said. "I need to retain control."

She took a deep, cleansing breath, her hand automatically going to the golden locket tucked under her shirt. Rubbing her finger over the embossed symbol on the outside of the locket, her mind began to empty and regain some semblance of normality. Her life had been starting to look up before all this, and her father had finally been letting her decide her own path instead of trying to persuade her to help run the Family. She'd been on a trip to tour the University of Missouri campus when the apocalypse began. She'd never been to college but had always wanted to as it was what normal people did.

Yet, all of that had fallen apart and here she was, left alone with her own thoughts, which wasn't the company she liked to keep. Her mind had still been hers when traveling with Emmett and the others, but that had changed when she was captured by that psychopath. It was all *her* fault, and when Ana found that monster, she'd end her once and for all. It was the only thing she was sure about anymore. After that, she didn't know what she was going to do, but she'd figure it out when she came to that road. Until then, she just needed to find the Reclaimers.

You had a chance to kill Jezz before, yet you hesitated. What's to say you really want *to kill her?* said a voice in her mind.

As that thought settled into her, she realized there hadn't been a real chance before. She'd barely registered that it was Jezz when she'd found the Reclaimers hiding out on that farm, and there'd been no time to take an accurate shot. But even though she knew that line of thinking was true, the doubt was still there, as was the voice in her head. It was all because of Jezz. The next time Ana saw that woman she'd be holding a crimson-dipped knife while standing over her bleeding corpse. That was the only way this would end. She *had* to kill Jezz. But how was she supposed to kill the woman who'd raised her? She was a monster, pure and simple, but she'd birthed Ana. What would her dad think?

"*Udalite etu mysl'!*" Ana screamed as she slammed the brakes. The Raptor skidded to a halt in the middle of the highway, a cloud of burning rubber around her. Throwing open the door, she jumped out and started pacing on the blacktop. "Remove that thought. *Udalite etu mysl'*. Remove that thought!"

She continued to repeat the phrase over and over again, alternating between Russian and English. Jezz was *not* her mother; her mother had died when she was little, but the similarities shocked her. The thoughts would not go away. *That* night came back to her with an intensity she'd never experienced before, and she was back in that hotel room once again.

It had been a cold January day in New York City. Her family was there for a business arrangement with the *Pakhan* of a rival family. Her father, Vadim, was out, meeting with the heads of that family, leaving an eleven-year-old Anastasia with her mother, Natta. The hotel was a nice one—The Plaza or something—she hadn't really been paying attention as she knew she had to be on her best behavior in public or it might trigger one of her mother's fits. Those were never good, but they'd been increasingly worse as of late, and little Ana was starting to accumulate the scars to show it.

Her mother wasn't the one to blame; she'd had a rough childhood growing up in her home country. Ana knew that, but it didn't help when Natta started beating her, sometimes with her hands, sometimes with whatever else was available. Like the family vase that had caused Ana to need thirteen stitches in her scalp. She'd been eight. That was when things had started getting really bad, when the darkness in her mother had begun to consume her. Now Ana was learning to recognize when her mother was building up to one of her fits. When that happened, she had to get far away and hide as she waited for it to pass.

Ana was sitting quietly on the red comforter of the fancy bed, watching the local news station. She wasn't allowed to watch cartoons; they would rot her mind, or so her mother claimed, and she never argued with Natta. Her mother had been in the bathroom when her father returned from his meeting, and Ana could tell it hadn't gone well by the way he walked. Ana let out an involuntary gasp as she rolled off the bed and hid between it and the wall, hunkering down in the corner. Her mother wouldn't be pleased.

"How'd it go, dear?" Natta asked, coming out wearing one of the hotel's white robes and her golden locket with their family portrait inside.

"Not good, *lyubimaya moya*," Vadim said, hugging his wife. For all her father's flaws, he loved her mother and got her the help she needed—or so Natta let him think. "Ivan won't budge. We're meeting again in the morning, but he wants control of the docks or he'll start another war, and we can't have that."

"No, we can't," Natta said, her eyes ablaze.

Ana quit watching then as she tried to crawl under the bed, yet the stupid hotels always had those boards stopping her from being able to hide underneath. Why couldn't she just go to her hiding spot back home? Why did they have to be here?

"I'm going to shower," her father said. "Where's my little Anastasia?"

"I'll fetch her," Natta said.

"Good," Vadim said as he closed the bathroom door.

Ana could hear the fan start and then the shower. That would muffle any noises she might make, but she'd learned long ago to stay quiet no matter the pain, and her mother knew how to beat her so it wouldn't show.

Thinking back, the rest of the night was a combination of blurry scenes interspersed with startlingly crisp vignettes—her mother beating her until she couldn't help but cry out and then her father coming out wrapped in a towel to see his daughter splayed on the carpet with a broken arm. It was the first time she'd seen her father strike her mother, but then her father was on the ground with blood caked on the back of his head as Natta stood over him with a knife. Ana couldn't see her mother's eyes, but she knew they held that darkness—that predatory look that wasn't satisfied until someone was in pain. But the hunger wanted something more that night.

Ana hadn't given the darkness a chance. Grabbing the Glock from her father's coat on the bed, she'd ended the monster, once and for all.

It'd saved her father's life but ended her own.

On a random highway in the middle of Alberta at the end of the world, Ana held the cool barrel of her Glock 19 to the side of her head. There was only one way to make the voice stop and end the torment. She would have control all the way until the end.

She squeezed the trigger.

1

THE QUESTION

Post-outbreak day 22, evening

A black armored vehicle pulled up to the small, two-pump gas station in Cynthia, Alberta. The LAPV was a monster of a rig that sported a custom paint job depicting a gray, three-headed wolf-dog on the front doors, along with streaks of red, white, and blue leading to the back where flames shot out behind the rear tires. Two young men decked out in black Kryptek uniforms and tactical plate carriers climbed out of the rig on each side and scanned their surroundings. The shorter one came around the front of the LAPV where broken chains were painted on its hood.

"Looks clear," James said to his brother, who still scanned the building that housed the gas station as well as a small hotel lobby.

"Yeah, but I don't trust it," Connor said. "They should've attacked by now. What are they waiting for?"

"I don't know, but this waiting sucks."

Connor nodded, not taking his eyes from the building or the trees surrounding them. The three vehicles following them pulled into the parking lot as James waved them over. Greg pulled in first, driving the blue Chevy truck with Troy and Lucas inside. Next came the blue van with Beverly driving, Neil sitting shotgun, and most of the group's supplies piled in the back. Finally, Emmett and Alexis pulled up in his souped-up black Ford F-450 complete with topper and shooting bench welded on top. James continued to scan across the road as they all pulled in, ready to bolt if they needed to get out quickly.

"Looks like they aren't here either," James said as Emmett rolled down his window.

"Seems like it," Emmett said, "but they could be anywhere."

"Agreed," James said. "We'll play it safe like the last time."

"Roger."

James walked back over to the LAPV. "Same as the last time," he told Tank.

"Gotcha," Tank said, pulling around to sandwich the two unarmored vehicles between Scourge and Emmett's truck.

The two middle rigs filled up while the people in them hopped out and relieved themselves while being covered by the armored vehicles. It wasn't a perfect plan and it didn't offer them much privacy, but it was better than pretending the Reclaimers weren't sitting out there right now, watching them. Once everyone was finished, Emmett had them pull behind the building to wait for him and Tank to fill up.

James walked up to Alexis, who was fueling the truck. "Hey darlin,'" he said, giving her a quick kiss. "Mind switching rides with me for a bit?"

"Why?" Alexis asked while smiling that dazzling smile of hers. "You got some secret plans with my dad?"

"You know it."

Alexis chuckled. "But really."

"I just wanna talk to him about some man stuff."

"Man stuff, eh?"

"Yeah," James said, smiling. "I want to see what he thinks we should do when we get to the lodge. He has the most experience with this kind of thing, and I want to pick his brain. I already talked to Neil back in Coutts."

"Well good, because I've wanted to talk to Chloe since we left."

Tank walked around the side of Scourge, zipping up his fly. "Drained one tank and filled another," he said, topping off the LAPV.

Alexis chuckled. "You just come up with that?"

"Nah," Tank said, "I always say that when stoppin' for gas on a road trip."

Alexis shook her head, smiling.

"You hoppin' in with Emmett?" Connor asked from the other side of Scourge.

"Yeah, gonna talk about plans when we get to Alaska," James said.

"Always the planner," Tank said. "You ever just fly by the seat of your pants?"

"That's all I've been doing since this started, but now there's finally something I can plan out instead of all these unknowns."

"This'll go wrong, too," Connor said.

"Yeah, but we'll get past it," James said. "I have faith."

Tank clapped him on the shoulder. "I'm glad to hear you got your faith back. Makes me feel better, plus now I can turn up the cynicism to offset your happy-go-luckiness."

James chuckled. "I wouldn't expect anything less. I'm just excited to be on the road again! The fresh air, wide open spaces—isn't it awesome?"

"Were you raised in the Shire?" Tank asked. "Thinkin' everythin's all parties and second breakfast and nothin' bad ever happens? We're in friggin' Mordor! This is the apocalypse. Something bad is bound to happen."

"Actually, I would make a good hobbit," James muttered.

"Just shut it," Tank said, winking at him.

"Nice reference," Connor said.

"Everyone ready?" Emmett asked, rubbing his shoulder where he'd taken the bullet the night before.

"Yes, sir," James said. "Do you mind if I hop in with you?"

Emmett looked at James, brown eyes piercing through him. Did Emmett somehow know already? He couldn't know; not even Connor or Tank knew.

"Sure," Emmett said and then looked at Tank. "You be careful up there, and take care of my daughter."

"Yes, sir," Tank said.

"Thank you," Emmett said, walking over and kissing Alexis on the forehead. "I love you, honey."

"I love you too, Dad," Alexis said. "It's not like I'll be far away."

"I know," Emmett said. "Now, let's mount up. We have a lot of ground to cover."

"Yep, we're burnin' daylight," Alexis said, grinning at her dad.

"That we are," Emmett said, smiling back.

James popped his head into Scourge. "I'll see you in a bit, my lovely daughter," he said, looking back at Olive.

The little girl giggled and rolled her eyes. "Okay, *daddy*. I love you."

"I love you too, sweetie," James said, and then he gave Alexis one more kiss. "Hands in, boys." James stuck his fist with the fresh tattoo over the center console.

"Really, James?" Tank asked. "Every time?"

"Yeah, it's too awesome not to."

"I'm beginnin' to regret this," Tank mumbled, placing his tattooed fist next to James's as Connor did the same.

It was the coolest fist bump ever.

"Let's do this," James said.

"Such a dork," Alexis said.

"Hell yeah," James said, walking over to Emmett's truck and climbing in.

Alexis climbed into the middle seat of Scourge with Chloe while Olive and Felix sat in the back seat. Olive waved at James with a giant grin on her face. He waved back, his smile growing. She hadn't stopped beaming since he'd "adopted" her that morning.

Was it just this morning?

This day was taking forever as they were all on edge, waiting for the Reclaimers to attack. The whole time they'd been filling up, his eyes had kept scanning the trees and other convenient hiding places, even as he joked around. Tank pulled out, and James smiled at Alexis through the window as she passed in Scourge. She returned it by blowing him a kiss, and his heart did a little flip in his chest. That was *his* girlfriend.

Maybe soon to be more than that, he thought.

"We're movin' out," Emmett said into the CB radio.

He received two confirmations in response as the van pulled out behind Scourge, followed by the truck with Emmett bringing up the rear of their little convoy. Some old George Strait CD played in the background, and James sighed a little. It wasn't that he didn't like country; he did, but being in Montana for the last few years he'd heard nothing else on the local stations. He much preferred his hard rock and metal, although if he *had* to listen to country, he could do a lot worse than the King of Country himself.

It was exhausting being ready for an attack they all knew would come. But maybe, just maybe they'd eluded the Reclaimers by snaking their way north on the backroads. They'd been able to kill two birds with one stone that way by avoiding the main highways going north *and* giving Calgary a wide berth. They were still taking the less obvious route and were almost even with Edmonton to the east. It was the best way to avoid a trap by the Reclaimers, but it also meant that it was taking them longer. If they wanted to make better progress, they'd have to get on the main highway soon.

James glanced at Emmett, who sat silhouetted against the sun setting through the window. This man had been like a father to him in the last couple of weeks. Even in the short time he'd known him, they shared a bond that was stronger than most people who'd known each other for years. It was the same for most of their group because with all they'd been through it was hard not to grow close. He'd found out it was a double-edged sword as it bred true friendships that were tested in the trenches, and yet when someone died, it made that loss even more piercing. He was still learning how to deal with that, but he didn't have to do it alone anymore.

"You wanted to talk?" Emmett asked after several minutes of silence.

"Yeah..." James said, his courage faltering. This was harder than he'd anticipated. Maybe he could stall a bit longer. "What do you think should be done once we get out to the bush?"

Emmett glanced over at him, and James swore he saw the man smile a little. *Did* he know?

"The first thing I'd do is shore up our defenses," Emmett said. "I know it's remote, but we still need to be ready for an attack. Next, we need to start sending out supply runs. Are there any roads out there?"

"No, it's only accessible by bush plane or a two-day horse ride. Maybe an Argo ATV or something could make it if the trail's not too wet."

"So, we'll want to take the plane in then. We should also have your brother start teaching someone else to fly because if something happens to him, we're screwed."

"He's started to teach Tank a little, but until he can have hands-on time, it'll be hard."

"Also, we need to get a couple of planes out there and secure one of the small airports or at least a landing strip somewhere out on the road system. That way we don't come back to a horde hanging out on our only way into town."

"Good idea. I hadn't thought of that."

"We'll also want to get some kind of power out there. That'll be important for water, cooking, and keeping the radios charged."

"We have a couple generators and some solar panels that can charge SAT phones and small electronics. The water is all gravity fed and just needs the water pump every few days to get it to the tanks. The cook stove, water heater, and refrigerator are all propane. It's set up to only need the generator every few days."

"That's a good setup."

"Yes, sir. We had to live up there for a few months solid, so we made sure it was comfortable. We also have the main lodge and six cabins that sleep four to eight each, as well as a sauna with a gravity-fed shower, a storage shack, meat shed, workshop, two woodsheds, two outhouses, an old corral, and a tack cabin as well."

"All the buildings are heated by a wood stove?"

"Yeah, and they're insulated very well. My family spent a couple winters at the lodge when my dad used to trap up there. It's not the most convenient way to live when it's brutally cold, but it's not bad."

"Who built this place?"

"The lodge was there when my parents bought it in the late eighties, but my dad and grandpa logged wood one winter. Then, the next summer, my dad and other grandpa used a chainsaw mill to make all the cabins. They all have metal roofs, and besides having to stain them every few years, the upkeep is easy."

"Sounds perfect. I assume with it being a hunting lodge, the game is plentiful?"

"Oh yeah, lots of moose around, and we can go after goats, Dall sheep, and bear, if we're getting desperate. Plus, we have a river that has quite a few King Salmon in the summer as well as two lakes that have arctic grayling, Dolly Varden and lake trout. Not to mention rabbits, ptarmigan, and other small game. We should be set on meat, and there are lots of berries around, too."

"You've given this some thought."

"Yes, sir. Even before the infection, my brother and I had a plan to go out to the lodge in case something like this happened. But I never dreamed we'd have to actually do it."

"Yet, here we are."

"Yeah, so you were already heading to Alaska before we met up. You have a place up there too?"

"Roger. I have a house northeast of Fairbanks. It's defensible, stockpiled with all kinds of supplies, and has a small shelter a hundred feet underground. The guy who used to own it built bunkers all over the country for the government. Apparently, he built his own personal one as well."

"Wow, that sounds nice. Why not head there?"

"The house wouldn't be comfortable for our whole group, and the bunker isn't somewhere I'd like to live the rest of my life. Plus, it's not that far off the road system and we'd have to drive through Fairbanks. Yours is more off the grid and sustainable in the long run. Although, my place is a good backup if things really get bad."

"That makes sense."

"Enough of this," Emmett said, turning to look at him square in the eyes. "That isn't why you wanted to talk to me, is it?"

"It was... part of it," James said, resisting the urge to scratch the fresh tattoo on his hand.

"Just go ahead and ask."

James was taken aback. "Ask what?"

"Son, it's written all over your face."

"Oh..."

James glanced out the windshield, mustering his courage. Their caravan was making good time, considering they weren't taking the most direct route. There didn't seem to be as many vehicles on the road as there had been in the U.S. The Canadians must have had more of a warning before the virus hit. He remembered back in Coutts that even a couple of weeks after this had started some of their big cities were still holding strong. Maybe the world governments *did* have a better handle on this than they all thought. There could still be hope for humanity.

Noticing Emmett glance over at him, James sighed. There was no point in trying to distract himself from asking. If Emmett already knew, what would it hurt to ask now? He thought of Alexis and how strong his feelings were. He loved her and wanted to spend the rest of his life with her.

"Mr. Wolfe," James began, steeling himself, "I'd like your blessing to marry your daughter. I know we haven't been dating long, and with everything going on maybe marriage is the last thing I should be worried about, but I love her and want to be with her. I promise you, I will do everything in my power to protect her and care for her, no matter what."

A small smile touched the corner of Emmett's mouth as his gaze stayed focused on the road ahead. That was a good sign, right? Or maybe it was more of a predatory smile.

"Before I answer your question, I want you to understand something," Emmett said after a few moments of silence. "What you're asking is bigger than just promising to love my daughter. As you said yourself, you will be charged with protecting her and taking care of her till death do you part. Normally, that would be hard enough in and of itself, but with the world falling apart around us, it takes even greater responsibility. You will not only need to love her and take care of her in sickness and in health, but you will also have to protect her from physical harm. You will have to *kill* to protect her and do things that may push you to your limits. She will need to be your number one priority in life over your friends and even the rest of your family. It's a daunting endeavor. Are you positive you want to take this on?"

James didn't hesitate. "Yes, sir, I am."

"Good. Because even though Alexis is one of the most capable women I know, she will still look to you to provide for her. You two will be a team, and a team is only as strong as its weakest link. Now, I'm not worried about my daughter being that weak link, nor am I doubting you, I'm just making sure you know the gravity of your request."

"I do, sir. I've given this a lot of thought and prayer over the past couple days."

Emmett glanced over at him and their eyes met. James could see the love for his daughter in those eyes as well as a deep determination to provide for her and keep her safe. He'd never gleaned so much out of a simple look before.

"You're a good man, James," Emmett said, returning his gaze to the road. "You have my blessing."

The smile that split his face would set a record for the world's widest smile. His heart felt like it was about to explode, and all he wanted to do was scream his victory into the sky. Yet he just sat there, smiling like a moron.

"I just hope you can do better than me," Emmett said, softer now. "I've made a lot of mistakes in my life, but my number one regret is the death of my son and the breaking of my family. I fought and bled for our country, saved lives, defended our freedom, and was one hell of a Devil Dog, but I'd give all that up if I could go back and be the father and husband I should've been. Remember that for when you have kids someday. They should be your second priority after your wife."

After God being first of course, James thought but didn't say. He still didn't know what Emmett thought of that and didn't want to disrespect him. James would take care of his family and be the best husband and father he could be with God by his side. That was the way he was going to live his life.

"Thank you, sir," James said, still smiling. "You won't regret this. I'll do my best to make Alexis happy and give my life for her."

"I know you will," Emmett said, smiling openly. "Now cut the 'sir' crap. We'll be family soon enough."

"Yes, si—I mean... sure thing," James said, his smile still wide enough to fit a boat in.

Emmett chuckled as they turned north onto Alberta Highway 43. The sun had set over an hour earlier, and the night was lit by the full moon. James could still make out the trees flashing by the side of the road and the pale light reflecting off the few vehicles scattered about. Things couldn't get any better. They were making great progress north, and he was about to ask Alexis to marry him. Maybe the rest of the trip wouldn't be so bad. The Reclaimers had to be long behind them, and after driving through the night, they should be far enough ahead not to worry about them as much. Even now, it would be impressive if they'd been able to follow them and anticipate their path throughout the day.

A loud thump broke the silence of the night as a bright flash in front of them temporarily blinded him. When his mind recognized that the van Neil and Beverly were in was nothing but a flaming husk, his adrenaline kicked in just ahead of the dread. Before he could process any more, a massive concussion turned his whole world upside down as the truck he was in blew up.

2

RECLAIMERS

Post-outbreak day 22, night

"They just turned onto 43 and are heading your way," a voice said through the radio.

"Set up the ambush!" Zeke yelled.

The Reclaimers burst into action as Max and another man ran across the highway to hide in the trees to the south. Two others went and crouched behind an overturned car on the left side of the road with another two behind a truck on the right side as Jezz, Zeke, and the last Reclaimer stayed where they were just inside the trees to the north.

"Scouts, meet us back here," Zeke said into his radio.

He received three affirmatives in response.

Their plan had been simple—get ahead of the survivors with scouts on different routes to anticipate their course. It turned out that hadn't been easy as the group was being extra cautious, but that just made the hunt all the better. They were finally limited to three main options unless the group had gone way off track. But their bet had paid off, and the timing was perfect, too. The night would hide the hunters and make sure the prey remained unaware.

It was finally time to repay the debt.

Joining the men by the truck ten yards off the side of the road, Zeke looked at the two other Reclaimers crouched there. "When I give the signal," he said to the Reclaimer holding their last RPG, "blow up that damned black truck and everyone else open fire."

"Okay," the Reclaimer said.

Zeke didn't even know the man's name—something like Bob, or Berry, or maybe Don—but it didn't matter; he was just a tool to be used. Glancing to the tree line behind him, Jezz nodded with an AK-47 to her shoulder and another Reclaimer by her side. It was time.

Zeke didn't have to wait long since the headlights from the group's caravan cut through the moonlit night a few minutes later. The LAPV would be leading as it had been all day. They needed to take that thing out first if they were to stand a chance. Holding a single grenade in his hand, he readied himself. He only had one shot at this.

"Get ready," Zeke hissed. "On my signal."

The man hoisted the RPG over his shoulder and nodded, positioning himself so the back blast wouldn't burn the others. The headlights grew closer, and he could hear the roar of the engines. Adrenaline began to course through his veins in anticipation. He'd been waiting for this day for weeks.

Light reflected off the truck they were hiding behind, and Zeke unconsciously crouched lower. The entire back side of the truck was cast in shadow even darker than the surrounding night. They would be invisible until it was too late. He could see the front end of the LAPV and began to count, trying to judge how fast they were traveling. The armored vehicle grew closer and he could make out the other vehicles trailing behind.

Now!

Zeke pulled the pin on the grenade and rolled it out into the middle of the road. It came to rest at a small pile of trash, and he counted down the seconds.

One. The LAPV was almost to the grenade.

Two. It was over it.

Three. The grenade shone in the LAPV's taillights. Zeke cursed.

Four. The next vehicle, a van, drew closer.

Five. The front end of the van was just over the grenade when the explosion lit up the night.

The front end was lifted off the ground as it was hit by the blast. Then the gas tank blew, and the van was consumed in a glorious inferno. The windshield on the vehicle they were hiding behind exploded inward from the concussion. Swerving, the blue truck in the caravan slowed as it went into the ditch and, barely keeping itself righted, managed to go around the flaming van.

"Now!" Zeke yelled as he opened fired on the passing blue truck.

The man with the RPG rose up and fired. The rocket-propelled grenade hit the pavement next to passenger's side of the black-armored truck. The explosion flipped the vehicle as the momentum carried it into a skidding roll, sparks flying from the roof as it scraped across the pavement.

The imbecile had missed!

The rest of the Reclaimers opened fire, and Zeke switched his aim to the upside-down truck as it slid to a stop, smoke billowing from the engine.

3

WITHOUT A FIGHT

Post-outbreak day 22, night

Blood leaked into Emmett's eye as a fire burned his thigh. Disoriented, his mind struggled to interpret what was going on around him as his instincts kicked in. He unbuckled himself, falling onto the roof of their Humvee, and then grabbed his M4 lying next to him. Luckily, it hadn't been damaged. He crawled out through the shattered side window as the ringing in his ears was greeted by quiet pops and flashes from all around.

It was an ambush. They were under attack!

He tried to stand but his leg wouldn't hold him, so he propped himself against the side of the Humvee and took aim at a flash of light from behind a car in front of them. The attacker's muzzle flashed again, giving him a perfect shot at the man only fifty yards away. His M4 barked as he quickly squeezed the trigger three times, and he was confident the man was down. More gunfire came from the tree line, but they were aiming farther down the highway. His mind struggled to comprehend what was going on. The trees on the side of the road were far from the desert landscape he should be seeing.

Suddenly, the situation returned to him with blinding clarity. It hadn't been an IED in Afghanistan; he was in Canada.

James!

Crouching down, he noticed James still in the cab of the truck, trying to kick open the passenger-side door.

"Over here!" Emmett yelled.

James glanced back at him and didn't hesitate as he dragged himself over to Emmett's window. He helped the boy to his feet outside, and James immediately stripped off his plate carrier that was smoldering where he kept his radio. Emmett took a second to look down at his leg that surely was on fire. It wasn't. Instead, the fabric of his pants was soaked in blood. Reaching down, he touched the piece of shrapnel sticking out of his thigh.

He murmured a curse.

It had cut clean through his femoral artery and he'd already lost a massive amount of blood. He didn't have long to live.

James shouldered his ACR and looked down at the older man's leg. "Emmett," James said, concern plain in his voice, "your leg."

Emmett just grunted and glanced at the taillights of their convoy up ahead. They'd be stupid to come back for them, and he wasn't going anywhere. That meant he needed to get James to the safety of the trees south of the road. Emmett didn't know if they could see him or not, but he waved at the rest of their group to go on. They'd just get killed by coming back there.

"Listen to me, son," Emmett said, firing at the muzzle flashes in the southern tree line. His hearing was beginning to return, and he could hear the bullets slamming into his truck from the opposite side. They were surrounded. "I need to you run as fast as you can for those trees. I'll cover you."

"What about you?" James asked, glancing down at Emmett's leg again.

He was already beginning to feel weak from the loss of blood. "My time is up, but I'll be damned if I go down without a fight."

"I can't leave you," James said, determination in his voice as he fired his rifle towards the trees.

"If you love my daughter, leave. I'm already dead."

James looked like he wanted to argue, but a bullet slammed into the truck between their heads. More bullets began to thump into the front of the truck as the enemies behind flanked them.

Emmett growled and stood up, using the side of his overturned truck as support. He popped above the underside and rested his M4 on the axle as he found his targets. Three men had broken from cover and were fifty yards out, circling to get an angle on them. The small red dot of his optic settled on one of them and he pulled the trigger. The man went down.

"Go now!" Emmett shouted as the remaining two men adjusted their aim and began to fire at him. "And tell Alexis I love her!"

"Yes, sir!"

He saw a flash of movement as James took off running in a low crouch towards the trees. One of their attackers moved to shoot at James, and Emmett put two neat holes in his chest. The last man had settled in his optic when pain exploded from his neck and he slumped down the side of his truck. Emmett crumpled against the vehicle as his M4 slipped from his hands. He fumbled to draw his Beretta as his other hand went up to his neck to stop the flow of blood. That last guy had shot him. He was able to draw his handgun from its holster but lost his grip and it fell to the ground. The strength was leaving his limbs as blood leaked from between the fingers held to his neck. Darkness closed in on the edges of his vision.

This was it.

The man who'd shot him came around the front of the truck, AR-10 held to his shoulder. One look at him and the man moved his aim to where Emmett had last seen James. After a dozen shots, the man lowered his rifle and looked back at him.

Darkness threatened to overwhelm his vision and he knew he was dying, but he wasn't scared. He just wished he could've told Alexis he loved her one last time—given her one final, lingering hug.

"*Da svee-dá-neeya*," the man said, and the last thing Emmett saw was the barrel of the man's rifle pointed at his head.

4

AMBUSH

Post-outbreak day 22, night

An explosion lit the back window as the van behind them blew up.

Tank cursed, slowing Scourge.

"Reclaimers!" Connor yelled as he grabbed his ACR and jumped into the back seat. He'd opened the hatch on the roof and was aiming back behind them when Tank saw Emmett's truck get blown over in the rearview mirror.

"Dad!" Alexis screamed.

Tank slammed on the brakes as he watched Greg drive around the flaming van. Neil and Beverly were both dead; he could see their bodies as the flames consumed the seats they were sitting in. Emmett's black truck slid to a stop, resting on the roof as all around them the night lit up with gunfire. Connor opened fire on the tree line north of the road, closest to them. Bullets began to slam into Scourge as the two groups in the trees started firing at them. Ricochets could be heard glancing off the roof, and suddenly Connor grunted and took cover inside. There was blood on the side of his cheek.

"What do we do?" Troy screamed through the radio as Greg pulled even with them. It looked like Greg was bleeding from his chest, but he nodded to Tank.

"You guys get out of here," Tank said into the radio. "We'll meet up ahead."

"Got it," Troy said as they sped off, continuing down the highway.

"We have to help them!" Alexis cried, pointing as her dad crawled out of his truck.

"I'm trying," Connor said, standing back up on the seat to shoot.

As Greg's truck drove out of range, more bullets peppered Scourge. They needed to do something, and soon. They couldn't just sit there. Tank glanced back at Chloe, who was sitting in the seat looking shocked, and then back to Olive and Felix, who had their ears covered and were hunkered in the back seat. It wasn't just him and Connor; he had other people he was responsible for. He couldn't go back to help and put all of them in danger.

Connor suddenly fell into the back seat like a ragdoll, his ACR clattering to the floor as he lay awkwardly in the seat between the two girls. Chloe screamed, but Alexis grabbed him and maneuvered him to the floor.

"Is he hit?" Tank yelled.

"He's alive," Alexis said. "He was hit in the helmet, but it didn't go through."

He glanced out the rear window to see James and Emmett by the truck as three Reclaimers moved to flank them. He noticed Emmett waving at them, but it wasn't for help. It looked like he was waving them on.

"We're goin'," Tank said as he moved his foot to the gas pedal.

"We can't just leave them!" Alexis said, looking back at her father and James.

Tank saw James take off towards the trees in his rearview mirror. He wished he could help his friend, but he knew James would want them to move on and get Alexis and Olive to safety, not put them at risk going back to save him. He drove on, all the while looking back in the rearview mirror as the flaming van grew farther away. Emmett had two of the Reclaimers down, and James had made it into the cover of the trees.

Suddenly, Alexis cried out. Tank glanced back to see Emmett slumped against the side of the truck. It looked like he was holding his neck as the last Reclaimer came around the side. Alexis made a break for the door.

"Keep her inside!" Tank yelled to Chloe, who moved quickly, grabbing Alexis to keep her from jumping out of the moving rig. His gaze was drawn back to the mirror as the man stood above Emmett and then the muzzle of his rifle flashed.

5

ESCAPE

Post-outbreak day 22, night

James crashed through the underbrush and into the trees. He'd made it without being hit, which was a miracle. His thoughts were buzzing too fast for him to pinpoint, but he knew that he was praying like crazy even if he couldn't form the words. Just past the tree line, he stumbled into a small clearing and noticed movement to his right.

After taking a quick knee, something splintered a tree behind him. He brought his rifle up and the chevron of his ACOG settled on the man's chest as he squeezed the trigger. A bullet threw dirt in James's face, and the man went down with a cry. James shot him again just to be sure.

Standing, James had taken a step forward when a branch snapped behind him.

"Don't move," a voice said.

James cursed, lowering his rifle.

"Turn around," the man said in a deep voice.

James slowly turned around, thinking of his options. He couldn't have survived that sprint to the trees just to get killed now. He had to honor Emmett's sacrifice. The Reclaimer behind him was a big man, holding a shotgun. At this range, the weapon would tear a nice big hole in James if he tried to move.

"You're him!" the big man said, surprise in his voice.

"What?" James asked in order to stall and maybe distract him. For some reason James got the impression the guy wasn't all there upstairs.

"The kid who was kissing on the bench," he said.

James had no idea what this guy was talking about. Was it when he and Alexis had had their first kiss back in Coutts? They'd been on a bench then, but how had this guy seen them? Had the Reclaimers been watching them the whole time?

The big man lowered his shotgun and James stood there, shocked. He should have lifted his rifle and shot the man, but he was too stunned to move.

"Go," the big man said. "Quickly. They'll be after you."

Was this a trick? He should just shoot the man and run, but something held him back. He was truly letting James go. James began to back up slowly, not trusting that the man wouldn't shoot him in the back.

"Why?" James asked when he was far enough away so the shotgun would be less effective.

"I used to be different," the man said. "Maybe this can make up for the bad I did."

James made it to the other side of the clearing. He nodded to the man, and then he turned and ran into the trees. The canopy was sparse enough to let some moonlight filter through, but he still had a hell of a time navigating as he tripped over branches and roots. His radio and plate carrier were gone, which meant all he had were his handgun with four extra magazines and his ACR with a partial magazine. He was heading south and he needed to go north, but first he had to get away from the Reclaimers.

Max stood alone in the clearing—the young man was gone. What had he just done? If Jezz or Zeke found out, he'd be dead. But wasn't he already dead? The way he'd been living lately was not a life; it was purely survival. He'd let a part of himself die these last few weeks, and by that, he was already dead. So, what did it matter if he died now? He shrugged. Maybe they wouldn't even find out.

Turning around, he began to walk back to the road when he jumped. Someone was standing just inside the trees. Max raised his shotgun as the shadow detached itself from the tree line. It was Zeke. He sighed, lowering his shotgun.

"I thought you were one of them," Max said.

"Of course not, you imbecile," Zeke said in his accented voice. "Did you see him go by?"

Max hesitated. "I didn't see him," he said.

Zeke glanced over to the body of Ron, his blood soaking into the soil on the other side of the clearing. Max had forgotten about the kid shooting him. Did Zeke suspect something? Should he just kill him now?

He didn't get the chance as Zeke raised his rifle in a split second and shot him.

Pain unlike anything he'd ever felt exploded in his stomach, and Max dropped the shotgun, grabbing his midsection. He fell to his knees as blood leaked through his fingers.

"You let him get away," Zeke said, slowly walking to him.

Zeke stopped in front of Max and raised a booted foot, kicking him onto his back. Max grunted as the impact sent a sharp pain into his gut. Zeke put a foot on his wound and pressed down, causing Max to cry out.

"Which way did he go?" Zeke asked.

Max didn't want to tell him, especially now, but after Zeke pressed harder, he pointed towards where the kid had run off.

"What is the meaning of this?" Jezz asked as she walked into the clearing with another dark-haired woman.

"This imbecile let one of them get away," Zeke said, not letting up the pressure on Max's stomach.

"What?" Jezz asked, her voice growing cold.

It made Max shiver. "I... I..." He tried to say something but couldn't get the words out past the pain.

"You what?" Jezz asked, walking to stand over him. Those cold blue eyes bore into his soul. How could he ever have followed her? She was bad—very bad. He'd known that, but until that moment he hadn't truly seen her for what she was.

Max shook his head. He would not apologize. Maybe letting the kid go would even out some of his badness.

Jezz shook her head and walked off. "Sam, you are my new lieutenant," she said.

"Yes, ma'am," said Samantha, the other woman.

Zeke looked down at Max and then let the pressure off his guts. "I'll radio our southern scout to try and cut him off. The other two should be here shortly," he said.

"Excellent," Jezz said. "The rest escaped, but we will find this one and then deal with the others."

Zeke nodded.

"What about him?" Sam asked.

Max realized she must be talking about him, but it was hard to concentrate through the excruciating pain.

"Let him bleed out," Zeke said.

"Make sure he will not survive," Jezz said.

A gunshot sounded as pain erupted in Max's left leg. Then another shot rang out, and his right leg was on fire as well.

"There," Zeke said.

Everything around him was taking on a dim quality, and Zeke's voice sounded like it was coming through a tunnel. Max couldn't even formulate thoughts as he was consumed by the pain radiating throughout his body.

"Let us reclaim our prize," Jezz said as they left the clearing, leaving Max alone with his pain.

Two more gunshots sounded and James instinctively ducked, glancing back. The shots had been far enough away that he didn't think they'd been aimed at him. The terrain started to slant downward and he lost his footing, falling forward and face-planting into the mud. Thankfully, he was able to keep enough composure to make sure he didn't shove the barrel of his rifle full of debris. Quickly getting up onto his hands and knees, James spit out the mud he'd eaten and took a deep breath. A large pond stretched out in front of him. He'd have to go around it, and that would leave him vulnerable.

He took off at a run, trying to get around the pond before he was caught in the open. He arrived at the far side of the water and went just inside the tree line—a perfect place to stage a quick ambush that would make those following him think twice.

Finding a thick tree, he took a knee behind it and rested his rifle against the trunk. It was only a hundred yards to the other side of the tree line. Were the Reclaimers even following him?

James cursed, a tear streaking down his face as he thought of Emmett's sacrifice. Everything had fallen apart and they'd only been back on the road for several hours. How were they ever going to make it to Alaska at this rate? But he wasn't going to give in to doubt this time; otherwise, he'd be right back in that same cycle again. Things may seem hopeless at the moment, but he had to hold on to hope because it was all he had. He took a deep breath. Maybe they weren't coming after him.

Movement on the other side of the pond pulled him from his thoughts. Someone was at the edge of the tree line. As he watched, he could see two shapes stop just inside cover. They stood there for several seconds, and James adjusted his aim, trying to make them out in the shadows. Finally, one of them moved, striding into the clearing at the edge of the pond. The figure was slender and looked to have long hair—a woman. She crouched down by where he'd fallen, and he realized that she'd found his tracks.

"C'mon, he's getting away," said the woman's voice, drifting across the pond.

That must be Jezz, James thought.

He took aim as the woman slowly walked around the edge of the pond, her gaze locked in his direction. He squeezed the trigger and the suppressed ACR belched fire. A dull thump could be heard as his bullet collided with flesh and the woman fell to the ground in a heap. He swung to the other silhouette still at the edge of the trees and noticed there were two people there now. One of their muzzles flashed and a bullet zipped by him. Aiming quickly, he let off a burst of three shots and then paused. He found what looked like one of the Reclaimers crouched by a tree and let off another burst of shots. Wood chips flew from the tree he was hiding behind, forcing him to take cover. These Reclaimers weren't like the rest—they could actually shoot.

He broke from cover and ran farther into the tree line, diving behind a fallen log as bullets smashed into the ground and trees around him. Those Reclaimers were *damn* good shots. If he stopped for even a second, he knew he'd be dead. Rising above the log, he aimed to where the muzzle flashes were coming from and let off a burst. Then he ducked back behind the log and crawled farther away until he lost sight of the pond. Bullets continued to fly through the forest around him, and then there was a brief pause. They must be reloading.

James stood up and took off with all his speed, running in a half crouch. The Reclaimers started to shoot again, but this time he was far enough away and out of sight. The ground was sloping downhill again, and he had to slow to keep his footing. He cursed himself for not grabbing his helmet with the NVGs before getting out of the truck, but it'd been hard to think past the pressure in his head. The ringing from the explosion was still there, but luckily it had subsided and he could mostly hear now. He'd never been blow up like that before, and he wouldn't be disappointed if he never was again. His head still ached, and his thoughts were fuzzy.

The ground dropped off in front of him, and as he slowed, he could see moonlight reflecting off a swift river. It was at least two hundred yards to the other side, and it looked deep. There was no way around it. He'd have to cross.

6

A HARD HIT

Post-outbreak day 22, night

Connor gazed out the windshield at the taillights of the blue truck. He was back in the passenger seat, having awakened a few minutes earlier with an intense headache. Apparently, he'd been hit in the helmet with a ricochet, yet it felt like his skull was splitting open. He'd been lucky that it hadn't been a direct hit or a few inches lower.

More like blessed, said an increasingly small voice in his head.

Blessed, sure.

They were all blessed—blessed to have Neil and Beverly roasted alive; blessed to have Emmett dead; blessed to have his brother on his own, running from a group of psychopaths. Oh yeah, they were _really_ blessed. Tank had filled him in on what happened after he'd been knocked out. Was James even still alive? But he couldn't begin to think like that. His brother was alive; he could _feel_ it.

The blue truck's taillights suddenly began to veer back and forth as the vehicle swerved in front of them.

Static came over the CB radio, followed shortly by Troy's voice. "We need to stop. Greg's hit."

Connor picked up the radio. "Roger that," he said.

The truck pulled to a stop and Tank parked Scourge next to it. Connor jumped out, ACR to his shoulder. He scanned the trees and behind them as Tank climbed out on the other side.

"Looks clear over here," Tank said, meeting Connor at the front.

Connor nodded as Alexis climbed out of the back seat, wiping tears from her eyes with one hand and holding their massive first aid kit in the other. She walked over to the driver's side of the truck as Greg opened the door.

"I..." Greg began and then took a wheezing breath. "Don't feel so good."

Connor could make out the blood on his chest, right about where his lungs were.

"Get him in the back seat!" Alexis said in a rush, setting down the first aid kit and rummaging through it.

Connor moved quickly, letting the ACR fall to his side as he and Tank grabbed the big man and laid him in the middle seat of Scourge. Alexis jumped in after they moved out of the way.

"He has a sucking chest wound," she said, ripping open the packaging on something. "Get his shirt off."

She handed Chloe a pair of scissors and she went to work. Alexis then quickly wiped the blood off and applied what looked like a large clear sticker with a tab on one side. Connor returned his attention to their surroundings.

"Everyone has a plan until they've been hit. Well, my friend, we've just been hit..." Tank began.

"The getting up is up to us," Connor finished, smiling a little despite the situation. Tank *would* quote the famous line from *Ghost and The Darkness* at a moment like this. "And we've been hit, hard."

"That ain't no shit."

Troy and Lucas walked over, carrying a bolt-action rifle with a scope and a Mossberg pump-action shotgun, respectively. They had a few scratches on their faces and arms but looked fine other than that.

"Either of you hurt?" Connor asked.

"No," Troy said. "I didn't even realize Greg was hit that badly until he started to swerve."

"I'm fine," Lucas said.

"Now what?" Troy asked, watching Alexis work on Greg.

Connor walked away from the group, kicking at an empty soda can in the middle of the road. They'd been played for fools. Somehow the Reclaimers had known where they were going and had set up a perfect ambush. He knew the explosion that had taken out the van was meant for them. It had somehow missed, but that was the only good thing that'd happened that night. Or maybe it would've been better if they *had* been in that explosion. At the moment, he was seriously considering death a good second option to living in this hell on earth.

Emmett was dead, James was being hunted, and they weren't even through Alberta, yet they were completely derailed. Who was going to lead the group? Greg was too wounded, Troy and Lucas would just get them all killed, and he sure as hell wasn't going to. Tank then? That could work, but what was their plan? Someone had to go after James. They couldn't all go after him; they may never find him, or they may find him dead. The group needed to keep going, but Connor didn't have to go with them.

He would go after his brother and the rest would continue on their way. They'd meet up later, but he needed to move now before the trail grew cold. Jogging back to Scourge, he grabbed their atlas and flipped open to the page that showed Alberta. They were just past Whitecourt and only a few hours from Dawson Creek, the start of the ALCAN.

Tank walked over. "What ya thinkin'?" he asked.

"We're here," Connor said, pointing. "As soon as you get to Dawson Creek, just follow the signs for the Alaskan-Canadian Highway. That'll take you to Tok, Alaska. We'll meet up there."

"What d'ya mean 'meet up'?"

"I mean," Connor said, ripping out the pages that held the maps for Alberta, British Columbia, and the Yukon, "I'm going after my brother."

"What? You want us to leave ya here?"

"Roger." Connor walked to the back of Scourge and opened the door. He grabbed his backpack that was already loaded with MREs, extra ammunition, a tent, and all the other supplies he'd need. He threw it over his shoulders and then put on his helmet with the NVGs.

Taking a small, clear, waterproof bag from their camping supplies, he put the maps in there with Alberta showing.

"There has to be a better way," Tank said.

"What would James want?"

"He'd want us to go on and keep the rest of the group safe."

"Then that's what you do." Connor stopped and looked at his best friend—his brother. "You have to take charge now. I know you don't *want* to, but we both know you can."

Tank sighed, looking at Connor with a sad smile on his face. "Take care, brother, and don't worry about the group. I'll keep 'em safe. When you find James, give him a hug and then a kick in the ass for gettin' separated."

"I will." Connor clasped Tank's proffered forearm. "We'll meet up in Tok or on the road."

"Get goin'."

Connor nodded and turned, heading towards a car in the ditch a few hundred yards back the way they'd come. It looked to be mostly intact, and hopefully it'd start.

"And Connor," Tank said after he'd made it a few steps. Connor stopped and looked back. "Make those bastards pay."

7

HUNTED

Post-outbreak day 22, night

James gazed up and down the river. There had to be a better way to cross, but there wasn't a bridge in sight, and he didn't have much time. The Reclaimers would be on him in a matter of moments. He had to cross, now. To his left there was a spot where the river braided out, splitting into multiple channels. Each of those channels would be shallower than where the river was just one big channel.

Taking off, he ran to the edge of the bank. It looked like he could wade through the first channel to a small island. Without hesitation, he splashed into the water, heedless of trying to stay dry. He'd be soaked by the time he got to the other side one way or another. The water was ice cold, but he didn't have to worry about hypothermia as it was at least sixty degrees out. Mud sucked at his boots, making it difficult to move, and the water flowed a little faster than he'd anticipated even though it was only waist high.

He made it to the island and quickly ran to the other side to find his next crossing. This channel looked deeper, but he should still be able to wade across it. He'd go to the next island, and then he'd just have to cross the main channel. That one was going to be tricky. Moonlight reflected off the water, temporarily mesmerizing him as he struggled to catch his breath. He was exhausted already, but he had to press on.

Something splashed into the water in front of him, followed instantly by a pop. He was being shot at! He lunged into the water and instantly realized he was in trouble. This channel was a lot deeper than it looked. With his feet on the ground, the water was all the way up to his chest. He didn't have a choice, however, so he waded forward as fast as he could as another bullet struck the stock of his ACR, which he held above his head.

James started to curse but was suddenly cut off as he hit the main current of the river. The water knocked his feet out from under him, and suddenly he was submerged as the river dragged him downstream. His head hit the bottom, and he was completely flipped over. He flipped again, unable to regain control. Then his feet hit the bottom and he kicked off, aiming for the surface. Breaking through, he took a deep breath right before he was sucked back under. This time he let the river take him instead of fighting it, and he was able to get his feet under him again. Kicking off the bottom to get more air, he was pulled back down as something constricted around his chest. The river rushed around him, but now he was stuck, water tearing at his clothing. He couldn't see in the murky liquid, so he felt at his chest. His tactical sling was pulling at him and he realized his ACR must be stuck on something, holding him down. Feeling along the sling, he reached his rifle and tried to dislodge it, but it held tight.

Lungs burning and his head swimming, he acted on instinct. Pulling the knife from his belt, he started to saw through the sling. He was almost finished when he lost his grip on the knife and it was pulled from his grasp. Unable to hold his breath any longer, he took a small gulp and swallowed nothing but water. Blackness closed in around him.

I'm going to die down here.

It was his last conscious thought as his sling ripped and the water took him. Blackness closed in, and he lost himself in it.

He stood at the edge of a crystal-clear lake, looking out across the calm waters. His bare feet were pressed into the soft sand and the sun warmed his back. A cool breeze blew against his cheek and he smiled, not knowing why. Things were just so peaceful. It was like none of the hardships or worries could touch him. In fact, he didn't even remember how he'd gotten there or what he'd been doing before. How long had he been standing on the shore? Maybe he should move, take a walk around the lake—yet he didn't. He just basked in the peace.

"Beautiful, isn't it?" asked a familiar voice.

James opened his eyes, not even realizing he'd closed them. Glancing over, he instantly recognized the man standing there. It was his father, Jack Andderson. Jack smiled at his son and then turned back to gaze out across the lake, or maybe it was an ocean. James couldn't see the other side, just an endless expanse of crisp blue.

"It is," James said.

He felt like he should be shocked to see his father, but he wasn't. This was where his father lived; he knew he'd find him here. Should that have worried him? It didn't, so he let the thought go.

"Where are we?" James asked, glancing at his father.

"I think you already know," Jack said.

"Does that mean...?"

"No, not yet. You have to go back soon."

"Then why am I here?"

"I don't have the answer to that question. But there's a reason."

"Is mom here, too?"

"Of course."

James paused, letting the warmth spread through him.

"What am I supposed to do, Dad?"

James didn't realize the depth of sadness he carried in his heart until he asked that question. Tears began to flow freely down his face, and he didn't try to stop them. He didn't feel ashamed of his emotion. They'd been through so much, and it was only natural to cry after everything that had happened.

"You do what you have always done, son. You trust. You believe that no matter what happens, He will be right beside you the whole way. When good things happen, celebrate. When bad things happen, lean in closer and grieve, but don't let the sorrow consume you. Toughness is not measured in the lack of tears but in the ability to press on through those tears."

His father gently grabbed his shoulders and spun James to look him directly in the eyes. Those were the same eyes James loved to look into. They held such deep strength and determination that it brought out courage in him. It was the effect his father always had on him when they'd had talks like this, few though they'd been.

"In short, don't lose hope."

James was wrapped in his father's embrace as the tears continued to flow from his eyes, and he noticed that a couple even streaked down his father's cheeks. Jack held his son as he cried out all those pent-up emotions—the sadness at losing so much, the guilt of those he couldn't save, the anger at the world and God for letting all this happen, and the fear that they'd never reach their destination without losing what made them who they were. The moment stretched on into eternity, and yet it was only a second before Jack broke the embrace.

"It's time," his father said, wiping the tears from James's cheeks. "Remember, don't be afraid to hope. I love you, son, and I'm so proud of the man you've become. I'll be seeing you around."

"Thanks, Dad," James said, more tears coming to his eyes. "I love you, too."

Slowly, James felt himself being pulled forward as he fell face first into the cool water of the lake.

James coughed up murky water and rolled onto his side. He was soaking wet, and it felt like he'd been tossed around in a washing machine. There wasn't a place on his body that didn't feel bruised. His legs were still submerged in the river, but the rest of him was lying on the muddy shore. Arms shaking, he dragged himself from the water and realized his legs were numb from the cold. Even though it was warm out, the water had still sapped the warmth from his body. He sat up once he was out of the river, shivering. Where was he?

He remembered getting sucked under and being stuck, but the rest of it was fuzzy. There were vague memories of a calm lake and talking with someone, and then he remembered being *pulled* from the river. Looking around, he realized there was no one else there, so maybe "pulled" wasn't the best word choice. Or maybe it was. James looked up at the night sky filled with glittering stars.

"Thank you," he whispered, coughing again.

It took a couple more minutes for the feeling to return to his legs. He knew that the Reclaimers were still after him, but at that moment he didn't even have the strength to stand. While he mustered his energy, he took stock of himself. Surprisingly, besides being cold, wet, and sore all over, he wasn't seriously injured. He figured he'd have at least a few scrapes or cuts, but he didn't. Inventorying his gear, he let out an involuntary groan. He'd lost his ACR in the river, along with his knife, tomahawk, and most of his handgun magazines. His Remington 1911 was still in its holster, and he had only one extra magazine for it.

When the feeling came back in his legs, he stood up shakily. He must've been washed downriver a ways as he couldn't see where he'd fallen in. He'd ended up on the southern side of the river, so that was good, at least. Not knowing what else to do, he set off to the south, hoping to find something to help him out of this situation. After stumbling the first fifty yards, he began to get his balance as his legs fully woke up and the blood started flowing again.

The trees ended up ahead and James slowed. There was a dirt road in front of him that turned to the northwest. Even though walking on the road would be much easier, it would also make him a better target. Plus, the Reclaimers would expect him to continue north after his group. Headlights shone on the dirt road as a vehicle came into view. James was still out of the light and he didn't want to be caught between the road and the river. Making a quick dash across, he crouched inside the trees on the other side, watching as the vehicle drew closer. It was a black single-cab truck that he didn't recognize. Fading back into the trees until he could just make out the dirt road, he crouched lower.

The vehicle drove over where James had crossed the road and then quickly stopped and backed up. A man jumped out of the driver's seat, armed with a shotgun. He walked up to where James had crossed and looked down at the wet boot prints. James cursed. He hadn't thought about the tracks he'd leave in the dirt.

The man pulled a radio from his pocket, his voice drifting to James through the trees. "This is Jax. I found his tracks."

"How fresh?" asked a voice on the other end that was hard to understand because of the heavy accent. Was that Russian?

"Not sure," Jax responded.

"Hold tight. We'll be there shortly. And be alert. He could be anywhere."

"Got it." Jax stowed his radio and raised the shotgun to his shoulder, looking into the trees where James was hiding.

He contemplated sneaking up and trying to take the man down, but he didn't have a rifle anymore, and he wouldn't pit his pistol-shooting skills against a man armed with a shotgun. Plus, more Reclaimers were on the way, and he didn't know how many would be with them. Taking the safe route, he decided to keep going and find a better place to hole up.

Sneaking away quietly, he continued to the south. He knew he should be worried. He was barely armed, a group of killers were hounding him, and he was separated from his group with no idea who was still alive. Yet, he couldn't shake the feeling that at the moment there was someone else running beside him in the night. Call him crazy, but he took comfort in that fact as he put more distance between himself and the road.

8

A BULLET NEVER LIES

Post-outbreak day 22, night

Ana dropped to her knees, and the handgun fell from her limp grasp. Tears streamed down her face as she knelt there, illuminated by the headlights of her truck. Unaware of anything going on around her, she curled into a ball on the blacktop and cried until the tears would no longer come. After a time, she sat up, wiping her eyes on the back of her sleeve.

The world had ended a few weeks ago, but it wasn't until tonight that *her* world had ended. She was no longer in control. She could no longer hold back the darkness that had grown inside her ever since she'd had to kill her own mother. Now that darkness was a part of her, not separate, and she was terrified that she wouldn't be able to keep from killing those she loved. Visibly shaking, she grabbed the Glock from the highway and stood up.

Why wasn't she dead? She looked down at the sleek black handgun resting in her palm. Working the slide, a bullet flew from the chamber and clinked onto the blacktop. She stooped over, picked it up, and examined it. The primer had been dented and the handgun should've gone off. She *should* be dead. Yet the round in the chamber had been a dud. In all her life, she'd never had that happen. Ever.

Taking a deep, ragged breath, Ana shrugged and pocketed the round. What did it matter now? She wasn't dead, and she sure as hell wasn't going to try a second time. She had things to do; it was time to end this. Jezz had to die. She was just like Ana's mother, and Ana would *not* allow her to live. She'd done it once, and she could do it again. There was only one outcome for someone that vile—a bullet. Once Jezz was gone, she could step up as leader of the Reclaimers. She hated to admit it, but they were just like her—people with darkness inside their souls that couldn't be shoved into a box. She was done hiding herself, and now it was time to take charge. And take charge she would.

Walking over to her truck that was still running, she climbed inside and sped down the highway, leaving the darkness in her wake. Yet, some of that darkness went with her, and it would stay with her until the end.

Connor drove back down the highway towards the ambush. The Chevy Impala that was sitting on the side of the road still had the keys in it and half a tank of gas. He was hoping for a more practical ride, but it'd have to work for now. Looking at the map, he noticed a road where he could pull off to the south, cross a bridge, and get on a dirt road that followed the southern edge of the river. He still wasn't sure what his best bet was, though he'd put money on his brother crossing the river. But even if he did find where James had gone that still didn't tell him whether he should follow him on foot or try to head him off.

He knew his brother well, so he might be able to anticipate where he would go. But at the same time, if James had to readjust or become purposefully unpredictable, Connor would have a hard time finding him. It might be best to just follow him, but that would put Connor on foot, chasing the Reclaimers who would be chasing his brother.

There was a chance the Reclaimers weren't after James, but they hadn't followed the rest of the group. That either meant they were all dead, had decided to let them go, or, more realistically, they were after the easy prey. Connor slammed his fist against the steering wheel, his fresh tattoo catching in the moonlight. He'd known something like this was going to happen as soon as they left Coutts. There was no way they could've stayed in the settlement after being kicked out by the town's leaders, and he'd wanted to keep going to Alaska anyway, but he'd just *known* this was going to happen. It was a simple fact of living at the end of the world. They were going to be facing hardship after hardship with no break until they got out to the bush.

As he turned south, driving over the Athabasca River, Connor found himself mouthing a silent prayer of protection for James, as well as the wisdom to find his brother. Did he even believe that would help? Yes... and no. His faith was still there, and it always would be no matter how hard things got. He'd faced too much to pretend otherwise. And yet, it was the smallest it'd been his whole life. Where was the *good* in this?

"James, can you hear me?" Connor said into his radio again. He'd tried to contact his brother as soon as he'd left the others, but James hadn't answered. Tank had told him that it looked like James hadn't had his plate carrier on when he took off, but he was hoping his brother still had his radio.

"Still nothin'?" Came Tank's reply over their channel.

"Nothing."

He turned onto the dirt road heading southeast.

"We're headin' out." Tank's voice was starting to sound scratchy. "Greg's stabilized and Alexis thinks he'll live."

"That's good to hear." Connor was only half listening as he scanned the road ahead for any sign that his brother had crossed.

"We'll meet up with you in Alaska."

Connor could barely make out the words over the static.

"Sounds good. Take care, brother."

"You... over... out." Only some of Tank's words came through.

"Over and out."

Headlights shining down the dirt road, Connor noticed a black truck fifty yards ahead. He slowed to a stop, bailing out with his ACR to his shoulder. Was that the Reclaimers', or a random vehicle? Fading into the trees to the left of the road, he made his way slowly over to the truck. There was no one inside. He rested his hand on the hood, and it was still warm. Reclaimers. Going back into the trees, he waited a couple of minutes, but no one returned.

Back at the truck, he opened the door, quickly switching the dome lights off and pulling his flashlight from a pouch on his plate carrier. He searched around inside and found nothing until he looked in the glove compartment. There was an owner's manual, proof of insurance, some napkins, and a sticky note. The words written on it were in a familiar, flowing script. Jezz.

Frequency 27.12500. Channel 14. Stay on at all times, J.

The Reclaimers were using radios!

Connor looked around, finding a set of boot tracks going across the road in front of the truck. Placing his foot next to one of the tracks, he matched the tread with his own Crispi boots. It was his brother's tracks. He'd crossed there, and the Reclaimers were hot on his heels.

Pulling the handheld radio from a pouch, he turned it on and tuned it to channel 14. There was nothing. He listened for a few minutes, but all was silent. He cursed. It had been worth a try, at least, but now he was back to square one. Did he follow on foot or try to cut his brother off? Neither sounded like a good plan.

"This is Dave. Do you copy?" came a voice over Connor's radio.

"We copy," said another voice, heavy with a Russian accent.

"I'm over in Windfall," Dave said. "If he cuts west or north, he should end up here."

"Stay there," the Russian said. "We'll contact you once we find him or need you to relocate."

"Got it. Do you know where he's going?"

"The last tracks we saw were heading south. But we lost him."

"Damn. Do you know where Jax is?"

"He's with us. Reid is heading south to watch there. We'll be in touch."

"Okay."

Connor couldn't believe his luck. It sounded like there were two scouts trying to cut James off, and the Russian had at least two others with him, probably more. Pulling the map from a side pocket, he found Windfall. It was barely a blip, so it would either be a very small town or potentially abandoned. He'd like to go after Reid, the Reclaimer to the south, but he had no idea where he was waiting. He did know where Dave was though.

It was time to do some hunting of his own.

9

STEPPIN' UP

Post-outbreak day 22, night

Allen Hook—or Tank, as he liked everyone to call him—glanced over at the passenger seat. Instead of one of the Andderson brothers who usually sat there, it was his girlfriend, Chloe. In most situations that would be an awesome thing. He had a girlfriend who was smokin' hot, but in this case, it was far from a good thing. James was missing, being chased by the Reclaimers, and Connor had gone after him. He didn't know if he'd ever see them again, and he wished he could've given each of them a proper goodbye.

What was he thinking? They weren't dead yet! He had to stay positive.

To make matters even worse, there was an injured man in the back seat, and they were down to eight survivors, including the two kids and the wounded Greg. Their most senior and competent member, Emmett, was dead, shot in the head by one of the Reclaimers. Without him, they'd lost their leader and a huge asset—not to mention a friend, father, and one helluva good man.

Damn those Reclaimer bastards!

They'd blown up Neil and Beverly, too, who Tank didn't know well, but they'd seemed like good people with their heads on straight. They were gone, along with over half of their total supplies. That left him with the two kids, two women, a wounded man, and two others he didn't know if he could rely on. It wasn't the start they'd hoped for and one that would make things difficult.

"Bloody hell," Tank whispered under his breath.

"What now?" Chloe asked, looking at him with tears in her eyes.

She was taking all this very hard, not that he could blame her. They'd been kicked out of Coutts and then ambushed in the same day. That was a lot to cope with. The only reason he wasn't cursing up a storm and beating the first thing he could get his hands on was because he was the leader now. Everyone was going to look to him. And sure, Lucas or Troy could try to lead, but he wouldn't let them. He didn't trust them fully, and he knew James would want him to take charge. Damn that guy for putting him in this position.

He'd briefly thought about letting Alexis lead. She was tough and her father's daughter through and through, but she'd just seen her dad shot and her boyfriend chased off by crazies. She wouldn't be in the mental place to lead, and even if she was, it'd just cause her undue stress. He knew Chloe wouldn't want to do it and probably didn't have the capacity. She was tough in her own way. She'd saved them from Bryce, but she wasn't the leader type. Then again, neither was he.

"We continue on," Tank said, resting his hand on hers. "We have to honor the sacrifices of those who've allowed us to get this far. It's time to finish this."

"But how?" Chloe asked. "There's so few of us."

"We'll make it work. There might not be many of us, but we're all fighters. We'll survive."

His girlfriend looked back out the window at the passing nightscape. He knew she'd get through this. It might take her a little more adjustment than the rest of them, but she'd be able to do it.

"It's good to see this side of you," Alexis said, kneeling on the floor in front of the middle seat. Her eyes were red and puffy, but for now she was holding it together well, probably due to the fact that her skills were needed to keep Greg alive. It was amazing what people were capable of when others depended on them.

"Eh, don't get used to it," Tank said, smiling. "As soon as Jamesy Boy is here, I'll go right back to my good ol' funny self."

"Nothing's wrong with that," Alexis said, a small smile tugging the corner of her lips. "It's just good to know we're in safe hands. My... my father was a good leader, and so was James. I know you'll do just as well as them." A tear escaped her eye, but she quickly wiped it away and went back to work, checking Greg's vitals.

Well, it was good that someone believed in him. That made a total of one, but he'd come around to himself as leader, eventually. He almost chuckled at that, but then the severity of their situation came crashing down again. While he smiled and acted confident on the outside, he was terrified inside—terrified that they were all going to die, that the brothers would never make it back, that the woman he loved would join the rest of his family in the grave, and above all, terrified that he was faking everything and he'd be found out. He was no leader.

He was a follower.

You're more than that, whispered a part of his mind.

He'd been hurt too many times, betrayed by those who were supposed to love and be there for him, starting with his real father and continuing on from there. It'd made it almost impossible to put himself out there, especially in relationships, but in some other areas of his life as well—actually, in all areas. He'd been living his life full of fear for so long that he didn't know how to do it any other way. The façade he put on was believable, but it was just a mask. Inside, he was terrified to trust anyone, himself included. He'd somehow failed his father as a son, and that had driven him away. What if he failed at this, too? It'd be the death of them all.

At least the stakes are low, he thought cynically.

This time things would be different; they'd have to be. He wouldn't allow his past or his insecurities to get the best of him. He'd push through and be the best damn leader he could be for these people. It was unclear how he'd do that, but he'd figure it out as he went. He'd always been a quick learner, and this would be no different. It was time to change things. He could do this, and to start, he'd stop bitchin' so much and get on with it.

I'd love some help down here, Big Man, Tank quickly prayed.

He didn't really know what he believed. Sure, there was a God; that only made sense. He remembered all those lessons from a youth group he'd been in, yet he'd only pursued his faith a couple of times. And after both of those had ended horribly, with life brutally knocking him down, he'd given up on it. Now, with everything going wrong, he might as well try, if just for the sake of believing in something beyond his own rotten circumstances. It was worth a shot.

"You planning to drive all night?"

The question came from the radio, and it took Tank a few seconds to recognize the voice as Lucas. He'd been zoning out. The tank on Scourge was just over a quarter, and they'd need to fuel up soon. Turning the music down, *Dead and Gone* by Trivium faded to a level where he could hear better. His passengers had gotten skilled at sleeping while he blared heavy music.

"Yeah," Tank said, taking a sip of Monster—his fifth one of the night. He could live on that stuff. In fact, he had in high school. That hadn't been the healthiest of choices, but it was damn good. As he set the can down, he noticed the fresh ink on the back of his hand. His pack was out there and he wished he could be with them, but he knew this was where he was needed.

"Troy needs some sleep," Lucas said. "Any chance we can stop?"

"I guess," Tank said, reaching for the atlas. Opening to Alberta, he noticed the pages were missing. He cursed. "You guys have an atlas?"

"Yep."

"Find us a small town to stop at."

The radio was silent, and he figured they were busy searching. Glancing at the clock, he was shocked to see that it was already four in the morning. He must've zoned out for most of the night. They'd decided to stay on the main highway now that they wouldn't have to worry about the Reclaimers, and it had helped them make good time.

"Didn't Connor say something about Dawson Creek?" Lucas asked.

"Yeah," Tank said. "It's the start of the ALCAN."

"Well, we're less than a half hour from there. Should we wait until then?"

"Affirmative. We'll stop in Dawson Creek."

$$10$$

FLYING MONKEYS

Post-outbreak day 23, early morning

James yawned and tripped over a small root as he took his eyes from his path. He reached out to keep himself from eating dirt again and barely caught himself. Pushing off the ground, he continued on his way. This was the sixth time he'd fallen in the last thirty minutes. It was early in the morning, and the sky was beginning to brighten. He'd lose the cover of darkness soon, not that it had helped him much in the last hour. They may not be able to see him well, but he was making enough noise that they could hear him from a long way off. It was time he found somewhere to hide out.

From the river, he'd gone southeast for over an hour—or he thought it was southeast. His running had turned into jogging and then into a fast walk, but now he was stumbling more than walking. Hopefully, he wouldn't run into any other survivors because they'd mistake him for a zombie by the way he was tripping over his own feet. After that first hour, he'd turned west and then more north, figuring they'd think he'd continue south for a while. The problem was they all knew he'd ultimately go north. He just prayed they'd be too busy trying to follow him to realize he'd changed directions until it was too late.

The Reclaimers would have a hard time finding him because *he* didn't even know where he was, and if it weren't for the eastern horizon, he wouldn't know which direction he was going either. But at least he knew which way he was heading now. Stumbling onto an old logging road, he unconsciously started down it as it cut a path north. It might not offer him as much cover, but at the moment he was too exhausted to care. It made walking a lot easier than trying to pick his footing through the forest.

After a time, he came to where the trees were nothing but stumps and he could see for a hundred yards. Before him lay what looked like an old gas plant or mine. There were large industrial buildings, huge tanks, offices, and other such structures. There were a few zombies stumbling around and only a couple of old vehicles. It seemed like this place had been a ghost town even before the apocalypse, and it would be the perfect place to hole up while he slept. Although getting there would be difficult without being seen, it was his best option. He said a quick prayer and drew his 1911 handgun. It was time to find a place to rest.

He did his best to sneak past the zombies. It wouldn't do to have corpses lying around, giving him away. Quietly going from cover to cover, he was able to make it to the heart of the compound without attracting any attention. There were quite a few buildings for him to choose from, but they were also the most obvious places to hide. Looking up at the sky, he saw that it was clear, and it looked like it would stay that way. He also noticed that most of the roofs on these buildings were flat, and a large one a little farther back looked like he could climb up onto it. It would be an unpredictable place to rest, and it would also give him a great view.

Jumping onto a dumpster, he was able to reach a small ledge. After hoisting himself up, he shimmied around the ledge to get to one of the large pipes going up to the roof with brackets every few feet—they would make perfect handholds. He finally reached the edge of the roof and pulled himself over, collapsing onto the other side. His arms were now as exhausted as his legs since he hadn't realized it was three stories high until he'd begun to climb. There was a small, three-foot wall around the roof and large green electrical boxes that he'd be able to hide behind.

The door to the rest of the building was locked from the outside, with a thin board across it. It seemed that someone had tried to make a stand there as there were spots of dried blood scattered around but no body. Maybe whoever'd been up there was now one of the zombies down below. But if that were the case, how had they gotten down without breaking all the bones in their body? Maybe they'd just dropped off, or the zombies were evolving and had grown wings. That would be terrifying—flying zombies. It would almost be like the flying monkeys from the *Wizard of Oz*.

"I'll get you, my pretty," James mumbled under his breath, then gave his best Wicked Witch cackle. The noise, though quiet, echoed around the roof, which snapped him from his daze. Had he really just said that? He must be more exhausted than he thought.

"I need to get some sleep."

Coming around the last electrical box, he stopped short and drew his handgun. On the edge of the roof, looking back towards where he'd come out of the trees, was a body. The man had been shot in the head, and his death was fresh as the blood pooling around him was still tacky. Getting a closer look, he confirmed that it had been a human and not a zombie. The corpse didn't even smell rotten yet, so he must've been killed in the last couple of hours. It had to be one of the Reclaimers, but who'd shot him?

James ducked down, realizing he was exposed up there. His slow mind finally registered that lying next to the man was a wood-stocked bolt-action rifle. It was an old Winchester .30-06 with a Redfield scope. Going through the man's pockets, he found six extra rounds, plus the five already in the magazine and one in the chamber. The man also had a handheld radio clipped onto the side of his belt. He pulled that off and turned it on, only to discover that the battery was dead. He couldn't catch too much of a break or he may begin to think he was just on a morning stroll instead of running for his life. His eyelids kept drooping as he checked the weapon, so he figured it was time to get some shuteye. Staying low, he found the nearest electrical box in the shade and set his back against it. No sooner had he closed his eyes than he was asleep.

11

DAWSON CREEK

Post-outbreak day 23, morning

They were in British Columbia now. That should be a happy thought for Alexis, but everything was weighed down by the reality that their progress had been paid for with yet another loss. Her dad was dead. Never again would he hold her and look into her eyes, lending that strength he always did with just a look. Never again would she be able to tease him and call him "daddy." Never again would she be able to hear him say he loved her. He was gone, and the thought nearly broke her.

Alexis sat in the middle seat next to Greg's feet, gazing out the window as the endless fields flashed by. It didn't look much different from what they'd been seeing for weeks, and she was ready for a change. All her life she'd wanted to see the mountains, and yet she never had. Sure, she'd seen some far off in Wyoming, but she was ready to be *in* the mountains. The thought brought James to mind. Not only had she lost her dad—the last surviving member of her family—but her boyfriend was gone as well. He may even be dead by now. The thought pressed down on her already weakened heart. How could she experience so much loss in a single day?

After her brother, Mason, had died she'd thought that would be the worst event of her life. But then she'd had to watch her dad shoot her stepdad and then fail to save her mom from the fatal bite of an infected. Now her own dad was dead, too, and she'd watched him die, unable to do anything. And the one person who could truly comfort her wasn't even here. She had no one.

A small hand gently rested on her shoulder. Alexis brushed the tears from her eyes and looked behind her at the dark-skinned, blue-eyed little girl in the back seat. That last statement wasn't entirely true—she wasn't alone. She was surrounded by her new family.

"I'm sorry about your dad," Olive said, sniffling. Her eyes were red and full of moisture.

Alexis rested her hand on top of Olive's. "Thanks," she said.

"I wouldn't worry about James."

"I'm trying not to, but with everything..." Alexis let the statement drop as more tears threatened to pour out. Would she ever cry herself dry? It'd been on and off all night.

"I know," Olive said, "but I've been praying. He'll be okay. Connor will find him, and they'll meet back up with us."

Alexis nodded. It was odd taking comfort from an eight-year-old, but Olive wasn't a normal kid. She'd seen plenty of death and heartbreak before the apocalypse had ever begun. Through it all, her faith had grown to something that would rival most adults, but that was the point of a child-like faith. She could trust God more easily than the rest of them.

"Thanks, Olive," Alexis said, moving to check Greg's vitals.

"You're welcome," Olive said as she leaned back.

"If anyone can make it," Felix said, "it'll be James and Connor."

She could tell that he'd been crying as well, but he tried to cover it up. The boy had looked to Emmett as a father figure, especially after Emmett had taken him out shooting a few times while in Coutts. Her dad had even given him a Springfield XD 9mm handgun, which Felix carried on his hip. Her dad had taken him under his wing, but that was over now. Would these kids ever get the chance at a normal childhood?

Greg's vitals had stabilized; she'd done all she could and now it was time to wait it out. If they could find a working hospital and an actual surgeon, they'd be able to do more, but she doubted there were any of those left.

"We're gettin' close," Tank said.

Alexis took a deep breath, glancing to the passenger seat. Chloe was taking this almost as hard as her. Alexis put her hand on Chloe's shoulder, just like Olive had done for her. It was easier to help others than to dwell on her own pain.

"How you doin'?" Alexis asked.

"Me?" Chloe asked, looking almost ashamed. "I should be asking you that, but here I am, crying like a baby." There was anger laced in those words, probably at her own "weakness."

"It's okay," Alexis said. "We all have a lot to cope with."

Chloe nodded. "I'm doing okay. It'd just be nice to get some sleep in something other than this seat."

"I second that."

"We really shouldn't be stoppin'," Tank said, stifling a yawn.

"Really?" Chloe asked, some of her normal sass returning.

Tank looked over at her, smiling slightly. "Yeah, I'm a man, so I can do anythin'. Like stay up for three or four days drivin' all the way to Alaska."

Chloe grunted. "Yeah right."

Alexis chuckled. It felt good to laugh. She could see how Tank's humor was much more than him just messing around. It was a way for him to cope with all of this but also to help those around him. The big guy really did have a big heart hidden under all that sarcasm.

"Is that Dawson Creek up there?" Lucas asked over the radio.

"Affirmative," Tank said.

"Good. Troy's about to pass out."

"Really? Tell him to grow some balls and drink a Monster."

"He's already had two."

"Two? That's for sissies. I'm on my sixth."

"Wow," Alexis said.

"You know that stuff will kill you," Chloe said.

"I have a sneakin' suspicion that a different kind of monster will get me before those chemicals do," Tank said to Chloe. Then he spoke into the radio. "Keep your eyes peeled. This looks like a decent-sized town."

"Will do," Troy said.

"Could you grab those for me?" Alexis asked, pointing to the M4 rifle and shotgun resting on the floor in the rear seat.

"Sure," Felix said, grabbing the shotgun first.

He took his time as he handed it to her, making sure to keep it pointed in a safe direction. She took the Benelli M4 semiautomatic tactical shotgun and loaded a round into the chamber. Then she took one of the shells Felix offered her from a bag in the back and refilled the tube. The shotgun also had six extra shells in a holder on the buttstock. She handed the weapon up to Chloe, who looked at it hesitantly.

"Here's the safety," Alexis said, pointing it out. "All you have to do is click it off and pull the trigger. It is a semi-auto, so it'll keep firing as long as you pull the trigger. New shells go into the tube down here and the action is here in case it jams. These are two-and-three-quarters-inch, four-shot shells, so within twenty yards you'll have no problem hitting an infected in the head, and the kick will be minimal."

"I—" Chloe started as Alexis handed it to her.

"I know you don't like guns," Alexis said, "especially after the last time, but if we get into trouble, you'll need to help. I know you can do it."

"Okay," Chloe said, taking a deep breath. "I can do it."

"Good," Alexis said as she leaned back and Felix handed her the fully outfitted M4 combat rifle her dad had given to her.

"Alexis," Tank said, "you good to clear the pumps with me?"

"Roger," Alexis said, steeling herself.

She'd just lost her dad and her boyfriend was missing, but there were people here who needed her. She could cry on her own time; there was work to be done. If there was anything she'd learned from her dad over the years, it was that when the time came to kick ass, she kicked ass. She could always cry later.

"Good," Tank said. "Chloe, you stay with the rig and be our backup."

"Okay," Chloe said with more confidence in her voice than before.

Alexis knew she was tough and would do what needed to be done. She'd done it before with Bryce, and she could do it again.

They entered Dawson Creek, and the town was overrun. Any hope they'd had of finding a hospital flew from her mind as she realized this place was just as bad as what they'd been through. They wouldn't catch a break here.

"Town is overrun," Tank said into the radio. "We'll look for gas on the far side."

"Got it," Troy said.

They came to a round-about, and Alexis noticed a sign with a large red arrow: *You are now entering the world famous Alaska Highway.*

"Welcome to the ALCAN," Tank said as he exited the round-about and started on the highway.

12

ON THE ALCAN

Post-outbreak day 23, morning

Tank pulled Scourge off at a small gas station—or as the Canuks called them, petrol station—on the outskirts of town. There were three pumps and the building looked easy to clear. He knew the others would like to get out and stretch their legs as they'd been cooped up most of the night. It might be risky, but he had to keep their morale up, especially with everything they'd just gone through.

See, he thought, *I'll make a fine leader.*

Stopping at the pumps, he grabbed his suppressed ACR combat rifle from beside his seat. The SAW was in the back as he'd traded it in for a more practical weapon in this situation. He also grabbed his new Frostmourne that Tom, the old mechanic back in Coutts, had made for him. The sword was relatively light and extremely sharp. Letting the rifle fall on its sling, he started to fuel up. Alexis came around with her M4 to her shoulder and handgun on her hip. He was glad to have her as she was now the most experienced shooter, next to him. Hell, with Emmett as a father, she was probably more experienced *and* a better shot.

Troy pulled to a stop at the other pump and Lucas quickly got out, his 12-gauge shotgun to his shoulder.

"Plan?" Troy asked, walking over.

"Fuel up both rigs," Tank said. "You and Lucas keep an eye out here while Alexis and I clear inside. Then we can take a quick break and grab anythin' useful."

"Sounds good," Troy said, glancing at Alexis. "I'm sorry about your dad... and James."

"Thanks," Alexis responded, not looking at him. Her eyes were scanning their surroundings.

She's good, Tank thought.

When James and Emmett were in charge, she was content to let them take the lead, but he could tell she had no trouble leading either. He almost wanted to hand the torch off to her, but she'd been through too much. She didn't need the added stress, even if she *could* do it.

"Ready?" Alexis asked, looking back at him.

"Yep, I'll lead," Tank said, hefting his giant sword. "You cover."

Alexis nodded as they headed towards the building. Tank stopped at the door and banged his fist against the glass. Shuffling and groaning could be heard inside, and Tank raised his blade above his head as Alexis readied herself to open the door. Tank nodded and she opened it.

Two undead stumbled out and Tank brought his blade smashing down into the first one's head. He was expecting the shock to jar his grip like when he'd used the old Frostmourne, but this was significantly less. The blade also didn't smash the skull and bounce off like before. It embedded itself a couple of inches into the thing's head. The undead dropped, taking Tank's sword with it. He had to let go as the other undead stumbled past its fellow and came at him. Blood exited out the back of the second undead's head as Alexis fired, her suppressed M4 barking behind him.

Quickly, Tank bent down, gripped Frostmourne, set his foot against the undead's head, and jerked his blade free. More groaning could be heard from inside the station, and he readied himself. He'd have to adjust his strategy as the blade wielded completely differently than his last one. The next undead exited the doorway, and once it was clear, Tank swung for its neck. The head flopped off as the body fell to the ground.

"Now that's kickass," Tank said, admiring the weapon in his hands. Tom really had poured his heart and soul into the sword, which was easy to tell by the detail of the work and changes he'd made to make it more practical. Aside from the congealed blood on it, the blade looked unmarred from smashing it into a human skull.

The inside of the station was now silent, and nothing else came out. Tank led the way as they entered and cleared the building. It was safe, but just to be sure, they decided that Alexis would escort the kids to and from the bathroom. He'd noticed that when she had something to keep her busy, she seemed to cope better. It probably took her mind off everything and helped her focus on the task at hand. He'd have to remember that.

While Alexis took Olive and Felix to the bathroom, Tank checked for any supplies. The place had been cleaned out, and all he found was a bag of half-eaten chips, which he left. He did find a case of Rockstar energy drinks in the backroom. They weren't Monsters, but they'd do in a pinch. With the supplies in Scourge, they should be able to survive for a few days between all of them. The truck Troy was driving had a couple days' worth as well, but the majority of their supplies, especially their food, had been in the van. If they could make good time, they'd have plenty of food to get there, especially if they drove straight through. He knew things rarely went as planned, but maybe this once they'd catch a break after the hell they'd just been through.

Ten minutes later, both rigs were filled up, and everyone had stretched their legs. Tank had cleaned off his blade and sheathed the weapon, which he rested on his shoulder looking back towards town. The undead were starting to make their way out there, and they were probably the same ones that had started following them when they'd driven by. With nothing better to do, the stupid things had just kept shambling this way even when they'd lost sight of the vehicles. Or maybe they weren't that stupid, just extremely slow. It seemed like the longer they'd been dead, the slower they became. They also appeared to be decomposing but at a decreased rate. Honestly, it was fascinating, and he wanted to study them more—if he wasn't in a fight for survival, anyway.

"Time to hit the road," Tank said, sticking Frostmourne back in Scourge.

"We're good to go," Lucas said, walking over to the truck. The blonde-haired man couldn't be much older than Tank, and he seemed to be a good egg.

Troy was already in the passenger seat, his red hair a mess and his eyelids drooping from driving all night. Tank didn't know what he thought of that one yet. He seemed nice but was almost too friendly. He acted like he was Tank's best friend, and Tank didn't like that, although he seemed to be doing well with everything that had gone down.

Tank stopped before climbing into Scourge. The LAPV was definitely the best vehicle he'd ever owned—not that there was much competition. Nothing else he'd owned had been bulletproof or this badass looking. He admired the awesome paint job. Yeah, this rig was the best.

Alexis was in the middle seat, checking Greg's vitals again with a look of concentration on her face. The kids were in the back seat playing a game of rock-paper-scissors. Chloe was in the passenger seat, looking like she was ready to pass out. That wasn't surprising as she spent most of the night alternating between staring out the window and crying.

"You okay?" Tank asked as he climbed in.

"Yeah," Chloe said, looking over at him with a small smile. "I'll live."

"Good," Tank said, starting the engine. "I don't know if I'd want to keep goin' without ya."

"You're such a sap," Chloe said with a chuckle.

"You know it, baby," Tank said with a wink.

"You want me to drive for a bit?"

"Are you kiddin' me? You look ready to pass out. I got plenty of energy drinks to keep me goin' all day!"

"Okay."

Chloe yawned and then rested her head back.

Well, that was an easy argument to win, Tank thought to himself with a chuckle.

He pulled out of the gas station, Lucas following in the truck. The undead behind them saw the movement and adjusted their course. How long would they follow? Until they couldn't walk anymore, or until they heard something else to distract them? What a crappy existence that would be, just following a basic instinct to kill and eat.

"How's Greg?" Tank asked, glancing back.

"He's awake and doing okay," Alexis said. "We need to find a safe place to stop so I can drain the fluids and then stitch him up."

"Got it," Tank said, "I'll keep my eyes out. You good, Greg?"

"Alive," Greg said, laying on his side with his back resting against the seat.

"Good to hear."

"I agree," Greg said with a chuckle that turned into a wet cough.

"Get some rest, bud," Tank said, returning his attention to the road.

Even though Tank acted like he was good, he was actually exhausted, and the energy drinks only did so much. It was going to be a long day, and he knew he wouldn't make it into the night. They'd have to find a place to get some sleep and then continue in the morning. *Walking Dead* by Decyfer Down began to play, and he turned the volume up a little. It was just another road trip through a decaying world.

13

THE CHASE BEGINS

Post-outbreak day 23, afternoon

James woke up to the sun shining in his eyes. He'd been asleep for several hours, and while he felt much better, his body screamed at him from all the abuse the night before. He'd swear that every square inch of his skin was one giant bruise. His hand itched and he scratched it but then stopped suddenly, remembering the tattoo. It was scabbing now, and he'd want to be careful lest he scar it. Stretching, he stood up and grabbed the Winchester rifle.

It was time he moved on. The Reclaimers could be right on his heels now. Peering over the lip of the roof, he scanned the surrounding area for several minutes. There was no movement other than a few zombies. It seemed like there were even fewer than before. Had the others moved on, or were they just out of sight somewhere? Shrugging, he spotted a couple of old trucks sitting by one of the buildings close to the paved road leading north. Hopefully, one of those would start and he could put some distance between himself and the Reclaimers.

He climbed down the building, which proved to be harder than climbing up. Landing on the ground, he took off at a crouched run towards the vehicles. Even though he didn't see any enemies around, he didn't like being exposed out there. One of the zombies between him and his target noticed him and began to shamble his way. Running around the thing, he reached the old truck and opened the driver's door, throwing the rifle inside. The keys weren't in the ignition. Not having enough time to look, he went around to the bed of the truck as the zombie stumbled past the open driver's door.

Climbing over the tailgate, James threw himself into the bed as the zombie grabbed at him. The tailgate stopped the zombie's torso and the flailing arms just missed him. Standing up, he grabbed a shovel from the bed and went to town. After a couple of swings, the zombie lay on the ground behind the truck with a crushed skull and James stood in the bed, breathing heavily as dark blood oozed off the shovel. Tossing it down, he hopped out and went back around to the cab. The noise of metal hitting bone must've been louder than he thought as two more zombies stumbled his way.

"C'mon," James mumbled to himself as he searched the cab of the truck for the keys. Flipping the visor down, a ring of keys fell onto the floorboard. "There we go."

He stooped down and picked them up, but the first zombie had reached him. James noticed the half-missing face on the other side of the driver's window as he stood there, holding the keys in one hand. He dropped them and stumbled back as the zombie ran into the door, slamming it shut. The thing was only two feet away. James was already drawing his handgun when the zombie's hand grasped him. It had a surprisingly strong grip as it seized James's shoulder, bringing its open mouth in close. The exposed teeth had chunks of flesh wedged in them, and its breath was worse than the smell of decay.

Unable to raise his handgun in time, he fired wildly from the hip. James started squeezing the trigger point blank, aiming the barrel up towards its head. The first shot took the zombie in the chest but did little to stop the thing. The next one hit it in the neck, splattering James with blood. The third entered the bottom of the zombie's chin when it was less than six inches from taking a bite out of his neck. The thing dropped, wrenching the handgun from his grasp in the process. A second zombie was right behind the first, reaching for him from only a few feet away.

His handgun was under the body of the first zombie, and the shovel was too far away to reach, so he resorted to the only other weapon readily available. Quickly picking up a large rock, he smashed it into the side of the zombie's head with all his force. It fell to the ground but was still moving, so James fell to his knees, bringing the rock over his head and then smashing it onto the thing's skull—once, twice, five times. He rose unsteadily to his feet, arms shaking, and blood splattered all over him. This was not how he was going to die. He'd made it too far. With the rock still gripped in his hand, he went back to the first zombie and smashed it in the head twice, just to be sure. Then he rolled it over and retrieved his handgun.

Three more zombies had come around the corners of various buildings and were heading his way, attracted to the gunshots. They were still a hundred yards out, so James grabbed the keys and tried the truck. Shockingly, it roared to life. He holstered his handgun and climbed in. The gas tank was a little over half and the engine seemed to be running smoothly. Since this was probably as good as it'd get, he didn't worry about checking the other truck and pulled away from the building. He would take the road north and hopefully hop onto a side road that paralleled the main highway after a while. He wasn't sure he wanted to get back on that just yet.

The driver's side window shattered, and James instinctively ducked as he heard the accompanying gunshot. Stepping on the gas pedal and staying hunkered down, he glanced out the window to see a man with an AR-style rifle, another man with a shotgun, and a woman with raven black hair and a wicked look on her face running towards him from the edge of the clearing around the compound. That would be Jezz. It had to be because her demeanor sent a shiver down his spine. Drawing his handgun, he popped off some shots at the three, and to his surprise, the man with the shotgun crumpled to the dirt. That must've pissed Jezz off because she raised an AK-47 to her shoulder and started firing. It was a legitimate AK-47, and the fully automatic weapon littered his truck with holes as he sped away.

Glass, foam, and plastic exploded all around him as bullets pierced every conceivable surface. Pain exploded in his leg as he rounded the nearest building and his attackers lost sight of him. He didn't fully sit up until he was on the paved road and the compound was half a mile behind him. His leg was bleeding, but that wasn't an immediate concern as it seemed to be a flesh wound. The road turned east, and he had no choice but to follow it since he didn't want to drive into a dead-end.

He could see a bridge in the distance. Glancing in the rearview mirror, he cursed. The truck that had been sitting next to his sped around the corner—with Jezz driving. He didn't need anyone to confirm his suspicions; he just *knew* it was her. He pressed his foot to the floor, but the old beater Ford reached its limit at 53 MPH. Even topped out, the Reclaimers were easily keeping pace with him. He wouldn't be able to outrun them.

$$14$$

HUNTER AND THE HUNTED

Post-outbreak day 23, afternoon

Why did I have to wreck my car? Connor wondered as he walked back towards Windfall.

The night before, he'd taken care of the sentry on the roof, and then he'd heard more radio chatter about the other sentry to the south. The man had given his location away, and Connor had gone hunting. He'd failed to get the jump on the guy, though, and he'd started shooting at Connor before he realized his location. With no choice, he'd hunkered down and opted for squishing the Reclaimer between the side of his car and Connor's Impala. It had taken care of the man but had also disabled both vehicles and given Connor a nice gash on his forehead. So now he was on foot, walking back towards where he'd seen a couple of trucks in the ghost town.

The sun was high over the tops of the trees lining both sides of the dirt road. He should be getting close, but he was seriously rethinking his choice to smash the guy. Not that he'd had much time to think when bullets started tearing holes in his windshield and smashing into the seat around him. He was lucky the man had missed him so many times. Connor hadn't even been grazed.

It wasn't luck, said a small part of his mind.

Ignoring that thought, he pressed on. The plate carrier wasn't making things any easier in the summer heat, but he was almost there—just a little farther. The drudgery of putting one foot in front of the other while keeping his head on a swivel was interrupted by three rapid gunshots.

Connor jerked his head towards the noise. The shots had come from up ahead in the direction of Windfall, which must be closer than he'd anticipated. He began to jog, his tired leg muscles protesting. The shots had been quick, which meant it was a semiautomatic, and it sounded like small arms fire. That could be James. He picked up his pace.

"Hold on, brother," Connor whispered.

If he had to go to the ends of the earth to find James, he would, and he'd let nothing and no one stand in his way. There was a fire burning inside that was fueled by pure rage at their situation. He knew if he let it, it'd consume him. Releasing it a little here and there allowed him to push on even when he didn't want to move anymore. He'd been up all night, yet that fire kept him awake and alert. He couldn't let his guard down because that would get him and his brother captured or killed.

Another gunshot went off, this one louder than before. It wasn't the same weapon; it sounded meatier. Then the rapid fire of a fully automatic weapon let off, and he knew his brother was in trouble. He sped up to an all-out run, huffing from the exertion. Someone was definitely shooting at someone else, and they weren't holding back. He could hear the bullets thumping into metal and glass shattering.

Breaking out of the line of trees, he could see the deserted compound of Windfall. By the smaller office building far to the west, movement caught his attention. A truck pulled around the building and started speeding down the paved road heading north. Connor took a knee and aimed through his ACOG optic at the vehicle a hundred yards away. He could make out two people in the truck before he lost sight of it as they rounded a turn in the road.

He cursed at himself. He should've taken the shot, but he hadn't identified his targets and didn't know if it was James or not. There'd been two of them, but his brother could've found a survivor, no matter how unlikely that was. He started running towards the compound. Nearing the office building the vehicle had left from, he noticed four zombies stumbling towards him. Four quick shots had them on the ground, blood oozing from the backs of their skulls. There were more dead zombies on the other side of the building but no more vehicles. Examining the spot more closely, he observed skid marks by where it looked like two vehicles had been parked and had pulled out at high speeds.

So, James had found a ride, but the Reclaimers were right behind him. There was a chance that it was some other random people, but that would be too much of a coincidence. Plus, something in his gut told him he was right, and he always trusted his instincts. Gazing around, he didn't notice another vehicle in sight. There could be more hiding behind some of the buildings, but he didn't have time to do a thorough search. He needed to go after them, and yet he couldn't run the whole way.

The large building where he'd shot the Reclaimer on the roof was the highest. If he climbed that, he'd be able to check the whole compound without having to run around. Jogging over to the door, he stacked up outside and for a second waited for his brother to open it. A second later, he realized just how foolish that was and shook his head. It was so ingrained in him to always have James around.

Opening the door and stepping back, he waited. A zombie came stumbling out, but it hit the dirt before it could take two steps—a suppressed gunshot sounding from his ACR. Another soon joined it on the ground, and then Connor moved into the building, taking his aviator sunglasses off and tucking them into a pouch on his vest. The immediate area was clear, and he moved to a big set of metal stairs. The bottom floor was open, with the next two floors consisting of catwalks. He didn't take time to register what else was in the room after scanning it for threats, and he took the steps two at a time.

At the top, a zombie with broken legs reached towards him. He pulled the trigger while still moving and the pathetic creature quit crawling. There were two farther down the catwalk, heading towards him. The first one dropped when a 62 grain 5.56 bullet tore its way through the zombie's face. The second one was hit before the first smashed onto the cold metal. That one careened over the side of the railing to smash through a wooden crate on the floor below. In a flash, Connor was past them and moving to the stairs that led up to the next level of catwalks.

This one was clear, and he moved directly to the door with an exit sign above it. It was barred and locked on the inside. He wasted little time throwing the bar to the ground and unlocking the door, but it still wouldn't open. Frustrated, he sprayed a few rounds into the handle and middle of the door, and then he kicked it with all his might. It slammed open with a metallic screech and he exited onto the roof, noticing a broken board lying on the ground. The sun was bright in his eyes compared to the dark interior, and he took the time to slip his shades back on.

The roof provided just the view he needed. He quickly searched below for anything that would help but came up empty. Running to the other side of the building to look north, he noticed nothing there either. Then, on the south side, he found the man he'd shot on the roof, but his rifle was missing. His brother must've come up here somehow and taken it. That didn't surprise him. James was always resourceful.

"Good," Connor mumbled to himself. "At least he's well-armed."

Going around each edge of the roof again, he noticed a few dead bodies on the ground below, mostly clustered around where the trucks had been parked, as well as a couple of others scattered around, but he couldn't find a single vehicle besides a large bulldozer. He had next to no knowledge about how to drive one, but since it was his only option, he'd have to try. Entering the building again, he made it to the ground floor after encountering only one more zombie. The yellow dozer sat next to one of the other buildings in the compound. Climbing into the cab, he glanced at the controls. There was a foot pedal, two joysticks, gauges, buttons, knobs, and other such things. At first glance it looked daunting, but he could fly a plane, so how hard could it be?

Turned out it wasn't *too* difficult and after a few minutes, he was turning onto the paved road and heading after the Reclaimers, going a whopping fifteen miles an hour. It was like the turtle trying to catch the hare.

15

MOTEL 9

Post-outbreak day 23, late afternoon

The late afternoon sun warmed Alexis's face, and she had to keep herself from dozing off. The rest of them were all sound asleep except Tank, who was still driving. Even Greg was out cold, breathing steadily on the seat next to her. She'd had to do an impromptu surgery on the side of the road when he'd started coughing and oozing fluids out of his wound. She'd cut him open and put in a tube from the extensive first aid kit they'd gotten from the military. The tube was hooked to a bag that was slowly draining the fluids from his chest. She'd sewn up the hole in his back after checking it, and she'd need to do the same to the front after it was done draining. It was the first time she'd done anything like that, and her paramedic training had only taught her so much, but having helped Dr. Nelson back in Coutts had given her more experience.

Now it was just a waiting game as she could do no more, except pray, which she'd been doing nonstop after Olive had encouraged her earlier. She'd prayed for her dad, not knowing exactly where he stood when... but she dismissed the thought from her mind lest it break her. Glancing out the window, she watched the greenery pass by in a blur. They were making extremely good progress, only having encountered a few large crashes. There were even some long stretches of highway with hardly any vehicles, and they could actually go the speed limit. It would be great if it weren't for the large hole torn in her heart.

Taking a deep breath, she said a prayer for James and Connor. If she lost James, too, she may never be able to heal from that. It'd be like taking her already fractured heart and tearing it in two. If that happened, she wouldn't give up, but in what capacity could she live on? She'd never have a whole heart again. That sounded kind of silly to her, but she knew it was true. At some point along the way, James had stolen a piece of her heart, and if he died, he'd take that to the grave with him. She realized that if James hadn't traded places with her in her dad's truck, it would be her out there. She shivered at the thought that it could be her being chased by Jezz. On one hand, she almost wished it was, but on the other—larger hand—she was glad that it wasn't.

She knew that was selfish to think, but Jezz had broken her hope back in the pole barn and she still had nightmares about it. James would want it like this, anyway. She knew he'd give his life to keep her safe, and even without knowing it, he'd put himself in danger and protected her. That was the way he was—just like her dad.

"Hey, man." Lucas's voice came over the radio. Alexis could hear the exhaustion in it. "We gonna stop soon?"

"I was considerin' it," Tank said, yawning. "I ain't got much left in me."

"Good," Lucas said. "Because neither do I."

"I'll be lookin'."

"What about over there?" Alexis asked, pointing to the north where a red barn sat at the back of a large cornfield.

"We should be far enough out of Fort Nelson," Tank said, yawning again. "Hell, it'll work."

He pulled off at a dirt road on the side of the field, driving back half a mile. They stopped outside the large white double doors.

"Let's check it out," Tank said, grabbing his sword.

Alexis climbed out, rifle to her shoulder. The surrounding area looked clear. She stopped at the large doors and then opened them for Tank when he came up. They waited, and after nothing came out, she went inside. There was a large combine harvester at the back, tools off to one side, and a few stalls full of hay. Other than that, the place was clear of any threats.

"Clear," Alexis said.

"Same," Tank said, coming out of the last stall.

"How's it look?" Lucas asked as they came out.

"Good place to rest," Alexis said.

"Sweet," Lucas said.

"Let's pull the rigs over in those trees," Tank said, pointing to where a few old cars and tractors were parked. "They'll be hard to see in there."

"Good idea," Lucas said as he climbed back in to move his truck.

Tank pulled Scourge in between an old Chevy and a tractor plow, turning the vehicle off. Without the sounds of engines running, Alexis admired how quiet it was out there. It would be almost peaceful if not for the situation they were in. She went back into the barn, made a bed with some hay, and covered it with one of the horse blankets hanging on the wall. That done, she walked back out to Scourge.

"Can you guys help Greg in?" Alexis asked Tank and Lucas, who were standing next to the rig, yawning.

"Sure," Lucas said. "Wake up, buddy."

"Where are we?" Greg asked, stirring.

"Just west of Fort Nelson," Tank said.

"We're gettin' there," Greg said, slowly sitting up.

"Yep," Lucas said. "Now, let's get you inside."

While Tank and Lucas helped Greg, Alexis woke up Olive and Felix.

"Are we there?" Olive asked, rubbing the sleep from her eyes.

"Not quite," Alexis said, smiling. "But we're stopping so we can all get some sleep."

"I've been sleeping," Olive said. "I'm good to drive."

Alexis laughed at the smile on Olive's face. "I don't think that's a good idea."

"Me neither," Felix said, stretching.

"Hey, you're supposed to be on my team," Olive said.

"I am, just not with this."

"Traitor."

Alexis laughed. "Let's get inside."

"Okay," Olive said, grabbing her little backpack.

Felix grabbed his also, and she noticed he rested his hand on the gun holstered at his hip. He was checking to make sure he had it. Smart kid. It was both good and sad that he was thinking like that—good because he was growing up fast and could help if they got into a bad situation; bad because he was too young for all of this—but she'd rather have him alive than living a "normal" childhood. They went inside and were soon joined by Troy. Tank went back out to retrieve Chloe and his bag.

"I thought you said this was as good as a Hampton Inn," Chloe said, crinkling her nose when she walked in.

"Did I say that? I meant a Motel 9," Tank said, closing the door. "There's the bed, and that corner is the bathroom. What else do you need?"

"It smells like moldy hay," Olive said.

"I guess as long as it doesn't have anything trying to eat or shoot us, I'm good," Chloe said.

"See, it's not as bad as a Motel 9 in that case," Tank said, "so it's just like the Hampton Inn."

Chloe laughed, and soon everyone joined in.

16

WRECKED

Post-outbreak day 23, late afternoon

A twinge of pain shot up James's leg and he glanced down. It began to hurt more and more as his adrenaline waned. Maybe he was shot worse than he thought. It would be nice to pull over and check, but he could still see the Reclaimer's truck behind him. So, while still driving, he examined his leg. He'd long since tied the arms of his once long-sleeved Kryptek shirt around it to stop the blood flow. It'd helped and the bleeding had stopped, but now it was beginning to throb. Eyes back on the road, he decided there was little he could do besides deal with it since the wound didn't look life threatening.

The increase in pain might be from using it to drive for almost an hour as he'd been using his left leg, but that had tweaked his back. He could put weight on the leg, so it hadn't hit the bone or anything important. Otherwise he wouldn't be able to use it, or he'd be dead already, and since it was neither, he decided to "suck it up buttercup," as his father used to say.

Thinking about his father brought a vague, dreamlike image to mind—him and his dad talking on the ocean shore with an intense feeling of peace. The feeling was almost tangible. Had it been a dream when he was on the rooftop or something more? Whatever it was, it brought a sense of peace, and he couldn't help but smile a little. So what if he was being chased by Reclaimers with a wounded leg, driving an old POS truck that couldn't even go 60 MPH? He was alive, and his friends were, too, and on their way north. It could be a lot worse.

Then something that he'd been trying not to dwell on rose to the front of his mind—Emmett. His smile faded and his heart fell. He'd given his life so James could get away. Tears came to his eyes, and he felt guilty. He shouldn't be smiling. Emmett was gone, killed by the very people chasing him now. The man had been like a father to him over the past few weeks and losing him was like losing his own father all over again. The tears came more freely and he had to wipe them away to clear his vision. Emmett had been one hell of a man, and James would never forget that he was alive because of Emmett.

Without him and Emmett, Alexis would be alone. She would be hurting right now, and he could do nothing to comfort her. He slammed his fist on the steering wheel. His semblance of peace had been shattered and the daydream was gone. Emmett was dead, not to mention Neil and Beverly, and maybe more, all because of those assholes following him. They'd done this to them, and he'd make them pay. They couldn't get away with this.

An hour later, James noticed his low fuel light come on. He was running out of gas, and there was no way he could stop and fuel up with the Reclaimers hot on his tail. They seemed content to just follow him, and he wondered why they weren't shooting yet. Maybe they wanted him alive. But in that case, why shoot at him and almost kill him earlier? Maybe they were hoping he'd take them all the way to the rest of his group so they could slaughter them all. He didn't know and it didn't matter, anyway. He was alive, and if he wanted to stay that way he'd have to act soon. There had to be *something* he could do. He busied himself with trying to think of a plan to lose them, but nothing seemed like a good choice. Trying to turn off on a side road wouldn't work with them so close. He could stop and start firing, but with only the bolt-action rifle and his handgun, he didn't like those odds. Another thought was that he could swing around and ram them, but that would hurt him as bad as them. There had to be *something* he could do.

He was deep in thought when he sped around an overturned semi-truck in the middle of the highway and saw a zombie stand up from a body it'd been devouring. There wasn't even time for him to think about swerving when he smashed into the thing at 45 MPH. The zombie was flung up onto the hood and crashed through the windshield next to him. With glass flying in his face, he put his arm up and was slammed into the steering wheel. He lost control of the truck as it swerved to the right and went into a ditch. Regaining some control, he was able to avoid hitting a tree by punching on the brakes. That slowed him down so the next impact didn't kill him as the front end of the truck smashed into another tree.

James's head snapped forward and collided with the steering wheel.

Ears ringing, James slowly opened his eyes. Everything was fuzzy and his head felt like it was splitting open. He reached up to feel his forehead, and his fingers came away bloody. As his vision began to focus, he recognized the truck he'd taken from Windfall and saw that smoke was rising from the engine. A tree had crushed the passenger side and reduced the zombie to a bloody pile of flesh. He reached over and unbuckled his seat belt; it was a good thing he'd had that on, or he might be lying in front of the truck right now and in a lot worse shape. Something clicked in his mind. The Reclaimers! Frantically, he fumbled to draw his handgun from the holster on his right hip.

"I wouldn't," said a heavily accented voice from the driver's side window, followed by cold metal pressed against his head.

James slowly raised his hands and turned to look. The man with the rifle against James's head was small, maybe five and a half feet, with short brown hair. He looked very plain except for his gray eyes; those were emotionless. James knew that if he so much as twitched, the man would blow his brains all over the cab of the truck.

"Good boy," the man said, his Russian accent obvious.

This guy wasn't just some random killer who was with the Reclaimers. He carried a confidence that bespoke he'd done stuff like this long before the apocalypse.

"Ah, we finally meet, my dear," a female voice said from behind the man. The black-haired woman walked over, and her smile made the hair on his arms stand up. She would've been a beautiful woman if her eyes didn't shine with predatory hunger. "I am Jezz."

"I know who you are," James said, containing his rage. It wouldn't do him any good here.

"And you must be one of the Andderson brothers, yes?" Jezz asked.

"Yeah." His emotions were raging. He didn't know whether he was angry or terrified—maybe a little of both.

"You are not very cordial, are you? I introduced myself, and now it is your turn."

"James."

"Nice to meet you, James. This is Zeke, my associate."

"Slowly get out," Zeke said, backing up but keeping the rifle pointed at James.

Zeke opened the door for him and then stood back. Jezz held her rifle at her side, like she wasn't worried in the least. In order to remain as calm as she was, she must trust Zeke, or maybe she was always like this. James slid out of the seat, careful not to put too much weight on his right leg when he stepped out.

"Get his gun," Jezz said, raising her rifle at his face.

They weren't stupid. They'd done this before. Zeke kept his gun trained on him with one hand as he took James's whole gun belt. James didn't flinch; this wasn't the time to act. If they just wanted to kill him, they would've already done so, unless Jezz wanted to do it slowly. That thought almost made him shiver. She was the kind of evil that would enjoy that. Maybe he *should* try something.

The moment passed as Zeke threw his gun belt into the bed of their truck that was parked a couple of yards away.

"What do you want?" James asked. "Why chase us all this way?"

"Why indeed," Jezz said. "You reclaimed some of ours, so I must return the favor."

She drew a knife from behind her back and started sauntering towards him. James couldn't help it this time—he did shiver. He could *feel* the evil in her. Jezz stopped just in front of him and caressed his cheek with the edge of her knife. It was extremely sharp, drawing a line of blood from his jaw. Willing himself not to move, he stared right into her crazed blue eyes.

"This one has a spine," Jezz said, grinning wickedly. "I like it."

"If you're gonna kill me, just do it," James said, acting braver than he felt.

"In time, in time," Jezz said, taking a step back. "I was hoping you would lead us to the others, but now…"

"We should kill him," Zeke said, the first hint of emotion showing in his voice.

"Not yet. We can use him to get the rest."

"I won't help you kill my friends," James said, clenching his fists. "No matter how much you hurt me."

"Oh, I believe you. We do not need to torture you. I know where they are going. We will use you as bait." Jezz smiled that smile of hers and walked back towards their truck. "Bring him."

Zeke approached him and James thought for a second to try to get the man's weapon, but before he could decide, the stock of the Russian's rifle collided with his forehead. For the second time that evening darkness engulfed him.

17

THE TURTLE AND THE HARE

Post-outbreak day 23, night

This was the slowest hunk of junk Connor had ever driven. While he knew it was faster than walking or even running, it still felt like he was moving at a snail's pace and he'd be better off on foot. He stayed in the dozer though as he "sped" down the highway at 15 MPH. The only good thing was he got to smash all the vehicles in his way. It became a way for him to get some of his pent-up anger out, and he may or may not have been going out of his way to push everything off the highway. That was the *only* positive of this thing. There was no music, it was loud as hell, and the AC was broken, which meant it was hot in the cab—really hot.

The fuel gauge was nearing empty. He'd fueled it up once but hadn't found anything after that. None of the pumps were working so he'd had to syphon some fuel, but that hadn't worked well either, and he knew he didn't have time to be messing around. On this entire stretch of the highway he'd only seen a dozen vehicles that looked like they worked, and yet they either didn't have keys or were out of gas, which only made sense. Why else would they be in the middle of the road otherwise? The passengers had either run out of gas or died, but he couldn't get any of their vehicles running. He'd gotten lucky with the Impala before, and he cursed himself for crashing that and ruining his chance of quickly catching up with his brother.

The dozer's dim lights shone on a truck that was in the middle of the highway fifty yards out, but it was on its side and he doubted it'd work. So he rammed into it with the blade. Glass shattered and metal bent as the truck was pushed off the side of the highway. He smiled a little. It felt good to break things and release just a fraction of the rage contained inside. His brother was being chased by the remaining Reclaimers and here he was going slower than a turtle. It made him feel useless, and he hated that. No matter what he tried, it always seemed to put him even further behind James and the Reclaimers. Why hadn't he just stayed in Windfall after killing the Reclaimer on the roof? He would've run right into his brother and they could've killed the last of the Reclaimers together, but he'd had to go after the man guarding the southern route and total both vehicles. Now he was in a bulldozer that was running out of fuel. Life just had a way of putting him in situations like this.

He wondered how the rest of the group was doing. They were missing five people now. Would they be able to get safely to Alaska with so few? He briefly wondered if this was the right call, but he dismissed that instantly. There was no other option but to go after his brother. James would understand that, and the rest of the group should, too. If not, then too bad. This was the way it had to be. He and his brother had started on this journey together, and they'd finish it that way.

Another thirty minutes passed without finding any vehicles to syphon fuel from, and none of them would start. That left him desperate as the dozer made a coughing noise, shuddered, and then went silent, grinding to a halt. The night was accompanied by a ringing in his ears as he collected his backpack and rifle and climbed out of the cab. Digging out his headlamp, he put it on as he began walking down the highway at a quick pace. There had to be something he could use to travel faster.

The minutes ticked by and still he could find nothing, and he had at least twenty miles until the next town. Finally, he spotted a minivan that had careened off the road and was sitting in a ditch. Feeling hopeful that this one might work, considering that it seemed in good shape, Connor ran over to it and looked in the window. His light shone back at him, but he could make out some of the interior. The inside was trashed and looked like a large animal had made its nest in there. Blood covered most of the windows and other surfaces. A hand smacked against the glass, and Connor didn't even flinch as he raised his rifle and shot the zombie in the face. Something else stirred in the back. Transitioning to his handgun, he opened the driver's door and the body limply fell out. He looked into the back and saw a baby in a car seat. It was moving, reaching towards him with little arms and groaning—a zombie baby. Connor shot it in the head and then checked the rest of the vehicle. It was clear.

Removing both bodies, he looked for the keys and found them in the adult's pocket. Sticking them into the ignition, he hesitated a second, sending up a quick prayer but doubting it would help. It didn't, and the van's engine wouldn't even turn over—dead battery. Connor slammed the steering wheel and then stormed out of the van. He raised his rifle and began to shoot the van as he screamed his frustration. The side windows shattered, stuffing flew into the air, and the metal was puckered with bullet holes. When his magazine ran dry, he pulled it out, shoved it into his vest, and slammed in another one.

He was about to empty that one into the van as well—because what the hell—but he stopped short. There was a bike rack on the top of the van and sitting there like a ruby on a pile of crap was a mountain bike. Climbing onto the roof of the vehicle, he unhooked the bike and lowered it to the ground. It was in great condition—a high-dollar bike with eighteen gears and a frame that looked to be made of carbon fiber. He'd be able to cruise with this thing. The only problem was his giant backpack full of supplies. He wouldn't be able to pedal well with that on his back. An idea popped into his mind and he ran over to the back door of the van. Sitting in the back was a baby trailer for the bike. It had a few bullet holes in the canvas cover, but other than that it was in working order. Cutting the canvas off and taking out the seat and the extra crap he didn't need, he stuck his pack inside and used a bungee cord to hold it down. It was perfect.

Soon, Connor was pedaling down the highway, his backpack in the small trailer behind him. The road was mostly flat there and he was actually making better time than in the dozer. He'd taken a quick break before starting off on the bike to eat a cold MRE and drink from one of his water bottles. It'd energized him, and he was ready to cover some distance until he could find a real ride, but at least he was moving quicker now.

Legs burning, Connor crested a hill and stopped pedaling to coast down the other side. He was doing his best to conserve strength and go as fast as possible while keeping a consistent pace. It'd been hours and he hadn't come across a working vehicle, but he was continuing to check each one quickly, just in case. Light shone on the highway from his headlamp, along with the bike's small front light. He even had a rear red blinking light. That way no one would run into him in the night. Ha!

He could feel his mind starting to stretch towards its breaking point—not only because of the situation, but he was running on very little sleep and food—so he used sheer determination to keep going. His light was reflecting off copious pools of blood in the middle of the highway, and suddenly there was a body right in his path. Jerking the handlebars, he regretted it instantly. He was going too fast, and the bike slid on the pavement as he fell onto his side. Scrapping across the asphalt, he careened into a ditch.

His helmet smacked onto hard ground, dazing him slightly. When he stopped sliding, he lay there for a few seconds collecting himself and then stood up. His left pant leg was shredded, but his pants had protected his leg from getting too chewed up. Feeling his shoulder, he knew it would be scraped up pretty badly. He checked the bike and was shocked to see that besides missing paint and the trailer's frame being bent, it was still in working order. He was about to hop back on when something caught his eye farther up. There was a truck in the ditch that tickled something in his memory. Riding his bike up to it, he saw that it'd smashed into a tree and there was blood on the front seat but no body—besides the mangled corpse of what looked like a zombie.

"Can it be?" Connor whispered. "No."

Examining the truck more closely, he could've sworn that was one of the ones he'd seen in Windfall. It wasn't the same truck he watched pull out with the two Reclaimers in it. But if so, that would mean... He noticed a rifle wedged on the floor. It was an old Winchester bolt-action rifle. That would have belonged to the Reclaimer who'd been on the roof, more than likely. This *was* his brother's getaway truck.

Looking up towards the highway, he noticed something lying there that reflected in the light. It was a chunk of blood-soaked Kryptek fabric. Picking it up, he recognized it as the long sleeve from one of the shirts the Wolf Pack wore. It had to be James's, and if he'd lost that much blood he wouldn't be running—maybe not even walking—away from this crash. Since his body was gone, that meant one of three things—he was either dead, a zombie, or the Reclaimers had taken him.

Any of those outcomes only left one option—find the Reclaimers and kill them all.

18

HARVEST TIME

Post-outbreak day 24, early morning

Tank was roughly shaken awake.

"Get up," Lucas said. "We're in trouble."

"What kind of trouble?" Tank asked, rubbing the sleep from his eyes.

"Uh, the kind where we're surrounded by a massive horde of zombies," Lucas said.

"What?" Tank asked. "You're supposed to keep watch!"

"I was..." Lucas said and then hesitated. "I may have fallen asleep, though."

Tank cursed, quite colorfully. He sat up, grabbed his gun, and listened. Sure enough, he could hear a cacophony of groans coming from outside the barn. Walking over to the ladder leading to the hayloft, he climbed it and carefully looked out the small window where the dim morning light showed a scene straight from a zombie movie. They were completely and utterly screwed—royally. The *entire* field surrounding the barn was filled with more undead than he could count. There had to be hundreds of them, as big as the horde he'd seen back in Fort Collins. This was bad; this was very bad. Where the hell had they come from? They seemed to be on the move, slowly ambling from the east, so maybe they'd come out of Fort Nelson, but what had caused them to start roaming? A lack of food? He'd figured it was only a matter of time until they started to horde up like in the movies. He'd just hoped his group wouldn't end up in the middle of one, like they were now.

Climbing back down, he quietly woke everyone else and told them the situation. They were all wise enough to stay quiet as they slowly packed up their belongings. Maybe if they stayed silent, the horde would pass by. He almost laughed out loud at that. There was not a snowball's chance in hell that something wasn't about to go seriously wrong and put them all in danger. It was time to come up with a plan.

"Huddle up," Tank whispered, motioning everyone to the middle of the barn. They didn't have to worry about the undead getting in easily. Before he'd dozed off, he'd secured all the doors and then had Alexis double check them. "We need a plan, and fast. Shit's about to hit the fan."

The fact that no one told him to watch his language around the kids was a testament to how scared they all were.

"Can we shoot our way out?" Lucas asked.

"No way," Tank whispered. "That'll draw more attention, and the rigs are a solid fifty yards away."

"We can't sneak out," Alexis said.

"Or run," Chloe added.

"Why don't we wait it out?" Troy asked. "They've passed us by so far."

"That won't last," Tank said.

To accentuate his point, glass shattered in the back window and a decomposing arm followed by a mangled face tried to fit through the way-too-small opening. The undead groaned loudly and quickly worked itself into a frenzy, which would just attract more.

"See," Tank said casually, pointing behind him with his thumb. "And the doors won't hold with hundreds of bodies pushin' against 'em."

"What about that?" Olive asked, pointing to the large combine harvester sitting in the back of the barn.

Tank was ready to shut the idea down when he looked at the thing again. It was basically a giant lawnmower with one large cylindrical rotating set of blades on the front.

"Oh, hell yeah," Tank said, a smile growing on his face. "Anyone know how to drive one of those?"

"My parents owned a farm," Troy said, moving to the large piece of machinery. "I'm rusty but should be able to get it goin'."

"Okay," Tank said, "I'll go with Troy and keep 'em from gettin' into the cab. The rest of you climb into the hayloft, and when you see an openin', book it to the rigs. Time to get some gears in motion."

"Be careful out there," Chloe said, walking over to him.

"I'm always careful, baby," Tank said, pulling her into a kiss.

"That's a lie."

Tank shrugged as he pulled the SAW machine gun from his backpack, tucked his ACR into the pack, and handed it up to Lucas. The undead were now frantically trying to get in. The two massive front doors shook from the bodies pressing against them. There was no way he could get them open to get the combine out. Oh well, it'd just make for a dramatic exit. The combine's massive engine roared to life, and Troy gave him the thumbs up.

"I love ya, babe," Tank yelled as he climbed onto the green beastie just outside the cab.

With one hand gripping the handle and the other holding his SAW, he nodded to Troy. The combine jerked forward and Tank gripped the handle tighter. The double doors loomed in front of them and he briefly wondered if he should've gotten into the cab instead of hanging outside. It was too late now.

The combine burst through the doors, pieces of wood flying into the air. As soon as they were clear of the doors, Troy started up the massive blades, and a half second later they hit the first undead. The thing died in a spray of blood and flinging body parts. It was a gorgeously gruesome mess. Encouraged by their success, they headed onto the field which was swarming with undead. It was time to harvest some walking corpses. The combine's blades may not have been designed to decimate human bodies, but it sure worked well.

Tank laughed as he looped his arm through the handle and started shooting his SAW wildly. Bullets smashed into undead bodies as others were turned into a red paste by the blades. Legs, arms, hands, feet, and all sorts of body parts rained down around them like confetti at a birthday party. It just made him laugh all the harder as they mowed down dozens of undead in the first few seconds.

Troy did an excellent job of taking out the ones between the barn and the vehicles. Then he started doing a circuit of the barn. The rest of the undead in the field were drawn to them by the horrible noise of the roaring engine, the shattering bones, and the squish of flesh being rendered into slush. They finished their circuit of the barn and saw that most of the undead were just pieces scattered on the field. There were a few here and there, but not many in their general vicinity. The SAW clicked empty as he continued to hold the trigger. Grabbing his second box of belted ammunition from his tactical vest, he began to reload during the lull in the action.

The rest of their group shot out from the barn, Alexis leading the way with her rifle to her shoulder, taking down a few stragglers. Lucas was helping Greg limp in the middle of the group with Olive as Felix and Chloe covered their six. His girlfriend had a look of pure determination in her eyes as she fired the shotgun into the face of a legless undead crawling towards them. His heart swelled with pride at his girl. She was a one-of-a-kind woman, that was for sure.

Slamming down the cover on the top of his gun, he worked the action. It was time to rock-and-roll. He noticed a huge group of undead through the trees to the east of their vehicles in the next field over. Their group wouldn't be able to beat them to the rigs.

"Over there!" Tank yelled, beating on the glass of the cab and pointing.

Troy looked and then adjusted the direction of the combine as they went around the northern edge of the tree line and into the neighboring field. The undead on the other side changed their course and started towards them, the more obvious attractant. These things were beyond mindless as they reached their arms towards the swirling blades of death. Even as the thing ripped their arms off, they continued coming. It was glorious mayhem, and he almost started laughing again when the combine belched smoke out the front. That wasn't good. They must have reached the maximum threshold for harvesting walking corpses as the blades slowly lost power and stopped rotating. He looked over and noticed that his group had made it to the vehicles.

"Let's go!" Tank yelled as he banged on the glass.

Troy left the combine running and climbed out of the cab as Tank aimed at the few undead between them and the trees. He mowed them down, but before he could jump to the ground, more undead came around both sides of the combine and blocked off their escape.

Tank cursed as he started picking off undead with his SAW. Troy stood next to him and started shooting his bolt-action rifle. The rigs started up and soon they pulled out, heading their way through an old dirt road in the trees. Alexis's head popped out of the top of Scourge and she opened fire. Between her, Tank, and Troy, they were able to thin out the undead enough for Lucas to pull the truck next to the combine as Chloe drove Scourge ahead. Tank jumped into the bed of the truck, followed by Troy, and Lucas took off, following Chloe. Alexis was taking out as many undead as she could in front of them, but she couldn't kill them all. Chloe didn't hesitate. She gunned it and Scourge smashed through the remaining undead, crushing them beneath the tires. They were clear all the way to the highway now.

Damn, I love that woman! Tank thought as Chloe smashed through a metal gate and bounced through the ditch to get onto the highway.

She pulled to a stop after a few hundred yards and Troy climbed into the cab of the truck as Tank ran up and jumped into the passenger's seat of Scourge. The horde was still slowly following them—not that they had much to worry about now. The undead couldn't keep up at 60 MPH.

"Well done, ladies," Tank said. "I'm impressed."

"Why? Because we're women?" Chloe asked with an odd smile on her face.

"Nah, just because you saved our asses," Tank said.

"Hey," Olive said. "Language."

"Oh, right," Tank said.

"You're welcome," Alexis said from the middle seat, reloading her M4.

"Why don't you pull off up here and we'll switch," Tank said to Chloe.

"Have you seen yourself?" Chloe asked. "You should be sitting on the floor."

Tank looked down; he was completely covered in blood and gore, and there was even an ear caught in his plate carrier. "Fair point. Stop at the next stream."

A few minutes later, they crossed a bridge and Chloe pulled to a stop. Tank grabbed a fresh Kryptek uniform and went out of sight under the bridge. He stripped down and washed himself off, along with his clothes and plate carrier. Putting the clean clothes on, he left his plate carrier off and walked back up to the road. He put a rock on his clothes in the bed of the truck to help them dry and carried his wet plate carrier back to Scourge. Alexis had cleaned off the seat where he'd been sitting, but she was now in the passenger seat and Chloe was still in the driver's seat.

"Hey babe, you can get out now," Tank said, going over to the driver's door.

"Nah, I like driving," Chloe said with that same smile from before.

It was like she was surprised that she enjoyed running over the undead—almost like she was discovering a new part of herself. He wasn't sure if that was good or bad since she wouldn't let him drive now.

"C'mon," Tank said. "It's my baby."

"No, I'm your baby," Chloe said with a wink. "Now, get in the back seat or I'll leave you."

Tank was speechless for the first time in his entire life. Who was this woman? She was like the old Chloe who wouldn't take any crap crossed with a new, more confident version of herself. Did this just come up from driving Scourge, or had it been building inside her? He walked around to the back seat, unsure of what he felt, but as he climbed in and Chloe glanced back at him with a grin on her face, he couldn't help but smile as well.

Okay, so maybe it isn't such a bad thing, he thought as Chloe stepped on the gas and threw them into the backs of their seats.

19

CAPTURED

Post-outbreak day 24, morning

The morning sun shone in his eyes and James stirred awake. The first thing he noticed was that his head felt like someone had driven a nail into it. Then, as he tried to touch it, he realized his hands were tied behind his back. Opening his eyes fully, he noticed he was lying on his side in the back seat of a truck. Zeke was driving, and Jezz was asleep in the passenger seat, a jacket balled up between her head and the window. When she was sleeping, she almost looked normal, but the memory of that look in her eyes kept him from believing that for even a second.

Zeke glanced back at him in the rearview mirror and grunted. That must be his version of "good morning."

"Where are we?" James asked through a dry mouth.

Zeke ignored his question and continued to drive, glancing back at him regularly. The man didn't trust him. While normally it would be good to have the respect of one's enemies, in this particular circumstance it just meant they'd be extra careful with him, and that lowered his chances of escaping. Anything could happen, though, so he'd bide his time and be ready when he got the opportunity.

Someone had bandaged his leg and it felt better than before. He was blessed that it wasn't anything serious although it was bad enough to make walking difficult and running near impossible. His entire body ached, and there were now bruises on top of his bruises. In the span of twenty-four hours, he'd been blow up, almost drowned, shot at, and then in a car wreck, and he felt every part of it. While no one thing hurt badly—like his side when he'd gotten hit with that piece of shrapnel—his *whole* body was extremely sore. He'd never been in a car wreck before, and while he'd almost drowned on a hunting trip in Alaska, it wasn't like the other night.

Thank you, Lord for keeping me alive, James prayed. *If you could continue to keep me that way, it'd be much appreciated. Amen.*

Even though he knew there was a reason he was alive here and now, he couldn't help the guilt he felt. So many of them had died along the way, and yet here he was—almost dead more times than he could count in the last three weeks—but he was still kicking. What made him special? It wasn't that he wanted to die; he just didn't know why the rest had to die while he lived.

He shook himself mentally. This line of thinking would get him nowhere. He was alive, and he'd make the most of it until he drew his last breath, whether that was today or in eighty years. As soon as he was able, he'd have a memorial for all those who'd given their lives to help them on their way. Their sacrifices would be honored—his parents, Felicia, Mila, all the others from Burns, Captain Miller, Neil, Beverly, Emmett, and the unknown Reclaimer who'd let him go and was more than likely dead now because of it. He would honor all of them, first and foremost by continuing to live and to fight until his last breath to get his group to safety.

Emmett's death was the most palpable at the moment, and James wouldn't let him down. He'd get them all safely to Alaska, and once there, he'd be the leader his group needed. It was up to him now and he wouldn't fail them. He would—

James caught himself, it was *not* up to him. It was up to God. *He* would be the one who got them safely to Alaska, not James. It would be good for him to remember that so he didn't fall into the same trap he always found himself in. Maybe his last breakdown had changed his habit of always trying to take control. The urge to take back the reins would always be there, but maybe this time it would be easier to rest on God's strength and not his own. That would be another sweet tattoo he could get: *By His strength.*

"Why're you smiling?" Zeke asked, and James noticed just how heavy the man's accent was. Last night he'd been a little too preoccupied to really notice. It made him think of Ana for the first time in a while. Was she still alive out there somewhere?

"Just enjoying the ride," James said, referring to a lot more than their current traveling.

"I can change that," Zeke said, a little emotion leaking into his voice.

James could tell the man was normally stoic and emotionless, but sometimes when he talked to or looked at James, he could see a deep rage buried below the surface. What had they done to piss the guy off? Well, they *had* killed a lot of his friends and decimated their entire group—twice. So yeah, he could guess why Zeke was so pissed.

"That's a Russian accent, isn't it?" James asked. Zeke ignored him. "Are you originally from there?" When he didn't answer, James continued, trying to get a response. "So, where are we? Did we drive all through the night?"

Zeke gripped the steering wheel tighter, and James decided to hold off on the questions for now. He wouldn't put it past the man to kill him while Jezz slept. It seemed that the only thing holding him back was the leader of the Reclaimers. He'd have to be more careful around him.

Zeke reached over and turned on the radio. There was nothing but static. Flipping down the visor, he began to look through the dozen CDs in the holder on the back. He picked one out and put it in the player. *Highway to Hell* by AC/DC began to play and Zeke turned the volume up.

James just smiled. Not only was the song fitting, but Zeke could have picked worse music, like some crappy pop. With nothing better to do, he closed his eyes and let his mind drift, which conjured images of Alexis, of course. A mind in love can do little else. He could see her smile as she sat across from him on their first date behind the diner in Coutts, the feel of her lips on his as they shared their first kiss, and the sound of her laugher as he said something stupid. It still amazed him that in the middle of the apocalypse, he'd found love. Then again, he'd always joked that it might take the end of the world for him to find a girl. Turned out that was exactly what it had taken.

He must've dozed off at some point because he woke up as the truck pulled to an abrupt stop, almost throwing him off the seat. Opening his eyes, he had a hard time looking over the dash at what had caused the sudden stop. Zeke was saying something in another language, probably Russian, and Jezz was staring straight ahead.

"We cannot get through," Jezz said in her weirdly stilted way of speaking.

"I saw a road back a kilometer or so," Zeke said, throwing the truck into reverse.

"Good," Jezz said. "We must be gaining on them. Something got these dead ones stirred up."

James caught a glimpse of a massive horde of zombies on the road as Zeke turned the truck around. Most of them were heading to the west, but the back few had turned at the sound of the truck.

Perfect! James thought.

While he'd love to catch up with his group and watch them kill his captors, he'd much rather that never happened. There was too high a probability that someone would get killed by one of the two villains in the front seat.

"Where are we?" James asked as they turned onto a road heading north. What *had* gotten the zombies all worked up? Hopefully, his group was safe.

"Just outside of Fort Nelson," Jezz said, glancing back at him with that smile of hers.

Fort Nelson? That was in British Columbia if he remembered correctly. That would mean they'd been on the ALCAN for a couple of hours. If his group had driven straight though since the ambush, they'd be quite a way ahead of them, unless they'd stopped to rest. Crap, maybe they were gaining on his group. Zeke was driving like a maniac at 70 MPH when he could, and James hated to admit it, but they were eating up the miles. He hoped his group was duplicating the Reclaimer's progress, but they seemed to hit trouble every few hundred miles. Then again, when the trouble happened to be homicidal maniacs, it made things even harder. But if he was *with* the homicidal maniacs, it just made logical sense that he'd be making better time.

"So, what's your plan?" James asked, taking a chance. Jezz seemed to like talking, so maybe he could get some information out of her.

"You will see," she said. "Be patient."

So much for that.

"We should kill him," Zeke said in a low voice. "We can reclaim the rest easily enough."

"Do you need to be reminded of how slippery they are?" Jezz asked.

"You won't catch them either way," James said. "They're ready for you now."

"I do not doubt it," Jezz said. "But with you as leverage..."

Zeke glanced back at him in the rearview mirror, and for the first time, James saw the emotion plain in his eyes—pure, unbridled rage. This man was going to kill him as soon as he got a chance.

20

THE ROCKIES

Post-outbreak day 24, morning

Alexis was dozing on and off in the back seat, and Chloe had finally let Tank drive after a couple of hours. Greg was doing better, so she'd taken his tube out and stitched him up, with instructions to be careful. He was asleep again as his body would need to heal. It was about time they stopped for gas and some food. They'd eaten last night when they'd stopped in the barn, but she was starving already.

The thought faded from her mind, however, as she dozed off again in the warm sunlight. She dreamed of James, as she often did now, but at the end of it her dad was there as well. She awoke with a feeling of loss and sadness that she had to shove down before she let it get a grip on her. This was no time to be weak. After they got to safety, then she could break down. It was how her dad always did things, yet it was harder for her, and soon a few tears were falling onto her lap. She quickly wiped her eyes as something caught her attention through the windshield.

"Are those..." she whispered aloud.

"The Rocky Mountains," Tank said. "Over three thousand miles of badassery."

"Wow," Alexis said, gazing around in wonder.

They were just like she'd imagined, but bigger. Their peaks reached up into the sky, and she admired their spruce-tree-covered slopes. A large river ran in the bottom of a valley to their left. This was what she'd been expecting when they'd driven through Wyoming, and it helped the despair gripping her heart loosen as she gazed at the sheer majesty unfolding before her.

"Should we wake the others?" Alexis asked, wanting them to see this too.

"Nah," Tank said. "Let 'em sleep. We'll be seein' bigger mountains in the next couple days."

"Bigger?"

"Oh yeah. These are just the little guys."

That was hard to believe. These seemed huge! She couldn't help but be in awe of the splendor. A smile split her face, despite her gloomy mood.

"Pretty awesome, aren't they?" Tank asked.

"They are."

"I loved livin' in 'em back in the day."

"You were in Fort Collins when all this happened, right?"

"Yeah, but I spent all of junior and high school livin' at nine thousand feet in the middle of the San Juan Mountains. It was awesome."

"What took you to Fort Collins then?"

"College, and I needed to get the hell outta that town." He must've seen the question on her face because he continued. "It was a small town with a lotta drama. I mean a *lot* of drama."

"But you liked living there, anyway?"

"For the most part. James, Connor, and my family being there helped, but I got out as soon as I could."

"That bad, huh?"

"Yep. I went back a few times each year, but when my ma died, I stopped visitin'."

"I'm sorry to hear that. How'd she die?"

"Cancer. It's a deadly bastard."

"I had an aunt on my mom's side. She died from breast cancer."

Tank nodded, then not so subtly changed the subject. "Is what the brothers told me true? About what you learned in the infirmary basement?"

"I'm afraid so."

"So your grandpa helped create this virus?"

"I'm not sure if he helped create it, but he had a hand in the whole situation, yes."

"And he thinks we're all infected and that when we die, we turn?"

"That was his theory."

"Huh, that blows."

Alexis unconsciously moved her hand to the pocket that held the note from her Grandpa Al. He'd somehow slipped it into her plate carrier before they'd left Coutts. It talked about how sorry he was to bring this on the world, and especially her. He gave her as much information as he could think of that would help them survive, but it was nothing new. In it, he also told her a story about her mother as a child, one Alexis had heard often but still brought tears to her eyes. He told her to tell Emmett he doesn't blame him for Jane's death and that he was proud of him. He finally ended by telling Alexis how much he loved her.

It had been a surprise when she'd found it, and at first she'd almost thrown it out the window. She still wasn't sure how she felt towards him being a part of all this. Given her ambivalence, she'd decided against tossing it out, and she was glad for it. The note was exactly what she needed to hear, and she would cherish it. He'd also enclosed the picture from his desk of the whole family, including a young Mason. It was the only picture she had of her family now.

"Let's get fuel here," Tank said into the radio.

"Got it," Troy responded.

They pulled off the two-lane highway. There wasn't even a town there, just a large square building that had fuel, a bakery, and boat rentals. She'd noticed an increasing number of signs for Muncho Lake, and she figured they must be close.

They came to a stop and everyone slowly stirred from their various states of napping. Alexis stepped out and was once again in awe of her surroundings. Miles behind the fuel station, a group of mountains rose into the sky like the teeth of some massive beast. Those must have been steep because halfway up there were no trees, just grey rock.

"Look at those!" Olive said pointing as she climbed out of Scourge.

"Wow," Felix said, after he'd scanned the immediate area.

"Pretty cool, huh?" Alexis asked, her gaze locked on the mountains.

"Enough droolin'," Tank said. "Alexis, I need you to keep watch while we fuel up."

"What about the bathroom?" Olive asked.

"You'll have to get one of the ladies to help you on the other side of the rig," Tank said, taking the fuel nozzle and sticking it into Scourge. "That buildin's too big to clear."

"I can help," Chloe said, walking up to Olive.

"Ah, hell," Tank muttered.

"What?" Alexis asked, jerking around to look at him.

"The pumps don't work," Tank said, hanging the nozzle back up. "Either no power or out of gas. I knew we'd come to this sooner or later."

"What now?" Lucas asked, coming over to them.

"Syphon some gas for the truck and diesel for Scourge," Troy said.

"Precisely," Tank said. "Smart kid."

Alexis glanced over at Troy and noticed he was looking at her, smiling. He'd always been nice to her but had grown more distant during their time in Coutts.

"Alexis and I can go check around back for some gas cans," Troy said.

"I'll stay here," Greg said weakly from the back seat of Scourge.

"Good," Tank said. "Lucas and I will look for a hose. And Chloe, you stay here and watch the kids."

"I can help," Felix said.

Tank looked at him and smiled. He walked over and knelt by Felix. "I know you can, kid," Tank whispered to him, "but I need someone to watch my girl. Can you keep her safe for me?"

Felix puffed out his chest. "Yes, sir."

"Good," Tank said, standing up. "Now, let's fill them tanks!"

Alexis smiled at the interaction. It seemed that being in charge of the group was really bringing out a different side of Tank. She joined

Troy as they walked around the building to check out the three sheds behind.

"How're you holding up?" Troy asked as they approached the first shed.

"I'm trying not to dwell on it," Alexis said, opening the door as Troy covered her.

"Makes sense," Troy said, lowering his bolt-action rifle when they didn't encounter any threats. "If you ever need to talk, I'm here."

"Thanks, Troy," Alexis said. "That means a lot."

She hadn't realized Troy was this much of a friend to her. It felt good to know she had someone other than Chloe because Alexis didn't want to burden her with all her problems when Chloe had enough of her own, although she seemed to be doing considerably better after the barn fiasco. Thinking of the barn made her miss Ana and those long hours together in the back of her dad's truck. Alexis hoped she was still alive but doubted she'd ever see her again.

"Here we go," Alexis said, finding two full gas jugs. "This'll work."

"I found these, too," Troy said, showing off a couple of axes and a shovel.

"Bring 'em," Alexis said, hefting the red jugs.

"Do you want me to get those?" Troy asked, jogging to catch up to her.

"No, thanks. Just keep me covered."

"Right."

She arrived back at the rigs and set the jugs down by the truck.

"Good find," Chloe said. "I'll start filling. You got us, Felix?"

"Yes, ma'am," Felix said, handgun held in a firm but not tight grip, his eyes scanning all around.

Olive stood next to Felix with a small pocket knife, watching his blind spots. They'd need to get the girl something a little more practical. Not a gun yet, but maybe a bigger knife or something. Even though she might not have the strength to use it, Alexis knew it'd be what James and her dad would do.

She and Troy returned to check the other two sheds, finding three empty jugs that she let Troy carry this time. Everyone was back by the vehicles when they returned. Chloe had already emptied the other jugs into the truck. Tank cut a clear hose he'd found into two pieces.

"Over here, ladies and gentlemen," Tank said, leading them to a truck with a camper that was parked by the building.

He then proceeded to show them how to syphon gas and had Troy and Lucas practice. Troy acted like he knew what he was doing, which brought some questions to mind, and Lucas got a mouthful of gasoline, which he proceeded to hack up. They were able to fill two of the jugs and empty those into the truck as well, which almost filled it up. There were no other vehicles around to syphon fuel from.

"I saw a sign for a lodge farther up," Tank said. "We'll stop there and do our tank drain shuffle."

"Our what?" Chloe asked.

"Tank. Drain. Shuffle. You know? Where you drain one tank and fill another?"

"You mean take a pee and fill the gas?" Olive asked.

"Yep!" Tank exclaimed. "You're a smart little girl. I see why James took a likin' to you."

Olive practically beamed at the compliment, and Chloe got an odd look on her face as she watched Tank.

"Well, we should probably hit it," Troy said, walking over to his truck.

"Yep," Tank said. "Load up, y'all."

"Y'all?" Alexis asked as she moved to sit in the back seat.

"Just tryin' it out," Tank said. "I don't like it."

"You should leave that to us Texans."

"Good plan."

"Why don't you say 'y'all'?" Olive asked Alexis once they were all loaded into Scourge.

"That's a good question," Alexis said. "I guess my dad never said it, so I just didn't pick it up. Not *everyone* from Texas says 'y'all,' just most of them."

"Oh—" Olive began to say but then cut off as the trees ended around them and Muncho Lake came into view. "Wow!"

Wow was right. They were high in a valley in the middle of the mountains and sitting in the bottom of that valley was a clear blue lake. Not only was the water pristine, but the lake was huge—at least a half mile across—and it went on past where they could see. It had to be miles long.

"That's gorgeous," Chloe said.

"I've never seen anything like this," Alexis said.

"Pretty cool, isn't it?" Tank asked.

"Don't tell me you've seen something like this, too?" Alexis asked.

"I used to live on the second largest natural lake in Colorado," Tank said. "At nine thousand feet."

"Not all of us had the chance to grow up in the mountains," Chloe said.

"I think," Olive said, "this'll be what heaven looks like."

"I could dig that," Tank said.

Alexis smiled at the pure childlike wonder in that girl. She was just an endless well of joy and faith. It was crazy how someone so young could be so influential to those around her.

"It's pretty sweet," Felix said, gazing out the window.

"You guys seeing this?" Lucas asked through the radio.

"Of course," Chloe replied.

The sunlight reflected off small waves as the wind moved the surface of the lake. Alexis didn't think she'd ever seen water that blue before. This was what she'd always thought the mountains would look like—pristine lakes, peaks rising all around, clear blue skies, spruce trees, and mountain streams. This was paradise on earth. She'd always loved Texas, but there was just something about the mountains that felt like coming home. Her heart was overflowing with joy.

"Alexis," Greg said, wincing. "I don't feel so good."

Her attention snapped back to the present, and she took in Greg's pale face.

"Okay, hold still," Alexis said, moving to check his pulse. It was racing. She felt his forehead and it was on fire. "Did you get out of the vehicle when we stopped back there?"

"Yeah," Greg said. "I had to take a leak."

"You probably overexerted yourself," Alexis said, moving from the seat. "Lie down and rest. I'll keep an eye on you."

Greg laid down, using their rolled-up coats like a pillow as he settled on his side. He closed his eyes and it seemed like some of the pain left his face.

"How's that?" Alexis asked.

"Better," Greg said. "I'm sorry for all this. I should've been paying more attention back there."

"Dude," Tank said, "you were shot. Not much you could've done. Plus, you got Lucas and Troy out safely. I'd say that's pretty damn brave."

"You did well, Greg," Chloe said.

"Thanks," Greg said, a small smile on his face. "Imma rest now."

"Good idea," Alexis said, checking his pulse again. It had gone down somewhat, which was good. He'd probably just over-worked himself getting out and walking around.

"Is he going to die?" Olive asked quietly.

"Shhh," Alexis said. "He's trying to sleep."

"Well, is he?" Felix asked.

"I honestly don't know," Alexis said. She knew she'd done all she could, yet it didn't stop the hopelessness from creeping in. "All we can do is wait and pray."

"I've been praying," Olive said. "For everyone."

"Good, keep it up," Alexis said.

"Looks like there's a lodge up ahead," Tank said. "We'll stop there and syphon off some fuel from all those RVs."

$$21$$

SILVER LINING

Post-outbreak day 24, early afternoon

"How did you let us run out of gas?" Jezz hissed.

"The gauge is broken," Zeke responded, keeping his tone calm.

They were standing off to the side of the truck with the hood up. They'd been there for a while as Zeke tried to figure out what had gone wrong, and apparently he'd just figured it out. James didn't know how the Russian kept calm with that woman screaming in his face. He'd seen how she could fly off the handle with little warning. Her being a heartless killer made for a bad combination with those around her.

Jezz's hand crept towards the knife she kept at her back as she eyed Zeke, who was bent over the engine again. James almost wished she'd do it. That way, there'd be one less of them to worry about. Then again, that might also mean he would be next.

Zeke wiped his hands off on the rag he'd gotten from the back of the truck and slammed the hood shut. "We're not going anywhere without gas," he said, throwing the rag on the ground.

"Then I suggest you find some," Jezz said, her voice as cold as a mid-winter's frost.

Zeke glanced at her, a dangerous light in his eyes. It seemed that his captors weren't set on who was boss, or maybe one was just tired of being bossed around. Either way, things were getting heated quickly.

Zeke turned away without a word and grabbed a gas can from the back of the truck. He glanced at James on his way back down the highway and the look made James shiver. The verdict was out on who had the deadliest light in their eyes. Jezz had the "crazy murderer" look to her, but Zeke had the steely determination of a professional killer—someone who excelled in the art of finding ways to end lives. In comparison, Jezz was just plain unhinged. Both were bad in their own rights, and James was trapped between the two.

Great place to be, he thought.

Jezz walked up after Zeke had left and opened the passenger door, grabbing her rifle.

"I need to piss," James said. He'd been tied up in the back all night and day, and his muscles were on fire.

Jezz glanced back at him and then walked around to the rear door by his feet. "If you try anything, I *will* reclaim you," she said.

"Sounds fair."

She untied his legs and then pulled him out. He stood shakily as his feet hit the ground, his muscles protesting after being cooped up for so long.

"Umm, my hands?"

"Nice try. Those are staying."

"Then how..." James let the question drop.

"You will figure it out," Jezz said with a smile.

"I guess you won't mind the smell of piss in the truck then."

James walked a couple of steps away.

"Stop."

He turned around and she ambled towards him with her knife in hand. The instinct to run overwhelmed him, and he barely managed to stand his ground as the image of a predatory cat entered his mind. She slashed out with her knife, cutting through his bonds.

"Try *anything* and you die."

"Yes, ma'am," James said, stretching his arms.

They ached something fierce. As he limped over to do his business, he noticed that Jezz kept her rifle on him the whole time. There was no cover for twenty yards, and she was standing only ten feet away. Even if she was a horrible shot, with a fully automatic weapon at that range he'd be dead before he ever closed the distance. This was definitely not the time to try anything.

It took him a while to relieve himself since he'd been holding it for hours and there was a woman watching him. Once he was done, he slowly limped back.

"Any chance I could get some water and food?" James asked. Without taking her eyes off him, she reached into the front seat of the truck and tossed him something. He caught it and looked down at the pair of handcuffs. "I guess that's a no."

He thought about trying to cuff his hands in front, but he had a feeling that wouldn't go over well. These people knew how to properly keep hostages, and so without any options and not wanting to get filled full of holes, he cuffed his hands behind his back. He even tightened them until they were snug.

"Get in the back," Jezz said.

James did as he was asked but waited for the right moment to head-butt and then overpower her. She never gave him the chance. Setting her rifle down, she drew her knife and pressed it to his throat while she reached over and buckled the seat belt across him. Then she pulled out all the slack on the belt so there was no give when it retracted. Removing the knife from his throat, she shut the door, picked up her rifle, and sat on the lowered tailgate to keep watch for Zeke's return.

The minutes turned to hours as the afternoon became evening and still there was no sign of Zeke. James thought he'd seen a few vehicles a couple of miles back, but whether they actually had any gas was a mystery. If they were abandoned in the middle of the highway, chances were good they'd run out of fuel. Zeke would probably be able to walk two to three miles an hour, so if he'd taken this long, it meant he'd gone farther than three miles. Or maybe he'd run into trouble. Maybe he was dead. The thought brought him some hope, but he realized how unlikely that was.

He had to look at the silver lining though. At least he was sitting up now and was in a more comfortable position even though his shoulders were killing him from having his hands behind his back for hours on end. But he knew it could be worse; he could be dead. He sent up another prayer, which he'd been doing consistently for the past few days.

Hey Jesus, I could really use some help here, but ultimately your will and not mine be done. I ask more so that you watch out for the rest of my group. Keep them safe and help them get to safety. I know you have a plan in all this, somehow. I trust you. By your strength, Lord. Amen.

He always felt a little better when he got done praying and this was no different. There was still hope, and unlike before, he wouldn't let this get him down. He didn't think everything was all sunshine and roses, but he wouldn't try to do everything on his own either. He'd trust and rely on God. Life was much easier that way. He'd attempted the other way too many times, and he'd learned his lesson.

With nothing better to do, James closed his eyes once again. At least he could get some sleep and rest up for when he'd need strength to escape.

Before long, the sound of an engine reached his ears from the south. Someone was coming. James opened his eyes and craned his neck, but he couldn't get the angle he needed. Could it be Zeke with a new vehicle? As he glanced around, he noticed that Jezz was nowhere to be seen. Now where had she gotten off to, and how long had he been asleep? The sun was still relatively in the same location in the sky, so it couldn't have been more than a few minutes.

Finally, the vehicle came into view on the highway, and it looked like a dark-colored Ford Raptor. He'd always loved those trucks. They looked badass, and whoever was driving had good taste. As the truck drew closer, he got a glimpse of auburn hair glinting in the sunlight.

22

NEW RIDE

Post-outbreak day 24, early afternoon

From his position in front of the Northern Rockies Lodge on Muncho Lake, Tank watched the undead drawing closer. He'd pulled past the lodge and up to the small gas station next to it. The pumps had been dry, so they were stuck with syphoning gas again—probably for the remainder of the trip. He stood in the middle of the parking lot with Troy and Lucas, each armed with an axe. Alexis and Chloe were behind them with their guns ready in case things got out of hand. There were only four undead coming at them, but he knew more were scattered among the surrounding RVs. They needed fuel and would have to get to those vehicles one way or another.

An idea hit him.

"You got these?" Tank asked.

"Oh, yeah," Troy said, hefting his weapon.

"Good, I'll be back," Tank said as he ran to Scourge. "Chloe, Alexis, get in the bed of the truck. Olive and Felix, open the hatch and get on the roof to watch our backs."

"Yes, sir," Felix said.

"What're you thinking?" Chloe asked as she walked up.

"We need to get to those rigs, and instead of runnin' into the undead at random, I'm gonna draw 'em out."

"Is that a good idea?" Alexis asked.

"We can see everythin' comin' for a ways. If there are too many, we'll fall back and thin 'em out with the guns."

"I mean, it *sounds* like a good plan," Chloe said.

Alexis nodded while climbing into the bed of the truck parked alongside the road.

Tank went over to Scourge and turned the engine on, then picked up his iPod. Flipping through it, he found the song he was looking for. *Already Dead* by I Prevail played through the speakers, and he turned it up loud. Moving away from Scourge, he listened and decided to turn it up even louder. He wanted to draw all of them from around the lodge. Returning to his spot by Troy and Lucas, he noticed they'd already taken down the four undead as several more started towards them from between the vehicles. This was about to get messy.

Hefting Frostmourne, he brought the sword down on one of the undead's skulls, careful not to swing too hard. The creature dropped in a heap at his feet and he took a step forward, swinging at another. A decapitated body fell to the ground, followed shortly by its head.

"It's nothin' to lose your head over," Tank mumbled between breaths as he took down another undead.

The surrounding area was soon littered with bodies and gore. Blood oozed onto the gravel, and brain matter splattered in unique mosaics on the ground. A few minutes later, Tank stood with his sword tip resting on the ground as he tried to catch his breath. There'd been quite a few more than he thought, but Chloe and Alexis had helped thin them so they weren't overrun. His plan had worked, however. No one was injured and they'd been able to take down all the undead in a controlled manner.

Tank walked back to Scourge. A Reason to Live by JT Music was playing and he let it finish to draw out any stragglers.

"Fifty-six," Lucas said, as Tank walked back. "We took down thirty-two while the girls handled the rest."

"That would've been a problem if they hadn't been so spread out," Troy said.

"But they were," Tank said, wiping his blade off with one of the undead's shirts that wasn't too bloody.

He'd have to clean it soon with the oil Tom had given him. Thinking about the grouchy old mechanic brought back memories. The man had made him promise to use the sword to make the world a better place for Tank's future kids. He was doing that now, but he couldn't help but feel that there was still something greater he'd have to do to make good on that promise. It was just a strange feeling in his gut. Or maybe the MREs weren't agreeing with him.

"Let's get the truck and drive around to each vehicle," Tank said. "We'll have one in the truck ready to cover and two gettin' fuel, just to be safe. Chloe, stay with Scourge and honk if we need to get outta here."

"I can do that," Chloe said, giving him a quick kiss before sauntering over to the LAPV. "But I want to join in the fun next time."

She really was an odd woman, but he loved it.

"Troy, drive us, and Alexis, cover us," Tank said, hopping into the bed of the truck with Lucas and Alexis.

"I *am* your best shot," Alexis said, smiling.

It seemed like a little of Chloe's sass was rubbing off on her. Maybe she was dealing with the losses better than he'd originally assumed.

They drove over to the first vehicle, and Tank and Lucas hopped out to begin the process. Twenty minutes later, they had both rigs filled, along with eight jugs, half of those diesel.

"Why don't we take one of the RVs?" Troy asked, tying the rest of the jugs tight in the bed of the truck.

"That's not a bad idea," Alexis said.

"No, it's not," Tank said. He looked at all the motorhomes scattered around and realized they had a lot of options. There were big ones, small ones, cheap ones, and fancy ones. He picked out one that was mid-size and newer looking. "Let's check it out."

He led the way to the RV, with Alexis and Troy behind him. Lucas stayed with the truck. Nodding to Alexis, she opened the door as Tank stood ready outside. A horrid stench assailed his nose, and he gagged.

"Shut it," Tank said through a cough. Alexis did so quickly, a look of disgust on her face.

"Not a good pick," Troy said, holding his nose.

"That one," Alexis said as she walked away from the foul-smelling vehicle.

Tank looked to where she was pointing and noticed another mid-sized RV that was about thirty feet long with a rack on the back that held a cooler and could fit the gas cans. This one turned out to be in pristine condition after they threw out the rotten food in the fridge. There was a bedroom with a queen bed in the back and enough space for someone to lay on the floor. There was a small kitchenette, a hide-a-bed, a dinette table with benches, and a cubby above the cab where a couple of people could sleep.

Troy climbed into the driver's seat and noticed the keys in the cup holder. "Nice," he said as he inserted them into the ignition. The RV started with little problem, and luckily it wasn't one of the vehicles they'd drained the gas from. "It even has a full tank."

"Drive it over and we'll load it up," Tank said.

23

FEAR OF DEATH

Post-outbreak day 24, late afternoon

Alexis sat on the couch of the RV. They'd moved Greg over to the bed in the back so he'd be more comfortable. Lucas was driving—after Troy had given him some pointers—and now Troy sat at the small table across from her. Felix and Olive couldn't resist the opportunity to ride in the cubby above the cab so they could look out the front windows at the landscape passing by. That left Chloe and Tank alone in Scourge, which Alexis knew they'd enjoy. Some alone time to talk was good for them after everything that'd happened. It wasn't, however, good for her as she couldn't keep her mind from bringing up thoughts of her dad or James, and it was too painful to entertain those for long.

Standing up, she walked back to check on Greg. He was still asleep but seemed to have the chills, and his breathing was ragged. She'd hoped that getting him to lie down on the bed would help, but he just seemed to be getting worse. There wasn't much she could do, however. He needed a doctor and some stronger antibiotics. She'd given him some pain meds so he'd at least be more comfortable. He'd barely awakened enough to take those, and then he'd passed out again. Maybe his body was just using a lot of energy to heal. She sat back down on the couch and sighed. It was always the people she couldn't help that hit her the hardest.

"You've done a great job with him," Troy said, looking at her from across the RV's small living space. "Better than any of us could've."

"I just wish I could do more," Alexis said, glancing up at Lucas. He was zoned out, listening to an Eric Church CD he'd found.

"There's only so much any of us can do in any given situation," Troy said, moving over to sit on the other end of the couch next to her. He was right, of course, but she always struggled with that. She thought she should be able to do more, to be able to help everyone. It rarely worked out that way though. "You saved his life. Even if something happens to him now, you did save him."

"I just want to keep him alive."

"You are. Now, we need to get your mind off this. I still know nothing about you. Where did you grow up in Texas?"

"Hill City, a small town in the eastern part of the state."

"How'd you like living there?"

"It was small, so growing up you knew everyone in the area. I didn't get a taste of the big city until I went to Lufkin for my paramedic training."

"Did you always want to be a paramedic?"

"After my brother died, I decided I wanted to be able to help people in life-threatening situations."

"I didn't know you had a brother."

"He died when I was young. I don't talk about it much."

"My little sister died when I was ten. We were best friends, and then one day I didn't have my best friend anymore." His voice got a little choked up, and a tear slipped down his cheek.

Alexis put a hand on his shoulder to comfort him. "What happened?"

"My mom was driving in a blizzard when a semi hit her. It was bad. It killed her and my sister. It was just my dad and I after that."

"That must've been hard. I lost my brother and my parents divorced, but at least I still had them."

"Divorce can be almost as bad as losing them, though; at least that's what I hear."

"It was hard."

"Well, so much for not talking about painful things," Troy said with a chuckle, wiping his eyes. "Thanks." He rested his hand on hers and then stood up. "You should probably get some sleep. I can keep an eye on Greg."

"I really shouldn't—"

"If you don't get some sleep, it'll just make you more prone to make a mistake. Trust me, I'll watch Greg and let you know if anything changes."

"Okay," Alexis said with a yawn, looking forward to sleeping on a real bed.

She pulled out the hide-a-bed and lay down. She was asleep as soon as her head hit the hard pillow.

Tank glanced at Chloe and she looked at him out of the corner of her eye. His pulse started racing with just that tiny look. This woman had successfully stolen his heart and in record time. He wasn't one to fall easily. He'd dated quite a few girls through the years, but he'd only ever thought he'd loved maybe two of them. This was different. It was like all the other times were just a preview of what was to come. He'd never felt this way about a girl. Hell, he'd rarely felt this strongly for anyone outside his family, ever.

Damn, I do love her, don't I?

She turned so she was fully facing him and smiled. A grin sprung to his lips in return.

"I love ya, babe," Tank said.

A small hint of surprise registered on her face, and then her smile grew.

"I thought I heard you say that the other morning," Chloe said, reaching over and resting her hand on his leg. "I love you, too."

Tank's smile grew so much it hurt his face. He didn't even know he *could* smile that wide. Finding love at the end of the world just figured. He couldn't have found her years ago; no, he had to find her when everything was falling apart. She'd even been in the same city as him before this, not that Fort Collins was a small city. They could've lived their whole lives there and never met. Just another reason the end of the world was a good thing, or at least a disaster that brought about something good with it.

"Allen," Chloe said, using his real name. He liked how it sounded coming from her lips. "If we do make it to Alaska, what'll our future look like?"

"Startin' this conversation with a light question, eh?" Tank asked with a chuckle. Then he grew more serious. He'd been thinking a lot about that lately. "We start a life together. That is, if you want to?"

"Of course," Chloe said. "This may be the end of the world and my options might be limited, but I pick you and that's not gonna change."

A tear slipped down Tank's cheek as her words warmed his heart. Luckily for him, it was on the left side of his face and he turned slightly so she wouldn't see. He still didn't know what to do with all this emotional stuff. Usually he just kept it hidden, but he was having a hard time doing that lately. It wasn't that his heart was three sizes too small, like the Grinch. He was just really good at hiding his under layers of cynicism. Now, however, it was coming to the surface, and he didn't have the usual desire to hide it.

What the hell's happenin' to me?

"Good," Tank said, looking at her after the tear had disappeared into his beard. "Because I feel the same about you. I don't want anyone else. I guess that means when this all settles down, we'll need to get married."

"Are you asking me to marry you?" Chloe asked, a sly smile on her perfect lips.

"Not yet," he said. "I want to do it proper. But yes, that's the next step I plan to take after I get you to safety."

"Well, once we get to safety, my next step will be to say yes."

Tank slipped his right hand off the steering wheel and took hers in his. Holding hands and smiling like only two people in love could, they continued down the ALCAN.

Troy sat on the couch watching Alexis sleep. He knew he still had feelings for her, but he was trying to keep them in check. She was with James, and he respected that—unless James didn't come back, which he probably wouldn't. He knew the guy was tough, but he was being chased by the group who'd outwitted them at every turn. James would only make it so far. When he never returned, Alexis would need someone, and Troy would be there for her. After enough time, she'd grow to love him, or she wouldn't, and he'd respect that too, although he hoped for the former.

Standing up, he pushed thoughts of Alexis from his mind. It was tough, but after a few seconds of scolding himself, he was able to. Glancing up at Lucas, who was still jamming out to his country music, Troy started for the bedroom to check on Greg. The two kids were still up in the cubby playing rock-paper-scissors. By the way they talked, they'd been playing this same game for weeks. Kids could be so easily entertained, but it wasn't that simple these days. Everything had changed over the past few weeks, and he was just now coming to terms with it. This was the way things were now and he had to accept that.

He walked into the bedroom, closing the door behind him to keep the music and noise of the kids out. Greg needed to get his rest, and Troy was worried for the big man. Greg always seemed to know what to do and was good at surviving, and Troy had learned a lot from him. Reaching down to check the pulse in Greg's neck, Troy stopped as Greg opened his eyes.

"How you feelin'?" Troy asked. Greg didn't respond; he just groaned. He must have been in a lot of pain. "Is there anything I can—"

He was cut off as Greg grabbed ahold of Troy's arm that was against his neck. Before he could pull away, Greg sank his teeth into the soft flesh of his forearm. Pain shot up Troy's limb and he tried to shake Greg off, but he bit down harder.

"What the hell!" Troy cried out, pulling out the knife sheathed on his belt. "Let go, man!"

Greg's eyes were bloodshot, and now that Troy really looked, he could see bruising under his skin.

He's infected!

Without a second thought, Troy slammed his knife down through Greg's eye. The big man's body went limp, and his head sank back to the pillow. Troy looked down at his forearm. Greg had put two perfectly shaped bite marks into his skin, and blood was leaking out.

"No, no," Troy whispered to himself. "This can't be happening."

He quickly found a bottle of water, rinsed the wound off, and then cut a strip from a pillowcase in the closet, tightening it around his arm. The bleeding slowed, and with the wound clean, maybe he wouldn't turn. They didn't know for sure that a bite caused it. It could be something else, or maybe Greg was too newly infected. Searching around, Troy found a long-sleeved flannel shirt in one of the drawers and threw it on over his T-shirt. The white cloth around his arm was stopping most of the blood. While the wound hurt, it wasn't bleeding too badly. Maybe he *would* be okay.

Pulling his knife from Greg's eye, he wiped the gore on the bed and then sheathed it. He couldn't tell anyone that Greg had bitten him. They wouldn't give him the chance to explain. Tank would just kill him, and he couldn't let that happen, not while there might be a chance he wasn't infected. Troy didn't want to die—not yet. Walking to the door, he hesitated. He needed to tell the others Greg had turned, but he wouldn't tell them the whole truth.

$$24$$

THE GIRL WITH AUBURN HAIR

Post-outbreak day 24, late afternoon

Ana? James thought, stunned.

That couldn't be her. He must be hallucinating from lack of water or food. That had to be it. But as the truck pulled closer and he got a better glimpse of her face, he knew it was indeed Ana. Where had she come from? She must've seen him, because her Raptor slowed to a stop behind the truck he was in. Ana climbed out with her AK-47 to her shoulder and slowly approached the truck.

"Ana!" James said. "Is that really you?"

Her eyes snapped to his as she drew even with the back seat where he was buckled. There was something different about her—the set of her face or the look in her eyes—or maybe it was just because it'd been a while since he'd seen her last.

"James?" she asked in her familiar Russian accent. Only something was different about her voice, too. "Why're you just sitting there?"

Jezz!

"You need to get out of here!" James said while looking around frantically. "Jezz captured me, and she's around here somewhere."

It was like someone had flipped a switch inside Ana. Suddenly she was in a half crouch, eyes darting at all the possible hiding places. She looked more akin to a wild animal than a person. Something had seriously changed in her, and he wasn't sure it was a good thing. This was not the same woman he'd seen last.

"Where is she?" Ana hissed.

"I'm not sure," James said, unable to take his eyes off her. What had caused this drastic shift? "She was here before I dozed off, but when I woke up, she was gone. There's another also, one of her Reclaimers—"

Gunfire cut off what he was about to say as the window in the open door by where Ana was standing shattered, raining down glass around her. She dropped even further into a crouch as another gunshot slammed into the front of the door. James could see Jezz now. She was coming out of the trees fifty yards away and walking towards them. Ana had moved to aim around the door when something scraped her in the leg and she grunted. Then she started firing rapidly at Jezz.

Jezz dove into a ditch as bullets threw dirt up around her. Ana moved back behind the door for cover, muttering something in Russian. Jezz stood up and fired a few more shots, but all missed their mark. Ana continued to fire wildly at Jezz's position, which kept the leader of the Reclaimers from being able to fire back as she jumped in the driver's seat and turned the key in the ignition.

"It's out of gas," James said in a rush as the windshield was peppered with holes.

He did his best to duck behind the seat in front of him, but it was hard because of being buckled in with the seat belt locked in place. Thankfully, the bullets missed both of them as Ana hunkered down in the front seat. Ana cursed loudly, firing blindly through the windshield. Without missing a beat, she ripped the magazine from her AK-47 semiautomatic rifle and slammed another one in.

"This is my last mag."

"Jezz has some in the glove box." James was hiding behind the headrest, even though it would offer little resistance to a bullet.

Jezz had quit firing. Maybe she'd run out of ammunition. That was the downside of a fully automatic rifle; it ate through ammunition quickly. James kept his eyes locked forward while Ana peeked out from below the dash.

"Where is she?" Ana asked quickly.

James was about to respond when he noticed movement out of the corner of his right eye. He opened his mouth, but it was too late.

"Don't move," Zeke said from just outside the truck. His rifle was pointed directly at the back of Ana's head. "I got her!"

Jezz rose out of the ditch, smiling despite the line of blood on her cheek. She sauntered towards the truck.

"Throw the gun outside," Zeke said. Then, when Ana didn't listen, he added, "Now!"

He didn't raise his voice, but his last word carried weight with it. How could he infuse so much command without yelling? Ana threw her rifle from the truck, but James could tell there was an uncertain set to her shoulders.

"Uncle Zeke?" Ana asked, slowly turning around.

"Ana?" Zeke asked, starting to lower his rifle.

"Do not underestimate her!" Jezz roared from in front of them, her rifle pointed towards Ana. "Get out of the truck, my dear."

Ana shivered when Jezz spoke to her, and she listened without hesitation. Zeke just stood there, shock plain on his face. It was the most emotion James had ever seen from the man.

"Get the other one," Jezz said, stopping in front of Ana. She'd been grazed with a bullet or debris across her right cheek, and the look in her eyes didn't speak well for them. "Are you deaf? Get James!"

Zeke flinched at the rage in her voice and opened the door, un-buckling James. Bringing him over to the other side of the truck, Zeke threw him down. James landed on his knees and barely managed to keep himself from face-planting.

"Ana," Zeke said. "Is that really you?"

"You *know* her?" Jezz asked, a gleam in her eye.

"*Da*," Ana said, looking up at Zeke. "How did you get here?"

"I was in Denver on a job for your father," Zeke said. "Then all this happened, and I ended up in Wyoming."

"Oh, this is precious," Jezz said. "Zeke, I would like you to meet the woman who freed our captives and helped decimate my men."

"Let her go," James said, speaking up. "You have me. You don't need her."

"Oh, you are correct," Jezz said, then looked to Zeke. "Get your gun on her!"

Zeke hesitantly raised his rifle to aim at Ana's head. The gleam in Jezz's cold blue eyes twinkled.

"Uncle?" Ana said, a tear slipping down her cheek even as her face was set in a stern mask.

"Shut up!" Jezz roared. "You have cost me everything, and I am going to reclaim you both. Zeke, shoot Ana, and I will take care of him."

"What?" Zeke asked, his eyes flicking to the unhinged woman.

"I said shoot her."

James could plainly see the emotions playing across the man's face. Ana meant a lot to him, and it surprised James that the man could feel anything other than hate. Jezz raised her rifle towards Zeke.

"You are weak," Jezz said, spittle flying from her mouth. "Do it or I end you."

Determination set in Zeke's eyes as Ana knelt there, a flurry of emotions on her face as well. It seemed like she was battling something inside that was consuming her. James couldn't let this happen. He had to do something.

Jumping to his feet in a flash, James roared and charged at Jezz, his hands still cuffed behind his back. Jezz swung her rifle over to him at the same time Ana lunged forward. Jezz fired three rounds at him before Ana was able to tackle her to the ground. The first round grazed his side, the next one clipped his shoulder, and the final whizzed past his face as he lost his balance and crashed to the ground.

Ana batted Jezz's rifle from her grip and it flew through the air as Ana drew her Glock. Jezz struck the handgun away and then head-butted Ana. The weapon fell to the grass and Ana sat back, dazed. Jezz drew her knife from behind her back and Ana shook off her daze, drawing a knife of her own. The two women slowly stood up, facing each other like a pair of hunting cats.

"Fine, I will do it then," Jezz hissed.

"Come and get some, bitch," Ana said, wiping the blood from her lip with the back of her hand.

Jezz lunged forward with a wild stab which Ana sidestepped. Ana had been trained by the killer standing next to James, watching the fight with his rifle pointed at the ground. Jezz tried another slash and Ana stepped to the side, slashing her own blade across Jezz's arm. The knife cut cleanly through the fabric of her green shirt and into the skin. This caused the woman to roar as she started slashing in a flurried rush. Ana countered each slash with one of her own, and when Jezz stepped back, she was covered in cuts while Ana just had two shallow ones. Jezz lunged again, rage contorting her face as she extended her arm straight out to stab Ana in the heart. The other woman batted it away from her with her left forearm and then jabbed her knife into Jezz's gut.

The leader of the Reclaimers glanced down at the wound with shock and then up at Ana's face, which was a mask of anger and pain. Ana held Jezz's weapon arm with one hand and gripped the knife that was plunged into the Reclaimer's gut with the other. Ana brought her knife up through Jezz's stomach, stopping only when she reached the sternum. Jezz's knife tumbled to the grass as her legs gave out and she fell to her knees. Ana let go of her arm and slowly walked behind Jezz as the crazed woman tried to hold her guts in, but it was a losing battle as blood and part of her intestines spilled out onto the grass.

"I have... been reclaimed," Jezz mumbled under her breath in an almost satisfied way right before Ana brought her knife across Jezz's throat.

25

ANOTHER FUNERAL

Post-outbreak day 24, early evening

Tank watched the sun as it sank into the sky before them, *Infection* by Beartooth playing in the background. They'd passed into the Yukon—the only territory standing between them and Alaska. If they kept this pace, they could be in Tok the next day. That thought brought a smile to his face. Things were finally going according to plan. If only the brothers were here, and Tank found himself missing Emmett as well.

"Will we have our own house at this lodge?" Chloe asked.

"I wouldn't call it a house," Tank said. "But we'll have our own cabin, yeah."

"Then how do we cook and do laundry? And shower for that matter?"

"I think they have some kinda sauna for showers and the lodge has a big kitchen. I'm not sure about laundry."

"I guess it'll be better than this."

"Oh, yeah."

"What'll we do out there? Just survive?"

"I'm guessin' we'll be plenty busy for the first few months as we get things up and runnin'. After that we'll all have our own jobs to keep the community goin'. Kind of like a commune."

"Before all this I would've thought that was weird. But now, with this group, it doesn't sound so bad."

Tank laughed. "Yeah, it won't be too bad."

"What're you most excited for?" Tank looked over at her, a twinkle in his eye. She giggled and slapped him on the shoulder. "Besides that," Chloe said with a smile.

"I hear there's a good stream to fish for salmon and two lakes that are full of graylin' and lake trout. I'm excited to get some fishin' in."

"I forgot you liked to fish so much."

"It was a way for me and Grandpa Carter to hang out and talk about life. I always felt at peace on the water. Like I was just a small fish in a big pond. Pun intended."

Chloe laughed. "Well, I'm excited for you to teach me how to fish. But I'm also excited to have my own space. I don't even remember what privacy feels like."

"Yeah, that'll be nice."

"Do you know how cold it'll get in the winter?"

"I'm not sure, but probably in the negatives."

"What? How are we going to survive in that?"

"The buildings are all insulated and have wood heat. That and lots of warm clothes when you go out."

"But I'll freeze the second I step outside!"

"How d'ya think our ancestors did it?"

"They weren't stupid enough to live in Alaska. At least, mine weren't."

Tank chuckled. "It won't be that bad. We'll just have to make sure we have enough supplies stockpiled for winter."

"So, what was that man saying to you when we left Coutts?" Chloe asked, randomly.

He could tell she'd wanted to ask this question for a while now.

"That was Tom. He's the one who built Frostmourne for me. When I took the sword, he made me promise to make the world a better place for my kids. His son died early on durin' this and I think I reminded Tom of him."

"Oh," Chloe said and then stopped as a voice came on over the radio.

"We need to stop," Lucas said, grief in his voice. "Greg's dead."

Alexis watched as Tank and Lucas carried Greg out in the bloody blanket they'd taken off the bed. She knew she couldn't have done anything for him, but it didn't stop her from feeling guilty. Troy walked out after them in a flannel shirt he hadn't been wearing before. He was sweating, and she found it odd that he was wearing long sleeves in the summer heat. Olive and Felix followed Troy out of the RV as Tank and Lucas laid Greg down on the side of the road in a shallow grave they'd dug.

A tear slipped from her eye as Tank shoveled dirt onto the body. Lucas brought over a large rock that they set on top to mark the grave. There wasn't much else they could do, given the situation, and they shouldn't waste too much time. It was just a body after all; Greg's spirit was gone. The rest was a vessel, but giving him a proper grave felt right. It gave the rest of them more closure than anything it did for the dead man.

Tank stepped back and took his helmet off. "I didn't know him well, but he was a good man. He did his best to help us along the way, and he died gettin' others to safety. May he rest in peace."

Alexis bowed her head and said a quick prayer as more tears came to her eyes. This was all her fault. All of it. Her dad was dead, James was dead, and she couldn't even save Greg. She'd become a paramedic to help people, not watch everyone she ever loved die while still being unable to do anything. It was just like Mason. Just like her mom.

Troy walked over and put an arm around her shoulder, and she leaned into him, crying. It was all too much. How was she going to go on without her dad? He was her rock, her shelter when life threw storms at her. He'd always known what to say to comfort her, always been there when she needed him, or at least he had been after he'd gotten out of the service. In fact, she now knew he'd left the Marines to be with her—to be a father. Now he was gone, and all she had left was an aching hole in her heart that nothing could fill. The person who'd always been there for her was gone, stolen away by a single bullet.

It wasn't fair. It wasn't right.

Why did he have to die? Why would God just let that happen? He should've done something, should've intervened and saved her dad, but it was too late now. He was gone, and there was no bringing him back. Alexis cried on Troy's shoulder as the rest of them said their own goodbyes to Greg. Then it was time to load up and move on. They couldn't even take the proper amount of time to mourn because they had to continue, to keep saddling up and pretending they'd somehow make it to safety. She was beginning to realize that by the time they made it there, nothing would be left of the people they'd been before—only hollow shells of who they used to be, if they even survived until then.

She wished James was here, but that wasn't even possible. She was kidding herself if she thought he was still alive. There was a very slim chance that he'd even lived the rest of that night, let alone a couple days by himself. He was alone, and she doubted Connor could find him before it was too late. It was useless, all of it. Nothing they did would ever change anything. She might as well just accept that. It would make life easier for the future, if they had a future past the end of the week.

"Come on," Troy said, gently steering her to the RV. "It's time to go."

She grabbed ahold of his arm as he led her to the vehicle, and he stiffened under the grip but said nothing. When she pulled her hand away to climb in, it was glazed with blood.

"Are you hurt?" Alexis asked, looking at him.

"What?" Troy asked, and she held up her hand. Troy looked down at his forearm and touched the blood. "Must've been from when I had to... put Greg down. I'll clean up once we're on the road."

Alexis just nodded, too torn to question him further. The world was truly ending around her, and there was nothing she could do to stop it.

26
CHANGE OF MANAGEMENT

Ana wiped her blade off on Jezz's shirt and then kicked the black-haired woman over, returning her knife to its sheath with a crisp motion. James watched as Jezz's blood drained from the gash at her neck, the crimson a stark contrast with her pale skin. The leader of the Reclaimers tried to catch her breath but couldn't since both carotid arteries and her windpipe were severed. It was like Jezz didn't know what to do as her hands moved from trying to shove her guts back into her body to trying to stop the flow of blood from her neck.

Ana never glanced back as she walked towards James and Zeke. James lay on his shoulder on the ground as Zeke stood above him. He couldn't see the man's face, but his rifle was still pointed at the ground.

Finally, Jezz's hands fell to her sides and the woman breathed her last. It was the end of a monster, a truly evil woman who had caused much pain in her life, but as Ana stopped before Zeke, he couldn't help but wonder: Had he traded one monster for another?

"You have grown," Zeke stated, and then he dropped his rifle and hugged Ana. She returned the hug, a couple of tears leaking from her eyes. She was quick to wipe those away when they separated. "I never thought to see you again."

"Nor did I," Ana said, a small smile on her face.

"How did you get caught up with this group?" Zeke asked, pointing a thumb in James's direction.

"Long story," Ana said.

"How's your leg?" Zeke asked.

Ana looked down, there was only a little blood. She examined the minor cut. "It's nothing," Ana said, bending down to look at James. "How do you feel?"

"It'd be nice to stop my shoulder from bleeding, but I don't think it's bad," James said, smiling at her despite the twist in his gut from looking into her eyes. The light they held looked eerily similar to Jezz's.

"We don't have to worry about that," Zeke said, picking up his rifle and pointing it down at James's head. "Step aside and I'll finish this."

"He's a friend, Uncle," Ana said, not moving. "Not an enemy."

"He and his group deserve death." Anger rose in his voice. "The debt must be paid."

Ana began to speak but stopped short. What was this about a debt? "We need him to get to the group," she said, looking away from James.

"That's what Jezz thought, too, but we don't need him."

"If we have him, I can walk into the group and they'll accept me back with open arms." Ana stood to look Zeke in the eyes. "Then we can kill them all. Otherwise you'll have another failed attack. I have no doubt you can kill some of them, but if you want them all..."

She let the statement hang between them, and James couldn't think of anything to say.

"It could work." Zeke moved his barrel back to pointing at the ground as he sighed.

"It *will* work."

"But if he so much as twitches to escape, I'll kill him."

"I won't stop you." Ana walked over and picked up Jezz's discarded AK-47, bringing it back to the truck.

"She'll come back unless we take out the brain," Zeke said.

"Let her rot," Ana said in a hiss.

That voice brought a chill to James's spine.

"I have two gas containers. We'll throw those in the back."

"I'll get James in the truck."

"Don't trust him."

"I won't."

Zeke moved off to where James now saw a red wagon that held two gas jugs a hundred yards back. Smoke rose from the truck he'd been riding in, so Ana lifted him to his feet and roughly guided him to the back seat of her Raptor, where she proceeded to buckle him in. Then she looked at his shoulder, wiping the blood off with a rag from the bed of the other truck.

"Ana," James said, "you're just saying that to get his guard down, right?"

She didn't respond immediately. "Your shoulder's fine, the bullet didn't even get to the muscle."

She wrapped one of the rags over his shoulder and then tightened it. He winced. "You're not going to lead him to the others, right?"

She slammed his door shut as Zeke arrived.

"We have kids!" James yelled. "You can't do this!"

Ana ignored him as she and Zeke filled up the truck and then threw the jugs into the bed. Zeke climbed into the driver's seat and started the engine while Ana climbed into the passenger seat, exchanging her AK-47 for Jezz's fully automatic one. He *had* traded one captor for another. When he'd first seen her, he'd been filled with hope. He'd thought she'd be able to help him and then they could go back to their group together, but that hope had been replaced with dread. Was her plan just a stalling tactic to keep James alive longer, or was she serious? Could she have gone that dark since she'd left the group?

"Ana," James began to say.

"Shut it," Ana said, her voice cold.

The answer to his question was plain to see in her eyes. She was going to lead Zeke to their group so he could kill them all.

Ana was going to betray them.

Tires screeched on the blacktop as the Dodge Charger, painted white and black with blue and red lights on top, careened around the abandoned Hostess truck. Too bad Connor wasn't looking for Twinkies because there was a pile of them scattered on the road. He was on a mission to save his brother, and nothing would stand in his way. He'd traded his bike for the police car back in Dawson Creek, and it'd been the perfect find. There was still a Benelli M4 12-gauge shotgun in the car, along with a first aid kit and a load of other good stuff. There were even three full gas jugs in the trunk, and it seemed most of the pumps were either down or dry.

This thing was a *lot* quicker than the bike or the bulldozer, and he felt like he was finally making progress. It helped that on the open parts of the road he was pushing 100 MPH, and the rest of the time he rarely slowed down past 70. Was it safe? Hell no. Was it his only chance to catch up to the Reclaimers who held his brother captive? Yes, and if that meant being a little reckless, then he'd be a lot reckless. There was only one thing on his mind now—finding his brother and killing any and all who got in his way, be they human, zombie, or otherwise.

This was his mission and he would see it through. As he drove like a madman down the ALCAN, he chugged a bottle of water and downed three power bars along with two Kickstarter energy drinks. He knew he needed to keep his body and mind energized because he'd been going nonstop for over seventy-two hours, starting with the Reclaimers' attack on Coutts.

It was starting to fray his mind, and he could hear quiet voices—the voices of his parents and his brother and his past drill sergeants; voices telling him to stop and ones telling him to keep going. He ignored them all as the landscape sped by. He was almost to Fort Nelson and would be through it in the next thirty minutes. There was no time to stop, no time to rest, no time to think.

It was do or die now, and he'd do just that.

27

TESLIN LAKE

Post-outbreak day 24, night

"Do you see that?" Chloe asked, pointing out the window. Tank glanced over, noticing the fading light reflecting off something large and metal sitting a hundred yards off the side of the road.

"It's an airplane," Tank said, realizing the long clearing was an airstrip. That's why they'd been seeing signs for Teslin Airport. "That looks military."

"Should we stop and check it out?" Chloe asked.

"Wouldn't hurt. They may have supplies."

He pulled off and drove across the airstrip and over to the plane. There was nothing in sight for a long way, with the airport buildings farther back down the airstrip.

"What we doin'?" Troy's voice asked over the radio. He sounded weak, like he was getting a cold. That was just what they needed—a cold going around in their small group, or even worse, the flu.

"Do you see the *giant* plane?" Tank asked.

"Yeah..."

"It's a C-17 or somethin' like it. Could be full of supplies."

"Oh, good call."

Tank mumbled a smartass remark without turning the radio on.

"We can't all be badass leaders like you," Chloe said with a wink and a kiss on his cheek.

Tank smiled, reaching over and gently cupping her chin. Then he brought his lips to hers and they kissed deeply. They hadn't had a lot of time to do this after leaving Coutts, and he missed the feel of his lips on hers. It also awaked other desires, but that would have to wait. A knock on the window ended the moment. Oh well, it had been amazing while it lasted.

"Yeah?" Tank asked, opening the door to glare at Lucas.

"I just... uh..." He stumbled over his words.

"I'm just messin' with ya, kid," Tank said, climbing out and slapping him on the shoulder. "Where's the rest?"

"Troy said he's feeling ill, so he'll stay with the RV," Lucas said, then hesitated. "Alexis hasn't spoken since Greg's funeral."

Damn, I'll have to do somethin' about that. Can't have Jamesy Boy's girl givin' up.

"Okay, Chloe get your shotgun," Tank said. "I need you."

She smiled at him as she grabbed the firearm. After drawing out all the undead at Muncho Lake, she'd been a lot more comfortable using it. Practice always made perfect.

"Ready," she said, shotgun to her shoulder.

"Now remember," Tank said, "watch where you're pointin' that and aim for the head."

"No shit," Chloe said, setting her face with determination.

"Good. Let's check it out," Tank said, shouldering his ACR.

It was getting dark and he didn't want to mess around with Frostmourne. Plus, without Alexis or the brothers to cover him, he felt less safe. Turns out he had nothing to worry about since the plane was clear of any hostiles *and* supplies. It looked like whoever had been there just abandoned the plane. In the cockpit, Tank noticed some papers shoved into the back of the seat. He pulled them out and started to read.

Apparently, this was an Army plane. Their mission was to resupply Teslin, and they were tasked with establishing a base of operations there because a nearby "secure location" was being filled with high-value personnel. There were instructions about how to take down the undead, along with what to do with anyone bitten, and there was something in there about more Intel to follow. It also talked about the whole state of the U.S., and it sounded hopeful but bleak at the same time. It seemed that they'd lost most of the country to the infection, but there were still a few large cities and many military bases holding out. They were told to hold tight but also prepare for the possibility of Operation Fallout. These weren't just orders for some random squad; he had the feeling this was for an elite unit, like Delta Force.

He refolded the papers and stuck them in a pocket, moving to join Chloe and Lucas at the back of the plane.

"Find anything?" Chloe asked.

"Just some orders for the soldiers who were in this plane," Tank said. "They were here to help out the town of Teslin."

"Didn't we just drive past that?" Lucas asked.

"Yeah," Tank said.

"Should we go back?"

"Have you already forgotten the last time? No, we're not goin' back. We're movin' on."

Lucas looked dejected but nodded as they walked to the rigs. Tank climbed in and they were on the road in no time. He yawned, glancing out the window as darkness encased the surrounding landscape. It would be nice to get some real sleep. He yawned again, noticing Chloe doing the same. It wouldn't help to switch out since she was as exhausted as he was. The RV behind him swerved a little and then righted its self.

"What the hell was that?" Tank asked in the radio.

"Didn't you see that deer?' Troy asked.

"Nope."

"Watch out!" Chloe said, pointing at the road ahead.

Tank hit the brakes as the mule deer stood there, like—well, a deer in headlights. The front-end of Scourge slammed into the poor creature, bowling it over. The tires bounced over it and Tank sped up a bit to give Troy enough space to stop without rear-ending them. Then he noticed a sign for a campground a kilometer ahead. Maybe it would be safer to stop for the night.

"Didn't you see that thing?" Chloe asked.

"Yeah," Tank said. "Didn't you see me brake?"

"Why didn't you swerve?"

"Haven't you ever taken Driver's Ed? You never swerve for an animal, especially when you're drivin' a bomb-proof vehicle. I think it can handle a deer."

"Then why do they do it in all the movies?"

"Because the movies are stupid, and they do it to add drama. Never swerve. There could be oncomin' traffic, or you could roll the vehicle. Just slow down and ram it."

"What about the deer? Is he alive?"

"Well, it was a doe, a female, but no, she's definitely dead. She's smeared over fifty yards of pavement."

"Poor thing."

"It was quick, at least," Tank said, pulling off at the campground. "Now, I think we need to clear this place and get some Zs."

28

ENIGMA

"Get up," Zeke said as he shoved James awake. He hadn't even realized he'd fallen asleep, but the rhythmic vibration of the vehicle over the blacktop had lulled him into slumber.

"Where are we?" James asked, blinking the sleep from his eyes. He must've been out hard.

"Let's go." Zeke shoved the barrel of his rifle into James's stomach.

"Back off, asshole." James climbed out of the back seat with his hands still cuffed behind his back. "I get that you're a dick, so no need to prove it all the time."

Pain flashed across James's face as the buttstock of Zeke's rifle collided with his nose. Blood ran into his mouth, and James spit it out, growling. He'd had about enough of this. Standing up, he readied himself to tackle Zeke or be shot.

"Quit it," Ana growled in a voice that made James stop in his tracks.

Was it him, or was she really beginning to sound *and* act like Jezz? What had happened to change her like this? Because one thing was certain: this was not the same woman who'd first joined Emmett's group all those weeks ago. Surprisingly, Zeke actually listened to her, muttering something in his language, but he was losing his control more often now, like a dam had suddenly broken open. Maybe he shouldn't egg him on, but James was tired, sore, bruised, hungry, thirsty, and just plain exhausted. If they were going to kill him, they might as well just do it now.

Zeke finally turned and walked down the road, the light on his rifle cutting through the darkness.

"What's going on?" James asked Ana as she swung a large backpack over her shoulder.

"Walk," she said, pushing him to follow Zeke.

James started moving. His leg was on fire, but as he continued to walk, it began to hurt less, or maybe he was just getting used to it. He glanced back at the truck. There was smoke curling out from under the hood. Something must've been hit in the shootout. It looked like they'd be walking now, and this would allow his group to increase their lead.

Falling into a limping rhythm, he followed a few steps behind Zeke, with Ana behind him. At first, he kept his head up and on a swivel, trying to figure out where they were. He noticed a sign for Watson Lake, but he couldn't make out how far ahead it was. After a half hour of walking and checking every vehicle they came across, however, he had to keep his eyes down and focused on his steps because his legs weren't responding like they should. When had he last eaten? It was over forty-eight hours ago, wasn't it? And water? He'd unintentionally drunk a boatload of river water when he'd almost drowned, but that was the last drink he'd had. He stumbled, trying to catch himself, but ended up falling onto his injured shoulder. Grunting in pain, he lay there, too exhausted to continue.

"Get up," Zeke said, kicking him in the stomach.

James curled into a ball to protect his vitals. "Tired," he responded weakly.

"When was the last time he ate?" Ana asked. Zeke shrugged, causing Ana to sigh. "If he doesn't eat, he won't have any energy."

"Then we kill him," Zeke said.

"No," Ana said firmly, "we *need* him if you want the rest."

Zeke started to say something, but Ana held up a hand and looked around. After another couple of seconds, the groaning reached James's ears as well. The ringing must be getting worse from all the explosions and gunshots lately because even now he could barely make it out. Ana disappeared into the night after the sound and Zeke watched her go. James just stayed on the ground, enjoying the relief of not being on his feet. He didn't even know how long they'd been walking.

The groans stopped and Ana returned a few moments later.

"There's a campsite in the woods that looks secure," Ana said pointing towards the trees. "We'll rest there."

Zeke grunted and started off in that direction while Ana helped James to his feet. He shakily stood up and mindlessly followed Zeke.

She was right; it was a good campsite. Someone had found where a semi had crashed through the trees and landed on its side. They'd pulled a couple more vehicles in to make a U-shaped barrier. The opening was only big enough to let two people in at a time and would act as a funnel if the zombies came for them. James stumbled to the back and collapsed against the semi-trailer.

Ana came up to him and reached behind him, un-cuffing his hands. Zeke sat ten feet away, his gun trained on him. James rubbed his wrists and stretched his arms and shoulders, which felt tighter than they'd ever been. It took him a solid five minutes of stretching before they felt somewhat better. Meanwhile, Ana had started a small fire in the pit in the middle of the campsite. The semi-trailer was positioned in such a way that it would block the view of the fire from the road. This was a good spot, and James would've been more appreciative if he hadn't been so beat.

Boiling some water on the fire while Zeke kept his gun unwaveringly pointed at James, Ana heated three Mountain House freeze-dried meals. She took one to Zeke and then brought one over to him, along with two bottles of water. He was so thirsty, he downed one right away and then took his time to eat, savoring the warm food. He also took his time because his stomach was messed up from not eating for so long. Once he'd finished, he rested his head back against the trailer and just enjoyed the simple things. He had a warm meal in his belly, his arms weren't wrenched behind his back, and the fire cast warmth across his face. Things could be worse.

"Put 'em back on," Zeke said roughly as the handcuffs landed in James's lap.

He looked up at his captor and smiled a genuine smile, obeying the man, and the smile seemed to affect Zeke even more than when he'd egged him on. Once he was cuffed, Zeke took a length of rope and secured his cuffs to the axel of the overturned semi-trailer. It left him enough slack to lay down, and that's exactly what he did. He was out in a matter of seconds.

29

CASUALLY DYING

Post-outbreak day 24, late night

Tank awoke in a layer of sweat. He'd had that dream again, the one where he had to jump in front of a train to save someone. The thing was, he didn't even know who the person was or why he was saving them. All he knew was that they needed help and he was the one who had to act. It was an odd dream he'd been having most nights since he'd made that promise to Tom. It must be his subconscious bringing what he'd promised the man to mind. The problem was the dream ended the same way every time; he was able to save the person, but he was hit by the train. He always ended up dead.

Looking around the RV, he saw that most of the others were asleep. Only Troy was up, and he'd be outside keeping watch while the rest slept. Grabbing his ACR, he walked to the door. Tank stepped out of the vehicle and took in a deep breath of fresh air. While it had been warm even during the night at the lower elevations, it was actually cool up there in the mountains. It reminded him of home, of his family, and of those nights spent outside with James and Connor getting into all kinds of shenanigans. It reminded him of better times.

"Troy?" Tank asked, looking around. He heard a grunt from the camp chair sitting next to the door. On second examination, he realized he'd mistaken Troy wrapped in a blanket for just something piled in the chair. "Dude, are you okay?"

"I feel like crap," Troy said. "This flu is killing me."

"Go lie down," Tank said. "I can keep watch for the next couple hours."

"I can stay," Troy said weakly.

"Get inside."

"Thanks."

Troy feebly stood to his feet and, with a hand on the outside of the RV the entire way, made it inside. He closed the door quietly as Tank hefted his ACR and walked over to Scourge, parked close by. Slipping on his helmet, he activated the NVGs and the world was suddenly bathed in green light. He began to walk around the campground. They'd already cleared it before deciding to stay there, but he might as well make a quick round or two.

This leadership role had been unwelcomed, especially considering how it'd happened, but he tried not to think about that too much. It was changing him though—he could see that—maybe not so much on the outside but on the inside. He'd never been responsible for this many lives before, only his own. His perspective wasn't the same on life, and he was beginning to understand how to put other's wellbeing in front of his own. It wasn't that he'd always been selfish; it was just different when he had people relying on him. Even if those people were responsible for themselves, he was still making decisions that would affect them all.

Now it was easy to see how James had come by his "episodes" after losing nearly one hundred survivors in the span of a single day, and Tank had a new appreciation for his friend. If he counted, he'd technically already lost one under his care, although Greg had been severely injured before. Now Troy was sick, but that should pass. The flu never hung on that bad for more than a few days. As a matter of fact, it was a good thing Troy had been in the room when Greg died, because if he'd come back after dying then he could've bitten someone before they knew what was going on, like one of the kids or maybe Alexis. That wouldn't have been good, and it could've—

The light bulb clicked on in his mind. Tank cursed, turning and running back to the RV. He burst through the door, not caring if he woke them all. "Troy!" he yelled

"What is it?" Alexis said, springing to her feet, handgun already drawn.

"Where's Troy?" Tank asked, glancing around at the lumps of people lying under blankets. He wasn't in there. Barging into the bedroom, he saw Troy's form under a pile of blankets on the bed.

"What's going on?" Alexis asked, following him.

"Troy's infected," Tank said, going over to the bed and throwing the blankets off.

Troy was lying underneath, and sweat covered his skin, which had taken on a sickly pale color. This was a lot worse than the flu. There was something glistening on the arm of his shirt. Tank pulled the sleeve back while keeping an eye on the unconscious man. A bloody cloth was wrapped around his arm, and when he pulled it off, there was a festering bite mark plain as day on his forearm.

"Oh, Troy," Alexis mumbled from behind him.

Tank shook Troy until he awoke, his eyes barely opening.

"Whass wrong?" Troy slurred.

"Come with me." Tank grabbed his unbitten arm.

"No." Troy jerked his arm back with surprising strength as his eyes fully opened.

"It's time for a walk."

Troy glanced down at his bitten arm, and his eyes went wide. "No! I'm just sick. It's only the flu. I don't wanna die!" He frantically glanced up at Tank and then looked over at Alexis. "Maybe... maybe I can beat it. We don't know if we haven't seen. Maybe I won't turn."

"Troy." Tank's voice was firm, and he gripped his ACR with white knuckles. "Come outside and we'll talk about it."

"No!" Something changed in his demeanor. "I can't!"

Troy made a quick move, reaching for something at his waist. Tank didn't wait to see if he was going for his handgun or not. In one smooth motion, his rifle came up and he squeezed the trigger. Troy's brains splattered over the headboard of the bed and his body went limp, his arm falling to his side, empty. The suppressed gunshot was loud enough in the RV to wake everyone who was still sleeping. Tank lowered the barrel, looking at the dead man bleeding on the bed.

He hadn't *wanted* to shoot him, but he wasn't going to let him endanger the rest of the group—*his* group. Glancing back at Alexis, he saw tears welling in her eyes but determination on her face. She knew it had to be done, and this group was used to loss by now. That didn't make it any easier though, not at all.

"What's going on?" asked a sleepy Olive, walking towards the bedroom.

"Don't go in there," Alexis said, turning and stopping the girl.

"What happened?" Chloe asked from back in the main room. Lucas was right behind her, axe in hand.

"Troy was turnin'," Tank said, turning around. "He was bitten by Greg and hid it. I had to put him down."

"Oh no," Chloe said, hand to her mouth.

"He…" Lucas began, but he couldn't finish his statement.

Olive and Felix just stared at the ground.

"Chloe, take the kids to Scourge," Tank said. "We'll load everythin' into there. No need for this now."

Chloe went to Felix and Olive, and the three of them left. Tank looked back at the body of Troy with a small hole under his left eye. He almost looked peaceful if not for the missing back of his head and the brains and blood on the white pillow. He'd done it to protect those he cared about, to protect the rest of his group. He was the one responsible for them now, and if this was what it took to be a leader, then so be it.

30

BROKEN LOYALTY

Ana walked between the trees as the early morning light streamed down through the thin canopy. The forest was peaceful, deeply contrasting with the landscape of her mind as two different sides warred within her. She didn't know which side was the strongest or which would win. She didn't even know which side was the *right* side anymore.

One thing was certain, and it brought a smile to her face. She'd killed Jezz. The woman who'd haunted her for the past couple of weeks was gone, and it felt good not to constantly be looking over her shoulder. When she'd driven the knife into the woman's gut, for just a second, she'd seen her mother's face instead. While that should've terrified her, it'd just made her feel all the more satisfied. No one was allowed to use her like that and live. She would not let anyone cause her that much fear ever again. Those days were over. She was done being afraid.

Circling back to their campsite, she walked through the gap to see Zeke standing in front of James as the two stared each other down. She didn't know what had been said, but her uncle looked furious.

"Time to go," Ana said, walking over and grabbing her backpack.

She decided that trying to defuse the situation would prove point-less. They'd just be right back at each other's throats again. Instead, she walked out of the campsite and headed to the road. They'd either follow or they wouldn't, but at the moment she had too much on her mind to care—like what she was going to do. She'd told Zeke about her former group to keep James alive, but she couldn't deny a part of her had meant it. That neither terrified nor excited her. It just was. Glancing back, she saw James limping slightly and Zeke walking behind him, his eyes boring holes into James's back.

As she traveled with the man who had trained her and practically raised her, she'd become aware that Zeke was no longer who he used to be. Once, he'd been a man of honor, even as a trained killer. She hadn't called him "uncle" just because he was basically a brother to her father but because he'd always been there for her. He'd never been a shoulder to cry on or to show weakness to—that was to be done alone in her room with no one the wiser—but he'd been there when she needed someone to help her control her mind and emotions, someone to train her body to be a weapon. He'd had a way of making everything else fade into the background as they sparred or trained with weapons. Then, when her dad had strongly encouraged her to be one of his advisers, she'd constantly had to go to Zeke for assistance. He'd been able to help her find her resolve and gain the confidence she needed to face her father's other advisors, who were ticked that a teenaged girl was showing them up. He'd been there for her all those years, and yet that wasn't the same man walking behind her now.

He'd lost most of his control, and that was something she thought she'd never see. He was the one who'd taught her to control her thoughts and emotions. It was because of him that she'd been able to get past the fact that she'd killed her own mother, burying those memories and moving on with her life. He'd been the one to help her get through life when her father grew increasingly hostile towards her over the years. And he'd been the one to tell her it was because Ana reminded him of her mother before she'd gone insane.

He'd known her dad since they'd come over from Russia, and he'd been his closest confidant and friend. They'd been through hell together as they forged the Romanovski family into what it was. But that man had died along the way somewhere, and the one following behind her was a different man who just looked like her uncle. Although, it shouldn't have surprised her that he'd lost his control. Wasn't she the same?

At every vehicle, Ana would stop and watch for any threats while Zeke checked them. They were all either in bad shape, out of gas, or had no keys, and hot-wiring a car was not one of her acquired skills, nor Zeke's. She doubted James would know how and didn't even ask.

After an hour of walking on foot, they arrived at the outskirts of Watson Lake. The closer they grew to town, the more infected they encountered, and their pace slowed. Finally, they found a gas station next to a grocery store that had a few vehicles parked close by.

"Keep an eye out," Ana said to Zeke, shrugging out of her pack. "I'll find us a ride."

"Make it quick," Zeke snapped.

She moved off towards a promising-looking truck. The battery was dead, so she moved onto the next one, checking half a dozen vehicles before finding a red Jeep parked behind the grocery store. It started right up, and she pulled it up to the fuel pumps. They weren't running, so she went to work syphoning some gas from the closest car. She was coming around the side of the gas station when she heard a gunshot and shattering glass.

What the hell?

Zeke shouldn't be shooting at any infected unless they were in some serious trouble. She ran over to the Jeep and stopped, shocked at the scene before her. James was lying on the ground amid fragments of the rear window. Zeke was standing over him, rifle pointed at his face. He'd just tried to shoot James! Emotions welled up within her at seeing her friend about to be murdered by one of her own family. Yet, she knew Zeke wasn't who he used to be, and now he was willing to do whatever it took to survive.

Not much different from us, said a voice in her mind.

"What are you doing?" Ana yelled, drawing her handgun and walking over to stand next to Zeke.

"Finishing this," Zeke said, the anger plain in his voice.

"I said we need him alive," Ana said, as calmly as possible.

Zeke just stood there, rifle pointed at James. He didn't respond, and she didn't like the look in his eyes. He'd lost what little control he had left. This was definitely *not* the man she'd known. She walked over and grabbed the barrel of Zeke's rifle, moving it off James.

"This is—" Ana didn't finish. Zeke jerked the rifle from her grasp and backhanded her across the face. Familiar pain seared her cheek, and suddenly she was a little girl again, her mother upset about something she'd done. A single tear slipped from her eye.

Zeke's expression softened as he looked at her. "Ana," he said, tenderness in his voice, "I—"

She didn't hear what he said next as rage roared to life within her, smothering all else. She would *not* be treated like that again.

Never. Again.

Zeke's eyes shone with realization, and they both moved at the same time.

"No one does that to me," Ana said in a low voice, her handgun pointed at Zeke's face as his rifle pointed at her chest.

"*He* is the enemy!" Zeke spat, furious again. "Not me! I trained you. Made you who you are."

"No," Ana said, venom in her voice. "You might've trained me, but no one made me who I am. I *chose* to be who I am."

She stared holes into his eyes, using every ounce of control she had not to shoot him in the face. He wasn't her Uncle Zeke anymore; he was just another monster who needed to be taken care of.

Just then, she thought she saw movement in the corner of her eye from back on the highway, but she couldn't risk looking. An infected was the least of her worries. The man who'd been like a father to her was holding a rifle aimed at her chest.

My uncle is still in there, said a soft voice in her head.

No, that man is dead. He's just like Jezz now. Just like our mother, said a different voice. A colder voice.

We can help him remember who he was.

End him!

No!

Kill him now before he kills us!

The voices continued, one vying for letting him live, the other wanting nothing more than to end him, then kill James and everyone else who might threaten her. Hands beginning to shake, the sights on her Glock wavered. Zeke's eyes were as intense as hers, but she saw something else in them. Something she recognized.

Loyalty to your family, Zeke's voice said in her mind, and she could see him sitting in their old training room, the same look in his eyes as now. He knew she could be more than what she was, and he was going to help her achieve that. *You must never betray one of your own. Family is first, always.*

Ana let out a long breath, lowering her handgun.

Zeke's face relaxed as he lowered his rifle as well. Holstering her Glock, Ana turned away and took a few steps, disgusted with herself. Yes, he'd never hit her before, but he was still her uncle. She couldn't just kill her own family. That wasn't who she was. She may be a killer, someone who would do anything to survive, and she may not even know which part of her was holding the reins at any given moment, but she was *not* someone who betrayed her own family.

But you have before. You can do it again.

The voice was persistent, but she had to ignore it. This wasn't who she was; it couldn't be. The two voices in her mind yelled at each other, and she flinched. Would she ever have peace within herself?

"I'm sorry, Ana," Zeke said from behind her, and she froze.

There was sadness in his voice that had nothing to do with him feeling guilty about hitting her, and it was accompanied by resignation. She drew her handgun and began to turn around while ducking. She wouldn't be fast enough. Zeke was the most proficient killer she'd ever known.

But before she could turn to face him, something thumped behind her and then Zeke fired. Pain flared to life within her.

31

OBLIVION

Post-outbreak day 25, morning

Alexis sat in the back of the LAPV in a daze—first her dad, then James, Greg, and now Troy. They were all dead. She'd been unable to do anything to help them, and she was directly responsible for two of them dying—no three. If she'd been in the truck with her dad, James would still be here and so would Connor. She'd forgotten about him in all this. He was probably dead now, too. They'd lost so many in just a few short days, and that wasn't even counting all the ones before—her mother, stepfather, Ana, and all the people from Burns. They were dead, too. Everyone was dead, and the rest of them would be soon. How had it come to this?

She watched out the window as they passed through Haines Junction. The town had been overrun, and everyone was infected—just like every single town they'd come across. It seemed that a few settlements had stood for a time because they'd had time to set up some defenses, but none of that had helped in the end. There had been signs around Whitehorse saying to head south to Carcross since it was safe, and there did seem to be few infected within the city, but they hadn't stopped. She didn't trust it. There weren't any safe places left. Coutts had probably even fallen by now. It was the way of the world.

As she stared out the window, she noticed the mountains rising above the spruce trees to the west. All around her, she saw the same—mountains rising into the sky. Varying shades of green stretched for miles in every direction. Pink Fireweed lined the sides of the road in clusters, adding a feminine touch to the landscape. Alexis emptied her mind and just enjoyed the scenery as there was so much to behold. She'd always loved Texas, but this was something else. It just screamed with rugged beauty.

This was God's country.

Feeling sorry for herself was wearing her out, and in that moment she realized that was exactly what she was doing. A lot of people had died, and she'd grieve them for years, but she was still alive, and as long as she drew breath that meant she had a purpose. God *was* still with her. Closing her eyes, she bore her heart out before him—giving over all of her worries, all of her fears, all of her hopes and dreams, and everything between. She gave it all over to the One who created it all. If He could make something this beautiful, He had the power to calm the storm within her. In fact, He'd done it many times before. Tears leaked down her cheeks as she continued to pray.

"Are you okay?" Chloe asked from the seat next to her.

"No," Alexis said, wiping the tears from her eyes. "But I will be."

Chloe scooted closer to her and wrapped her in a hug as more tears streamed from Alexis's eyes, and soon Chloe's joined hers. They'd all lost so much—not only the people closest to them but parts of themselves as well. She knew that no matter what happened, no matter how much life went back to "normal," they'd never be the same people again. Stronger, if they allowed God to use this for their good, but not the same—never the same.

"We're gonna stop here and fuel up," Tank said. There had been fewer and fewer vehicles lately, and she was amazed at how barren this part of the Yukon was.

Alexis broke their embrace and smiled at her friend. "Thanks," she said. "I needed that."

Chloe chuckled, wiping her eyes. "Me, too."

Not all was lost, not everyone dead. She still had her new family around her, and determination replaced her earlier hopelessness. Her dad wouldn't be wallowing in self-pity if he were in her position. He'd fight until his last breath to help them, to keep her and the others safe. That would be what she had to do to make him proud. Then and there, she decided to do whatever it took to keep these people safe, to keep her friends alive, even at the cost of her own life—or someone else's.

Tank pulled Scourge off to the side of the highway and noticed there was a larger opening past the line of high brush along the road. Driving down through a gap in the brush, the LAPV came to an abrupt stop.

"What the hell?" Tank exclaimed, his gaze glued out the windshield.

Alexis gripped her M4 tighter. Before them, in a large gravel clearing two hundred yards across and five hundred long, was a city of tents. There had to be dozens of them of all sizes, from large canvas-walled tents to small multi-colored backpacking tents. People of various ages, sexes, and skin colors moseyed around among them. Some were cooking meals at campfires, while others sewed clothes, collected firewood, sharpened stakes, and strung cans together on ropes. Not a single vehicle was in sight, and only a few of the people closest to them looked up at the massive armored vehicle. Most went back to their chores, paying them no heed.

An older woman with a kindly smile broke from the rest and strode to them, a walking stick gripped in her hand. She waved as she drew closer.

"They don't look like a threat," Lucas said.

"No, but looks can be deceivin'," Tank said.

The woman reached Scourge and stood by the driver's door. Her mouth moved but her words were indecipherable through the thick bulletproof glass.

"Well, hell," Tank said. "Cover me, I guess."

Alexis opened the top hatch and stood up on the seat. Tank opened the door and stepped outside, rifle in hand but pointed non-threateningly at the ground. Alexis kept her eyes on the rest of the group of tent-people while Tank talked to the woman below.

"Hello there," said the woman. "My name is Pam Jones, and this is our little community." She stretched her hands towards the tents.

"I'm Tank, and these are my people," Tank said.

"Would you like to come in and rest, maybe get some food and water?" Pam asked, "Your people look weary."

"No, thanks." Alexis could tell Tank was suspicious of all this. She was, too.

"Okay... What brings you through here?"

"We're tryin' to get to Alaska."

"Ah, what a beautiful place. We were just there a couple of months ago."

"How d'ya get here? I don't see any vehicles."

"We don't use vehicles or any form of technology, for that matter. We believe in living a simpler life."

"So you're Amish?"

Pam chuckled. "That's what a lot of people think, but no. We're more like... gypsies, if you will. We travel around the country, stopping where we can and living for a while, enjoying what that place has to offer, and then we move on."

"That sounds... different. How are ya still alive?"

"We eat, sleep, and procreate just like you. We sometimes have to go into town and sell our wares to buy food, but most of the time we live off the land and whatever people bring with them when they join us. Our people are free to come and go as they choose. Some stay for years while others just join us for a vacation from the hustle and bustle."

"No, I mean how are you alive with all the undead and the end of the world?"

"End of the world?" She chuckled at that. "What do you mean?"

"I mean the walkin' dead people tryin' to eat you and whole towns decimated. How have you missed that?"

"We've been here for over a month, and no one has needed to go to town since this place is abundant with all we need."

"So, you haven't noticed the dead people walkin' around?"

"We have had a few encounters with the diseased, but it's just another disease like the bubonic plague. It's not the end of the world. Are you sure you wouldn't like to get some rest? You may need it."

"Thanks for the offer, Pam, but we need to be goin'. We shouldn't have stopped this long as it is."

"I understand. If you ever find your way back, we'd love to host you. Guests are always welcome."

"Thanks, and good luck with survivin'," Tank said, climbing back into Scourge.

Pam smiled at them and waved as he backed the LAPV away from the tent-city and its unaware people. Alexis wanted to help them, to warn them about what they didn't understand, but that would put her current group in danger, and if these people were happy then who was she to upset their way of life? They seemed to be able to handle themselves. She could tell from her vantage point that they were building a wall of spikes around their camp, along with cans used to alert them. Maybe they didn't need help after all.

She climbed back down through the hatch as they turned onto the highway. "That was odd," she said.

"Yep," Tank said. "They did seem happy though."

"Maybe living in oblivion is better than facing reality," Lucas said.

"It'll only get 'em killed," Tank said.

"But has knowing really helped us?" Lucas asked.

He had a very good point.

32

RESCUE

Post-outbreak day 25, morning

Blood sprayed out of Zeke's chest as a bullet tore through him. Slumping to the ground, he pulled the trigger, and as his AR-10 fired, Ana dropped to the dirt. What had just happened? James glanced at Zeke and saw the light leave his eyes. The shot had taken him right in the heart, but who had fired it? The bullet had hit Zeke at an angle and exited out his back, meaning the shot had been fired from down the highway to the south. But from where James was lying on his back, his vision was blocked by the Jeep.

He got to his feet, hands still cuffed behind his back. He went over to Zeke first, and the man was indeed dead. That was good, because if he'd killed Ana like he tried, James would've been next. He was walking over to check on Ana when he saw movement from the road. There was a police car speeding towards them on the highway. James dove to the ground, hoping the driver hadn't seen him. Where were the keys for the handcuffs? Ana had them last, so he crawled over to her.

Tires screeched as the car came to a stop twenty yards away. James wouldn't have time to get the keys and get un-cuffed. The car door opened, and he prayed it wasn't someone hell-bent on killing. He'd just lost his captors, and he didn't want any more. Scrambling faster to Ana, he stopped as someone spoke.

"James," called a familiar voice from the cop car. "Are you okay?"

"Connor?" James asked, gawking at his brother who was standing there dressed in his black Kryptek camouflage with his ACR to his shoulder. "Brother!"

"Is he dead?" Connor asked, slowly walking towards Zeke.

"Yes, but he hit Ana." James stood up and walked over to the red-haired woman.

"What's goin' on?" Connor walked over and shot Zeke in the head twice.

"Long story," James said and knelt by Ana. There was blood on her upper arm near the elbow, and it was dripping onto the ground. Her eyes were open.

"He was going to kill me," Ana said softly. It seemed that she was in shock.

"Yeah," James said, "but he didn't get the chance." He helped her slowly sit up. "Do you have the keys to my handcuffs?"

Ana looked at him for a few seconds and then rummaged around in her pocket, using her left hand to bring them out. His brother walked over as she un-cuffed James.

"How do you feel?" James asked, looking at Ana's arm hanging limply at her side.

"It hurts, but I think I'll live," she responded with a grimace of pain.

"Ana," Connor said, "good to see you. Now, anyone want to tell me what the *hell* is going on? I've been following you for the last three days, and I want some answers."

"After we get this wound taken care of," James said. "Bro, mind going into the station and getting a first aid kit if they have one?"

"No need," Connor said, walking back to his car.

"Let me do the talking," James whispered to Ana as his brother started back to them carrying a first aid kit he'd retrieved from the trunk.

Ana looked up at him, emotions playing across her face too fast for him to follow. When Connor was back, James carefully cut the sleeve of her shirt off at the shoulder. When the fabric fell off, he gasped. The hole in her upper arm was bad. There were bone fragments sticking out of the torn skin where the bullet had disintegrated it. This was not good. As carefully as possible, he used one of their last water bottles to wash off the wound, but it did little to clean it. Then he put a large bandage on and wrapped it tightly with gauze, ignoring the sounds of grinding bone fragments. Ana groaned as he put her arm in a sling to keep it from dangling at her side. She'd surprisingly stayed conscious the whole time, though he could tell it pained her greatly. He'd done all he could, but it was only a temporary fix. Something would need to be done soon.

"Better?" James asked.

Ana shook her head.

"It'll stop the bleeding at least, which is our main concern right now."

Her eyes held a faraway look and she didn't answer. She'd gone through a lot, just like he had. And even though Zeke had been an asshole, he could tell that he and Ana had once shared a strong bond, but it seemed that bond hadn't survived the end of the world.

"Let's get you into the car," James said, helping her up. Before he could put her in the back seat, Connor took her knife out of the sheath on her side. "What—"

"I don't trust her," Connor stated. "And until I hear the full story, she stays in the back, unarmed."

Ana didn't even seem to notice as James buckled her into the back seat of the cop car. She was completely out of it—whether from the shock of the bullet wound or her emotional wounds, he didn't know. James and his brother gathered up the guns, ammunition, and fuel cans. They also syphoned the gas out of the Jeep and into the cop car. Then they were on the road.

After driving in silence for a few minutes, Connor spoke. "I'm glad you're alive, brother."

"Thanks for the assist," James said. "I wasn't sure if I was gonna make it."

"From what I've gathered of your flight, you barely did."

"That's true enough."

James rubbed his leg, which was doing better but still ached, as did his shoulder, but those were just flesh wounds. The tattoo on his hand was also aching since he hadn't been able to lubricate it and the scabs had scrapped off. It would definitely scar some now, but that was the least of his concerns.

"You mind giving me the lowdown?" Connor asked.

He could tell that his brother was relaxing by the minute. When he'd first shown up, he'd had a wild look in his eyes. He'd been ready to take down any threat that should arise, but now he was calming somewhat. James told his brother about everything—from the truck getting blown up, to Emmett sacrificing himself for James, to the Reclaimer letting him go. He told him about almost drowning, then Windfall and almost being shot, then wrecking into the tree, being captured by the Reclaimers and Ana coming in. After that he made sure to tell it in a way that made Ana seem as though she was just going along with it to save him.

He wasn't sure himself what he thought about what she'd done. At first, he'd been sure that she was going to betray them, but as time passed, he picked up on her kindness towards him and the battle that seemed to be raging within her. He didn't know what it was all about, but for some reason he trusted her and didn't think she meant them any harm. That didn't mean he would completely let his guard down, but with the showdown and Zeke almost killing her, the least he could do was give her a second chance. She'd almost died on account of him.

"So, all that blood on the grass back by the shot-up truck," Connor said. "That was Jezz?"

"Yeah," James said, "Ana took care of her."

"There was no body."

"No one destroyed her brain." Now that he was out of harm's way and his story was told, he realized he was starving. After his stomach rumbled loudly, he spoke up. "You got any food?"

"In the pack."

Connor pointed to the large pack resting on the floor by James's feet. Rummaging around inside, he came out with an MRE and the last two bottles of water, one of which he gave to Connor. He didn't even take the time to heat the meal; he just opened it and stuffed the food into his mouth. When he was done, he ate a protein bar as well. They would have to ration, but right then he needed the nourishment.

"You need anything, Ana?" James asked, glancing back at her. Her eyes were closed, and her head rested against the seat. She must have been asleep. James shoved the last of the protein bar into his mouth. "So, what's the plan?"

"We're gonna meet up with the group in Tok."

"Who's leading them now that... Emmett's gone?"

"Tank. Greg was hit during the ambush. Not sure how he's doing, but it was pretty bad."

"And Neil and Beverly?"

"Gone. The first explosion took out the whole van."

"How's Olive? And Alexis?"

"They're both alive. I can't answer for much other than that."

"Well, that's somethin' at least. We may be hurting, but God is watching out for us."

"How can you say that?"

"How can I not? I was blown up and lived, Emmett making the ultimate sacrifice. That Reclaimer let me go. I almost drowned but didn't. Then I got shot up and came out with only a flesh wound. I wrecked but survived and was a captive for days to two psychopaths. And finally, you came in when you did. How did God *not* have a hand in that?"

"And what about the rest?"

James shrugged. His mind had asked the same thing, multiple times, but he told his brother what he told himself. "I don't know. But I know I'm alive and there has to be a reason for that. So I'll do what I always need to do—trust."

"You do that and I'll keep doing things myself because that's the only way to get them done."

Oh, Connor, how wrong you are, James thought.

He knew better than to say it, though. Glancing over at his brother, he finally saw the exhaustion on his face. Connor had been after him the whole time, never stopping. That was over ninety-six hours without any real sleep. James didn't even know how he was still coherent.

"Pull over," James said. "I'll take a turn driving."

"I got it," Connor responded without taking his eyes off the road.

"Just do it, bro. We both know you need it."

Connor sighed and slowed down. It was amazing how fast he'd been going—the fastest they'd been able to go since this all started because the roads had been growing increasingly clear of obstructions. There was still the odd vehicle here or there but nothing that caused them to have to get off the road. Apparently, not many people had been traveling this way when it all started, which was just another sign that Canada had been more prepared than the U.S. People had been able to get to where they needed to go before this had all gone down. But it still hadn't saved them all.

James got out of the car and walked around the front, meeting his brother. "Thanks again, Connor," he said, quickly embracing him.

Connor half-heartedly returned the hug. "I'm just glad you're safe," he said. "I don't know what..." His face hardened and he didn't finish the statement. James knew what he meant, and it pained him to see his brother burying his feelings like that.

"I know," James said as he broke the embrace.

He walked around to the driver's side and climbed in. The Dodge Charger was a nice ride, and after testing how crisp the pedals and steering were, he headed down the ALCAN at 70 MPH.

33

STEFAN LEAR

Post-outbreak day 25, early afternoon

The dream kept playing itself over and over in the back of his mind, and he couldn't dismiss it for long. What had it truly meant when Tom had told him to make the world a better place? His mind immediately went to killing all the bad guys and undead, but that was just silly. That'd never happen. Then he thought about what the future _could_ be like if they were safe, somewhere where they could rebuild. He knew that to make the world a place like that, it would take him doing things he normally didn't—stepping up when he'd rather stay in the background. He was now the leader of the group, and that was something he never would've picked. Yet here he was.

Tank said a quick prayer as they continued down the ALCAN. He wasn't even conscious of the action; it was just something he was increasingly doing when he began to feel overwhelmed. They were making pretty good progress because the roads were mostly clear, but he was making sure to drive like a grandma. It was getting more difficult to find diesel fuel, so he was doing his damndest to get the best mileage they could. He hated it. Driving like this was for old people. He turned the music up as _Trying Times_ by Demon Hunter began to play. At least that was one thing he could still do.

"Time to switch," Chloe said from the back seat.

Turning the music down, he glanced at the clock on the dash. Sure enough, it was time. Letting out a sigh, he pulled Scourge to a nice, slow stop. It felt wrong to drive this big beastie so delicately, but it was better than running out of fuel. Chloe climbed into the driver's seat and he kicked Lucas out of the shotgun seat. Leaning his head back, he stifled a yawn. Maybe it wasn't such a bad idea to switch so he could finally get some rest. They'd run out of energy drinks and he was starting to feel all the exhaustion of the last couple of days.

"What you got there?" Lucas asked from behind him.

"Nothing," Olive was quick to respond.

"Is that a snake?" Lucas exclaimed.

"No!" Olive said.

"A snake?" Chloe asked, looking towards the back.

"Road!" Tank said as the passenger-side tires hit the gravel on the side of the highway.

Chloe quickly looked forward and adjusted their course with a jerk of the wheel.

"Baby, I really think I should drive," Tank said. "You are a female after all. We wouldn't want to get in a wreck."

"Oh, shut the hell up," Chloe said, clearly not in the mood.

Tank chuckled, looking back at the small, soft-sided dog kennel that sat on Olive's lap. Sure enough, the ball python, Squeezer, was coiled inside. How did that little girl get the snake they'd left in Coutts all the way here?

"Olive," Alexis said, looking back at her.

"I know," she said, her eyes downcast. "But I couldn't leave him. He's as much a part of the group as any of us."

"He's a snake," Lucas said.

"And?" Olive asked, looking up with fire in her eyes.

Tank chuckled and glanced over at Chloe. "We can't leave him," he said, "which doesn't give us much of an option now."

"Yay!" Olive exclaimed. He could hear her unzip the kennel, and he looked back to see her taking Squeezer out. "I got all of his stuff in my backpack, and as soon as we get to the lodge we can get him a real cage."

"What about food?" Lucas asked, eyeing the snake with clear suspicion.

"There'll be plenty of mice out there," Olive said.

"How did you get him in here?" Alexis asked.

"Before we left, I put him in my backpack. Then I found this kennel in the RV and thought it was perfect."

Tank chuckled again while looking at Chloe out of the corner of his eye. She was fuming. He'd have to apologize for his last comment to her. It'd been a joke, but maybe he'd taken it too far. Or instead of apologizing, he could find a toy snake and put it on her lap while she slept. That would be a good one. Then again, did he really want to piss her off even more? Probably not. He'd just apologize and make things easy. No need to make them worse. He rested his head back again as Olive informed Alexis all about snakes and how they could taste the air. It brought a smile to his face to see such a small thing changing the entire mood in the rig. That snake may come in handy after all.

"We're at a quarter tank," Chloe said, jerking Tank awake.

Rubbing his eyes, he looked at the clock. He'd only been asleep for thirty minutes.

"The jugs are all empty," Tank said, yawning. "We'll have to stop." He looked out the window and noticed they were already stopped. There was a road going off to the left with a cluster of buildings a half mile back. "Well, check it out."

Chloe pulled off the road and Tank gripped his ACR. It was locked, cocked, and ready to rock. He could hear the rest of them checking their own weapons. It was nice not having to tell them to get ready.

The buildings looked like a large lodge with a couple of cabins around it. There was a shed out back and a carport with a tractor and a truck in it. Next to that was a fuel tank sitting off the ground with its own hose and nozzle.

"Bingo," Lucas said.

"What? You guys are playing a game without me?" Tank said, looking back.

"Huh?" Lucas asked.

Chloe just rolled her eyes and Alexis smiled. Nothing like a little joke to break the tension. They pulled to a stop by the tank and he was the first one out, scanning for threats, with Lucas and Alexis following. Searching the shed and carport they found nothing, so he went over to the fuel tank and emptied some out on the ground. It was diesel so he began to fuel up.

"Hey, guys," Alexis said, "I'm hitting the head behind the shed."

"That rhymed." Tank chuckled.

"Whatever," Alexis said. "I'll be right back."

"Take your time," Tank said, resisting the urge to wink. He didn't want to give her the wrong idea. It was just a habit of his.

She walked behind the shed thirty yards away, and Tank went back to fueling up. This wasn't a commercial-grade nozzle, so he had to keep the lever pressed down to keep the diesel flowing.

"Why are you always joking?" Lucas asked, lowering his rifle.

"Haven't I been over this with all of you already?" Tank asked, exasperated.

"Not me."

"Okay. Well, ask one of the others. I'm busy."

"You're just standing there."

"It takes immense concentration to hold this lever down."

Lucas mumbled something and walked over to the other side of Scourge. Tank finished fueling up as Alexis came back around the shed.

"I have to go, too," Olive said, opening the back door.

"I'll take you," Alexis said.

They went back to the shed, and Tank walked over to the other side of the LAPV to stand next to Lucas, gazing back at the lodge.

"I joke around because it lessens the tension. It helps us all cope with everythin' goin' on. But don't ever take my jokin' for me not takin' things seriously," Tank said.

"I guess that—" Lucas began but was cut off.

"Howdy, boys," said a voice from their left.

Tank turned and raised his rifle to his shoulder.

"None of that, now," said the man standing beside one of the cabins forty yards away. "Look behind you."

Lucas cursed behind Tank, and he knew that there was indeed someone behind them.

"And over there," the man said, nodding to the lodge.

Two men were coming around the lodge and walking towards them.

Tank cursed under his breath. They were practically surrounded and in the open. He looked back to the man who was talking. He had to be the leader, and if Tank could take him down... they'd be killed by the others. Damn. The leader was an older man, but he had a mean look to him and a crazy light in his eyes. He held an old wooden-stock Thompson submachine gun and was dressed in plain clothes.

"Now that we have that settled," said the man with a smile, Tommy gun aimed at Tank's chest, "lower your guns."

34
PROGRESS

Post-outbreak day 25, early afternoon

"That looks like a freshly dug grave," Connor said from the passenger seat, pointing ahead.

"It does," James said, slowing the car. "Let's check it out."

Pulling to a stop, Connor hopped out and walked over to a mound of dirt. It could've been just a filled-in hole, but the shape and the rock sitting on one end told the full story. There were some aggressive tread marks in the soft soil next to it. He could be mistaken, but it looked a lot like the LAPV.

"Check these out," Connor said.

"Scourge?" James asked.

"Maybe."

"Who would this be?"

"Probably Greg. I told you he wasn't doing good."

"I just hope…" James turned away.

"Don't do it, bro. It *is* Greg. I know it."

"Okay." James took a deep breath. "Well, nothing we can do here. Let's head out."

"I can drive."

"Get some more rest. I pretty much slept for the last two days."

Connor sighed but didn't want to argue.

"Mind if I get out?" Ana asked from the back seat.

"Oh, yeah," James said, opening the door.

Connor gripped his rifle a little tighter. No matter what James said, he didn't trust her. Not yet. Some things didn't add up with James's story, and until Connor was sure, he'd keep a close eye on her. James grabbed an MRE and water from the pack and set it in the back seat while Ana went into the brush. She came out a little while later, looking pale. Her wound was really taking a lot out of her. James went over and helped her to the car while Connor watched from the front seat.

"Did you tape the taillights?" James asked, climbing into the driver's seat.

"Yeah," Connor said. "Makes it harder for anyone to follow."

"Good idea," James said, buckling his seat belt. "You good, Ana?"

"Yeah," she said, quietly.

"Let's hit it."

Connor rested his head against the window and watched the landscape pass them by as James sped the car up. He should be happy. He'd found his brother and rescued him, but things just felt wrong. The whole situation pissed him off. His brother was alive, and that was the important thing, but the hell they'd both gone through was slowly eating away at what little faith he had left. How was he supposed to go on after everything? He tried to fight it, but soon his eyelids drooped and sleep took him.

James climbed back into the car, shutting his door as quietly as possible, but it wasn't quiet enough. Connor's eyes snapped opened and he looked over at James.

"Sorry, bro," James said, putting the car in drive.

"What were you doing?" Connor asked, looking out the window.

"There was a large military plane on the airstrip back there," James said, getting back on the highway. "I thought I'd check it out real quick."

"Without backup?" Connor asked.

"It was in the middle of nothing and very empty. I wanted to let you sleep."

Connor grunted.

His brother was in a foul mood and James didn't understand why. He'd come in at the last second and saved him. Hadn't that been his goal? But maybe that was the problem. He'd been single-mindedly focused for the past few days, like he could get sometimes. Now that he no longer had that driving factor, all the emotions he'd shoved down would come to the surface. His brother was just processing everything, and he couldn't blame him.

It was hard enough for James, and he was leaning on God as much as he could. It must be even harder for his brother right now as he was trying to do it all on his own. That could be a dangerous thing. James said a quick prayer for his brother, Ana, and the rest of their group. If they could just get to the lodge, everyone would be able to fully work through their emotions instead of all this unfinished processing before the next disaster.

That terrified him though. He knew there was a lot more for him to process, and even though he was trusting in God, once they stopped, everything would come back—just like in Coutts but worse. When they finally made it to the lodge, it would be the true end to their long journey, not just a false one like in the border town. Just being still for that long had brought a lot back to him. Once they were truly home, it would be even worse, but there was a promise there as well. They would be safe, and they could start anew.

Once they were at the lodge, things could finally move forward. They'd been on the move for weeks now, going from one thing to the next, barely holding on. That would all change soon. They couldn't be far behind the rest of their group, and as long as they didn't run into serious trouble, they could get there by this evening. It felt good to be getting this close. Once in Tok, they only had a few hours to Glennallen. Then Connor could fly them to the lodge and they'd be home, at their final destination—their last hope.

35

THE HARD CHOICE

Post-outbreak day 25, afternoon

Alexis peeked from around the shed, Olive safely behind her. As soon as she'd heard the unfamiliar voices, she knew there was trouble. She could see the man who was talking, as well as the two coming from the lodge, but not the one who was presumably facing Lucas.

"What do we do?" Olive asked in a whisper.

Alexis shushed her.

"What d'ya want?" Tank asked, his rifle pointed at the ground.

"My name is Mr. Lear," said the man who was talking. "I want that vehicle and all your stuff."

"Ah, hell no," Tank said angrily.

"Is all that stuff worth your lives?" Mr. Lear asked. "What about the lives of the others?"

"Stefan," said one of the men who came from the lodge. He was now standing thirty yards away from Tank and Lucas, who were five yards from the LAPV. "What about the other woman and the girl?"

"Don't worry about them," Stefan said. "Hey! Tell that one in the vehicle she better not move or you both die!"

"Chloe," Tank said loudly, glancing out of the corner of his eye. "Stand down."

Alexis felt Olive stiffen behind her, and she quickly turned to see a man lunging at her with a knife. Her training took over, and she pushed the knife aside with her forearm and kicked him in the crotch. He dropped the knife with a grunt and fell to his knees, grasping his manhood. Then she brought her boot to the side of his head. It wasn't enough to kill him, she hoped, but it was enough to knock him out.

"Did you hear that?" one of the other men asked.

She'd made too much noise.

"How about this," Tank said loudly. "You get the vehicle and we keep enough supplies and our guns."

"Ya think I'm stupid, kid?" Stefan asked.

"No," Tank said. "But without anythin', we might as well be dead, anyway."

Stefan took a moment, like he was thinking about it.

Olive picked up the man's knife and held it in a white-knuckled grip. She was too young to have to use that, so Alexis needed to do something. There was only one choice, but she dreaded it. She'd have to kill someone, and the decision might get one of her group killed as well, but that was better than all of them. Emotion rose up within her as images of Evan's face being blown off came back to haunt her. The same thing had happened to Troy. She'd killed plenty of infected before, but people? She'd never killed a person. Would it be different, and could she even *do* it? Then she remembered her conversation with James about how she was afraid her inaction would cause the death of someone she cared about. This was that exact moment, and she was hesitating.

"Okay," Stefan said. "I figured it out. I'll give ya each a shovel for when ya get in deep shit. Kinda like now."

His other men laughed.

Teeth gritted, Alexis carefully leaned out from behind the shed on her knees. The grass was tall enough to hide most of her, but her rifle was above the grass, and she took a bead on their leader, who was preoccupied with keeping his gun on Tank. It would be risky, but she was out of time and options. She could see in the group's demeanor that they were growing tired of talk. Settling the crosshairs of her scope on the man's chest, she made the hardest decision of her life.

Tank looked at the leader, Stefan Lear, and knew that no matter what they did, they'd be dead. This man didn't want just their stuff; he wanted their lives. It was plain to see in his eyes, and even worse, he may keep the women alive—for a time. The thought sickened him, and he wanted to shoot the bald man right in his smug face, but he knew he couldn't get the drop on him.

Help us, Big Man, Tank prayed.

His plea was answered almost instantly when a bullet smashed into Stefan's side and exited out the other. He fell in a spray of blood, an incredulous look on his face. Tank didn't hesitate. He took a knee, swinging around to face the two men to his right. Aiming quickly, he let the chevron of his ACOG rest on the one to his right and pulled the trigger quickly. The man went down. The other man was able to get two shots off, but the bullets slammed into Scourge behind Tank. Before Tank could get a clear shot to finish the job, the man was on his knees, grasping his neck. Then another shot took the wounded man in the head and he fell backwards to the gravel. Turning fully around, Tank saw that the fourth and final man behind him was also bleeding on the ground.

"You good?" Tank asked Lucas.

"Yeah," he responded. "That guy *just* missed me."

"Alexis, was that you?" Tank asked loudly, looking around them for any more threats.

"Yeah," Alexis answered, hurrying over to the LAPV with Olive in tow.

"Nice job," Tank said. "You saved our asses."

She nodded as she ushered Olive into the LAPV.

"Lucas, fill up the gas cans, quickly," Tank said. "I'm gonna get their weapons. Alexis, watch us."

"Roger," Alexis said.

"Got it," Lucas said, rushing over and getting the cans off the small rack they'd hooked up to the hitch on Scourge.

Tank walked over to the leader, keeping his gun trained on him. The man was weakly trying to grab his Tommy gun that had fallen just out of reach. Tank picked up the gun and then looked down at the leader. The man stared up at him, pain on his face and hatred in his eyes.

"Sorry, mate," Tank said. "I'll make sure to get ya a shovel."

Stefan chuckled, blood leaking from his mouth. "Smart ass," he said past the glob in his throat.

Tank took the man's knife and handgun and then moved on to the rest of the men, leaving Stefan to his dying.

Alexis sat in the back seat next to Lucas. She'd just killed some-one—and not just one but two. They had been bad guys, just like her dad said, and she didn't doubt that. But it didn't make dealing with it any easier.

It was them or us, she thought to herself. She had to believe that.

Taking a deep breath, she looked out the window. The moun-tains had a calming effect on her, and every time she began to feel overwhelmed, she'd look outside. They spoke promises to her that the world wouldn't always be like this, that there was a creator who cared about her and had more going on than what she could see. There was a whole world outside of her mind, and while it was tough to deal with the losses, she needed to keep going for the sake of those they'd lost. So, she decided to do just that and keep moving forward, even when she felt like giving up.

"Hey, Alexis," Tank said from the driver's seat, "good job back there. You gave us the chance we needed."

"I just did what I had to," Alexis said.

"Precisely, and sometimes that's the hardest thing to do."

She looked up towards the front seat and noticed Tank earnestly watching her in the rearview mirror. Chloe was also looking back at her with a knowing look on her face. She'd had to do the same thing with Bryce.

"Thanks," Alexis said.

"I think it was badass," Olive said, "the way you took them down. Bam, bam!"

"Olive!" Alexis said, taken aback.

"I know killing is bad, but they were bad, and it's okay to kill bad people."

"I would've done it, too," Felix said.

Alexis was about to say something when she realized they were right even if it shocked her to her core. Even though it wasn't something two young kids should be talking about, it was the belief her dad and the rest of them held, and she'd just proven it. If it was her life or the life of her family, then the bad guys had to die or it would be her family dying instead. She hated the messed-up world they lived in. It was just so *wrong*.

"While that's true," Lucas said, "you still shouldn't talk like that."

"Yes, sir," Felix said. "But I mean it."

"Okay," Olive said, chastised. "I was just trying to help."

"Thank you," Alexis said.

"Look!" Olive exclaimed suddenly, pointing out the window.

Out in a swampy flat was a large animal. The thing was huge, with dark brown hair and massive antlers.

"That's a bull moose," Tank said.

"Wow," Olive said. "He's huge. Why are his antlers fuzzy?"

"They're in the velvet and growin' now in the summer," Tank said. "Then, he'll scrape them off in the fall when the antlers harden."

"That's so weird," Felix said.

"He looks funny," Olive said as the moose passed from view. "What's that thing hanging from his neck?"

"It's called somethin' special," Tank said, "but I just call it his neck flappy flop."

Olive giggled. "Flappy flop!"

"I bet he'll taste good," Felix said.

"Oh, yeah," Tank said.

"I can't wait to eat one," Olive said.

"There'll be plenty of those at the lodge."

Alexis chuckled. While Olive was mature in some areas, she was still a kid, and that made Alexis happy. Maybe Olive *could* still be a child in a world like this. Alexis hoped so because eventually she'd want to raise a child of her own. That made her think of James and a tear slipped down her cheek. She might not get that chance after all.

36

TOGETHER IN TOK

Post-outbreak day 25, early evening

"Here we are," Tank said.

"Really?" Chloe asked from the passenger seat.

"Welcome to Tok, Alaska."

"Where're we supposed to meet up?"

"Not really sure."

As the town came into view, a large red hangar stood out to their left. He knew there should've been bush planes parked outside, yet there were none. The people in rural Alaskan towns had been the most prepared for something like this, and a lot of them probably had similar ideas to head into the wilderness. He had yet to even see a single undead since they'd crossed the border an hour and a half earlier. That was a good sign. Maybe this place was so remote that the infection hadn't really hit there.

"We finally made it," Lucas said, stretching.

"I wouldn't count those chickens just yet," Tank said. "We still have to get out to the lodge."

"Yeah, but that'll be easy, right?" Felix asked.

"Hopefully, but it all depends on which planes are available," Tank said. "It'll be a whole day of flyin' for sure, and that's if Connor shows up."

"That long?" Lucas asked. "What kind of planes are we flying on?"

"Bush planes," Tank said. "Some only hold one passenger, and the bigger ones still only hold four or five."

"Oh, that wasn't what I imagined."

Tank pulled Scourge off the highway and into the small airport with the red hangar. "This'll be as good a place as any," he said.

Alexis was out first, rifle to her shoulder as she scanned their surroundings. She was becoming increasingly better at all this, and she'd been good to begin with. He was still surprised but pleased that she'd gotten the jump on Stefan Lear and his men or that would've turned out a lot worse for them. Tank walked towards the door to the office on the west side of the hangar.

Chloe got out behind him, her shotgun in hand. She was also getting a lot better at this and was truly accepting and dealing with it. Ever since the barn, it seemed as if she'd found some semblance of peace in what had to be done. When he'd first met her in Fort Collins at the stadium, he hadn't thought she'd last the week, but she had, and he sure was glad about that. In the beginning, she'd lived in denial, but then Bryce had been the tipping factor for her. It hadn't been easy, though, because she struggled with that decision daily. Leaving Coutts had only made matters worse, and he'd been worried about her, especially after they were ambushed by the Reclaimers—again. But then they'd been surrounded by undead in that barn and she'd had to step up. It'd culminated there. He still didn't know exactly what had done it, but ever since then she'd accepted that the world was a horrible place right now but she still had to press on. He was beyond proud of her.

Tank entered first, Frostmourne leading the way. They cleared the building quickly and he was shocked that the place looked untouched. He hadn't been in a building in who knew how long that didn't look like it'd been ransacked. It was almost like they'd just closed for the weekend and had never come back. He almost believed that, except everything was missing. Whoever had been here had cleaned house before leaving, and it didn't look like they'd be coming back anytime soon.

Back in the main office, he heard static crackle over a radio and then a voice came through. He moved back into the room and found Lucas behind the office counter next to a radio with the antenna up.

"What d'ya do?" Tank asked.

"Shhhh," Chloe said.

Lucas turned up the volume.

"This is 96.9 KYSC, The River, Alaska's classic rock authority. We're happy to stick with our listeners even during a time such as this. If you're receiving this message, then know that Eielson Air Force Base outside of Fairbanks is safe. I repeat, the air force base southeast of Fairbanks is safe. We have beds, warm food, and the military protecting us. There is more room and extra supplies for survivors. Every day, patrols are going out and beginning to clear the surrounding area, and officials say we can come back from this.

"I know to some of you this may sound a little too good to be true, but it is. All are welcome at Eielson. Now, let's get back to the music and play some more kick-ass classic rock."

The DJ quit talking as *Simple Man* by Lynyrd Skynyrd began to play. Lucas stood there, looking at the radio like it held a brick of gold.

"I'll be damned," Tank murmured.

"Maybe this *can* be beat," Alexis said.

"I didn't think..." Chloe began. "Do you think it's real?"

"I don't know," Tank said. "We'll talk it over when the Anddersons get here."

"How long are we gonna wait for them?" Lucas asked.

"As long as we need to," Tank said.

"But what about the base? We should head there as soon as possible."

"We stay until I say so," Tank said, staring the other man down. "Or you can find your own ride and leave now."

"I just—"

"I don't really care." Tank turned from him. "Let's find somethin' to let James and Connor know we're here."

James watched out the windshield at the familiar landscape around them. He was very familiar with this stretch of the highway between Northway and Tok. They'd almost reached their final destination, and the whole plan was becoming a reality. He could hardly contain his excitement. Even in that, though, there was something that kept ahold of his mind—that grave on the side of the road. They weren't sure that it was one of their group or that the tracks had been from Scourge, but more than likely they were, and that meant someone was dead. Connor said it was Greg, but even in that they weren't sure. It could just as easily be someone else.

His mind wouldn't let him rest. What if it was Alexis or Olive in that grave? How could he go on if it was one of them? After all they'd been through, to lose either one of them at the end of the journey would be devastating. Each time his mind began to run wild, he didn't try to control it; he surrendered it to God. He was tired of always trying to do this on his own, and he wasn't going to revert into the cycle he always found himself in of not trusting. There would be times when that happened, given that he was far from perfect, but he was going to make sure they were few.

Ana was in the back seat, and she was groaning to herself. She'd been doing that for the last hour or so, and he knew her arm wasn't doing well. The bleeding had mostly stopped, but they'd been able to do nothing permanent for her. The bone was definitely shattered, and something needed to be done to fix it, but neither he nor his brother knew how to help. Ana was in immense pain, and he just hoped Alexis would know what to do.

If she's still alive, said a voice in his head.

He would *not* think like that. She was alive, and once they met up with the rest of the group, she could help.

"How are you feeling?" James asked Ana.

"Alive," Ana said through gritted teeth. "Barely."

Connor glanced back at her in the rearview mirror. James knew his brother was having a hard time trusting her. He could tell by how much he watched her every move, and even though James wasn't sure about her loyalty, he just somehow knew she wasn't a danger to them—although there was a small part of him that remembered the look in her eyes after she'd killed Jezz.

"How are *you* doing, Connor?" James asked.

"Good," Connor said, taking a deep breath. "I'm sorry if I came off a little harsh before. I was runnin' on very little sleep."

"I know," James said. "Don't worry about it. That intensity was what saved us."

Connor nodded, a smile playing across his lips. "It's good to have ya back."

"It's good to be back. There were a few times when I didn't know if I was gonna make it."

"Well, we did, and we're almost there."

"Actually, here we are."

James looked out the windshield as the familiar sight of Tok came into view. It didn't look much different than it always had. In fact, they'd only seen a couple of zombies in Northway and very few vehicles along the highway. It seemed that the infection hadn't hit as hard up there, but he didn't have any delusions; it had still ravaged The Last Frontier. These Alaskans were a tough people, though, and if anyone could survive this, it'd be them.

The large red hangar that was the main hub of the airstrip came into view. The white words *40 Mile Air* were hanging on the side of the building like always, but below that was something new. A very crude representation of the three-headed dog, Cerberus, was spray-painted in orange on the side of the hangar.

"There!" James exclaimed.

"I'll be damned," Connor said, turning the cop car into the driveway heading to the hangar.

They pulled up, going around the side of the building by where the office door was. Sitting there was a glorious sight—the LAPV with all its painted badassery. Scourge. Their group was here.

They'd finally made it to Alaska!

37

REUNION

Post-outbreak day 25, evening

James jumped out of the car before Connor even had it parked, and he winced as he put his full weight on his wounded leg. Quickly checking his surroundings, he made a beeline for the office door. It opened before he was up the steps, and all his aches and pains from the last few days faded. He'd been blown up, drowned, shot, wrecked, held prisoner, and more, but all that was gone the instant he saw her face.

Alexis stood there, tears in her eyes and a rifle in her hands. She was the most beautiful thing he'd ever seen or would ever see. In all the hours he'd been apart from the group, he'd trusted and prayed but hadn't dared to hope for this moment. Yet there it was in all its glory, and he couldn't find a single thing to say. So, he didn't speak. Lunging up the steps, he pushed her rifle aside and wrapped Alexis in his arms, holding her like it was the first and last time he ever would, and he was unable to stop the tears that came to his eyes.

She stood there for a few heartbeats and then wrapped her arms so tightly around him that he thought he would pop. She began to sob in his arms, and the world faded around them until they were standing in the middle of nothingness—just two people pouring out their hearts in time's oldest expression of reunion, of pain, of loss, of happiness, of the inexpressible emotions that were a mystery even to the people who felt them.

James pulled her back to look into her bottomless hazel eyes and smiled. "I love you," he said in a whisper. "I've known that from the first time I met you. It just took my brain a little to catch up with my heart."

"I love you, too," Alexis said, still crying even though she smiled.

Pulling her close, he brought his lips to hers. They shared a passionate, salty kiss for a few seconds, but then James pulled away as he felt something wrap around his waist.

"My little munchkin!" James exclaimed, looking down at Olive as she hugged him. He bent down and picked her up, hugging her tightly. "I'm so glad you're safe."

"I knew you'd make it," Olive said with a sniffle. "I was praying."

"That is the only reason I survived," James said, "God helped me out—a lot."

With one arm he held his adopted daughter and the other his future wife. This was all he needed in life. Everything just felt *right* in that moment. They were together, and soon they'd all be one big family. It was perfect.

"Glad ya found him," Tank said, walking out and gripping Connor's forearm.

"It was tough. He's mighty squirrelly," Connor said with a chuckle, gripping Tank's forearm back. "But I got it done."

"Glad to see you made it, man," James said. "How's the rest of the group?"

"We lost Greg and Troy," Tank said, "but we got here."

"Good job," James said, releasing the girls and going over to give Tank a big hug.

"Is that Ana?" Alexis asked, incredulous.

"Oh, crap," James said. He'd completely forgotten about the woman. "Yeah, and she needs help."

Alexis walked around to the back door of the car and opened it. Ana climbed out, grimacing as her arm brushed the back of the seat.

Alexis didn't hesitate, giving her a massive hug while being careful not to touch her wounded arm.

"I'm so sorry for what I said," Alexis said. "I wish I could take it back."

"No need," Ana said, her voice hard.

"Ana, I'm serious," Alexis said, more fervently. "I was out of line. You did what you had to do, and I respect that."

Something flashed in Ana's eyes, and she seemed to relax just a little. "Thanks," she said, then grimaced again.

"We need to get you inside so I can look at that," Alexis said, leading her into the office of the hangar. "Could someone get the first aid kit out of Scourge?"

"I can," Felix said, hurrying outside. "Hey, James, glad you're alive."

"Thanks, Felix," James said, patting the kid on the shoulder as he passed.

Felix returned a few seconds later with the massive first aid kit. James was amazed that he could even carry it. The thing had to weigh more than the kid, and it was almost bigger. Felix passed Lucas in the doorway, taking the monstrosity inside.

"Hey," Lucas said to James, "Tank tell you about the air force base?"

"No," James said, glancing over at Tank.

"It can wait," Tank said. "Let's get everyone inside first. We have a lotta catchin' up to do."

"Shouldn't we get on the road?" Lucas asked. "The base—"

"Lucas," Tank said, giving him a look. "We'll talk inside."

James looked at Tank, who just shrugged and then followed Lucas in. Connor grabbed his pack from inside the cop car and brought it inside as James followed.

They were all together again.

"Damn, those bastards," Tank said after James had finished his story. "At least they got what they had comin'."

"Yeah, they did," James said.

His mind was still trying to grasp everything Tank had told him. They'd been through a lot as well, and it pained him that both Greg and Troy were dead. They'd lost so much since leaving Coutts, and that wasn't even counting all the ones before. People's faces flashed through his mind and he felt his skin flush with heat. He hadn't had an episode in days, but he could feel one coming on now. Instead of fighting it, he prayed and surrendered it over to God.

After a minute, the feeling passed and he opened his eyes.

"An episode?" Connor asked.

"Almost," James said, wiping his forehead. "But it passed. I haven't had one in a while."

"Good," Tank said. "Maybe you're cured."

"That'd be nice."

"So, what's the plan?" Lucas asked impatiently.

"Well," James said. They'd had the radio on while they were swapping stories, and he'd heard the DJ talk about Eielson. He knew what his gut was telling him, and he'd been listening to it for years. No reason to stop now. "This isn't a decision any one of us can make. We all need to agree, but I know what I think."

"It's not worth it," Connor said. "The message was prerecorded, and it may not even be standing." Lucas opened his mouth to speak, but Connor continued, cutting him off. "Even if it *is* safe, it won't be for long. The lodge is our best bet. We'll have everything we need there, and then, if they do get this mess cleaned up, we can always check it out. But I'm done trusting other people; we need to fend for ourselves. No matter what, I'm going down to Glennallen and flying out to the lodge tomorrow."

"And I'll be with you," James said, "as will Olive."

"Yeah," Olive said, sitting next to James.

"Me, too," Felix said, sitting across the office by Tank.

"Chloe and I will also," Tank said. "No reason to change the plan now for a potentially false sense of hope."

"I know Alexis is with us, too," James said, glancing down the hall. "And Ana."

Alexis and Chloe were in a room helping Ana with her arm. He should go check on them and see what Alexis had found out. Maybe it wouldn't be as bad as he thought.

"You guys can't be serious?" Lucas asked, standing up. "There's a safe base, and you want to just go out and stay in some cabins in the woods?"

"Exactly," James said.

"Pretty much," Tank said.

Lucas shook his head as he walked over to the door and went outside, slamming it shut behind him. James looked at Tank, who shrugged. Tank said that Lucas had done well, but after Troy's death it was like he'd almost given up. The two of them had gotten closer over the last couple of weeks, and James could understand where he was coming from. To someone who didn't know the way of life in the bush, it would be a big adjustment, but it was far better than anything they'd had lately, other than Coutts. That had almost been good enough for him to want to stay. If not for the feeling that it wouldn't last, he could've seen that place as home.

"We need some help in here!" Chloe said, coming into the hall, her hands covered in blood.

James quickly stood up and ran down the hall, the rest of them at his heels. Ana was on a long conference table with her shirt laying in two pieces on the floor, exposing her arm. The wound was worse than he remembered. It was bleeding again, and he could see bone fragments poking through the torn skin like a shark's teeth. There was a tourniquet on the upper part of her arm above the wound. That didn't bode well.

A makeshift IV was hooked up to a coat rack, and Ana looked to be out cold. The first aid kit lay open on a small table next to Alexis, who was digging around in it. The thing was more like a small mobile hospital than a first aid kit. It had a defibrillator and a bunch of supplies as well as other tools that weren't in most. She came out holding a scalpel and a piece of wire with a loop on each end—a gigli saw. This wasn't going to be good at all.

Olive and Felix stood in the doorway.

"What can we do?" Felix asked.

"Search this place," Tank said. "Don't leave anythin' unchecked and stay together. We need any supplies you can find."

"Yes, sir," Felix said, moving off.

Olive gave them one last look and then followed. Tank had really taken charge of the group and it was awesome to see the growth in his friend. Never before would he have taken on something like this, but not only had he done it—he'd done it well. Alexis rubbed something on Ana's arm and then stared at the scalpel in her hand.

"Are you..." James began, but couldn't finish his thought.

"If it's not amputated, she *will* get an infection," Alexis said, steel in her voice. "Her humerus is shattered above the elbow where the bullet impacted, and it's nothing but a mess of bone fragments and torn muscle. If we don't take the arm, she won't live."

"I trust your judgment," James said, resting a hand on Alexis's arm.

"It's the only way. We have to take the chance," Alexis mumbled under her breath.

"You got this, honey."

"What do you need us to do?" Connor asked.

"I need more hands to stabilize her arm," Alexis said. "And all the prayers we can get."

38

FLYIN' RYAN

Post-outbreak day 25, late evening

Alexis pulled off her gloves, throwing them into the trash can as she exited into the hallway. Sighing heavily, she leaned against the wall, purely exhausted. There was nothing more she could do now; it was all up to Ana and God. Everything had gone as good as could be expected and the bleeding was under control. They were blessed that the military had given them such a comprehensive first aid kit when they'd left Coutts. She'd already had to use it twice, and it would get more use before all this was over.

Her exhaustion went far beyond her physical body. She'd been stretched in a hundred different directions in the past few hours. The amputation had gone well, and she prayed that Ana would recover, but her mind kept bringing up images of her mother bleeding out on the pavement. Her dad had done everything he could to save her, and Alexis had helped, but her mother had still bled out. This time had to be different.

"How's she doin'?" James asked, coming out of the bathroom. They'd been able to get the water that was still in the top of the toilet to wash off with. It wasn't the most pleasant idea, but it was water and helped get the blood off before they sanitized their hands.

"We've done all we can," Alexis said as James came over and wrapped her in his arms. She felt that the world had grown brighter now that James was back. "She's laying on one of the cots the military gave us. We'll have to stay here tonight. No way can we move her yet."

"We were thinking about it anyway since it's safe and we don't know what the airport by Glennallen will be like," James said, resting his cheek on her head.

"Is there a hospital here?"

"A clinic. Why?"

"We should get all the supplies we can and anything else we can find."

"They'll probably have taken most of it, but it won't hurt to look. I'll get the guys together."

"I'll stay here and watch Ana. Chloe and Lucas can stay here, too, and keep an eye out."

He didn't pull away when the conversation ended, and she leaned into him further. Wrapped in his arms, she almost felt the same security she'd had with her dad. It did feel good to have him back, and she felt much better than she had a few short hours ago. The future wasn't as bleak as it had been, but her dad was still gone—and with him a piece of her heart.

"Have I ever told you that you're an amazing woman?"

"No."

"Well, you're the most amazing woman I've ever known."

"You're just saying that."

"No, I'm not." James pulled away enough to look into her eyes as he gently tilted her chin. She looked back into his eyes. "Not only are you great at helping people, and you care, but you're not afraid to do what must be done to save those you love. You're strong and yet tender, determined and yet kind. Wrap all that up in such a beautiful package and that's what I call the real deal."

She giggled a little even as a couple of tears came to her eyes. "Thanks."

"Tank told me what you did," James said, still looking her in the eyes. "I'm proud of you. I know it wasn't easy, but you saved them."

She would never be able to tell him how much those few words meant to her. It felt like a burden had been lifted from her shoulders.

It wasn't only James telling her that, but she felt it resonate within her soul.

"Thank you," she said, burying her face in the crook of his neck.

Tank sat outside on a bench with Chloe, looking past the airstrip and the trees to the mountains rising in the distance. He watched as Connor moved around the other hangar to check for any useful supplies. Whether a result of his new insightfulness or the extremity of Connor's emotions, Tank could tell something was up with his friend. He was stressed, like a rubber band about to snap.

"Look at those mountains," Chloe said from beside him, her head resting on his shoulder.

"Beautiful, aren't they?" Tank asked.

"Yeah," Chloe said.

"But not as beautiful as you."

"You cheeser." Chloe chuckled.

Tank laughed. "Cheeser?"

"Someone who's super cheesy. A cheeser."

"Okay, it's official, you're weird as hell."

"Have to be to put up with you."

"Ouch."

"Eh, I got used to it."

She turned to him, smiling. Her eyes were sparkling in the light of the setting sun, and those lips... They were luscious, and he couldn't restrain himself. Leaning in, he kissed her, and she kissed him back.

It got very passionate, very quickly.

Someone coughed and Tank pulled away, blushing at what was surely an epic make-out session. He didn't even know how long they'd been kissing, only that his leg was numb from Chloe sitting on his lap. As a matter of fact, when had she gotten on his lap?

Ah, never mind, he thought with a smile.

Chloe moved back to the bench next to him, her hair a mess.

Tank looked up but didn't see anyone around. "Hello?" he asked.

"Ya done?" James asked, poking his head around the corner of the building.

"You know, we're all adults here," Tank said.

"I know." James walked over to them. "I just didn't want to barge in on such an intimate moment."

"Bah, and yet ya did."

"Yeah, we need to go check the clinic for supplies, and I have another stop, too."

"Won't everything be gone?" Chloe asked, not looking directly at James. Her cheeks were tinted red, which made Tank smile a little. She was sure cute when she blushed.

"Probably," James said. "But even if we can get a few items, it'll be worth it."

"How dangerous is it?"

"No more than anything we've done yet." James glanced around. "In fact, it's probably a lot safer because there don't seem to be many zombies around."

"A cake run then," Tank said, standing up and stretching. "We'll be fine, baby."

"I know." Chloe stood as well.

"Goin' on a run?" Connor asked, walking up from across the tarmac.

"Yep," James said. "Find anything?"

Connor held up a small toolbox. "Just this."

"Better than an undead while you're on the crapper," Tank said.

"What?" James asked.

"I got tired of sayin' 'stick in the eye.'"

"That's as bad as a sittin' chicken!" James laughed.

"That one's a classic." Tank smiled.

"You're such a child," Chloe said with a wink, and Tank laughed.

Connor just shook his head as he walked to Scourge. Tank did see a small smile on his face though. He'd have to move forward with Operation Fire Water tonight. That guy needed to get some things off his chest, and alcohol was the best way to do that. Giving Chloe another kiss, he walked to the rig as she picked up her shotgun and went inside with the others. Lucas stood outside by the door with his shotgun.

"You got this?" Tank asked him.

"Sure," Lucas said. After seeing Tank's reaction, he added, "Yes, I got it."

"Good," Tank said, "because half my heart is in there, and if somethin' were to happen..."

"I got it," Lucas said, standing up straighter. "Trust me."

Tank nodded. "I do."

Walking over to Scourge, Tank thought about Lucas. He still didn't know if the guy had what it took to survive, but he'd made it this far, and Tank did trust him—mostly. It helped that he knew both of the women inside were tough as nails. Connor was already in the passenger seat, and James sat in the back with Tank's ACR.

"It's good to have the Pack back," Tank said, making a fist with his tattooed hand and putting it over the middle console. The other two did the same with their tattooed hands. It was the most epic fist bump ever.

"Let's do it," James said, smiling widely.

Connor climbed out of Scourge and scanned the parking lot of the Tok Clinic. Even here there didn't seem to be any zombies. They'd passed several on the way, but nothing like he'd come to expect. These people must've had more warning than the rest, which made sense. The infection had broken out mainly in the central lower forty-eights and then popped up on both coasts. He hadn't heard anything about Alaska, and even Canada had had more warning than them.

"Let's take it nice and easy," James said. "No need to get sloppy now."

"No shit, Jamesy Boy," Tank said. "I didn't make it this far to end up a large happy meal."

"I don't know if you'd be a large anything anymore," James said. "Maybe a medium."

"Thanks, dude. I don't even know how many pounds I've lost."

"Well, you're lookin' good."

"Um, sorry man, but I already have a girl. And I don't swing that way."

Connor chuckled despite himself.

"And *there's* the asshole side," James said, also chuckling. "Just wanted to make sure you hadn't grown out of that."

"Oh, I'll never grow out of that," Tank said as they stopped at the front door.

"I'll take point," Connor said, and the other two nodded.

They cleared the clinic quickly as there were no threats inside. This place looked like the buildings they were used to clearing. Things were scattered everywhere, and most of the examination rooms had blood in them. A few even had bodies—or what was left of them in their advanced state of decay. Tok had definitely been hit with the infection; it'd just weathered it better.

"Gather all the loose supplies," James said, grabbing a trash bag from under the counter and handing some out.

"Ladies and gentlemen—Cpt. Obvious," Tank said.

James smiled. "It's good to have you back, brother."

"Yeah, yeah," Tank said, moving off.

"How you doing?" James asked Connor before he could leave.

Connor looked at his brother. James was just trying to help him, but he was in no mood to share his feelings right then. They'd have plenty of time for that out at the lodge. They weren't out of the woods yet.

"I'm good," Connor said. When his brother didn't move, he added, "We can talk later."

"Good," James said, clasping him on the shoulder as he moved to the chaotic supply room.

Connor went down the hall to the office and started collecting the random batteries and such. They had all the necessary supplies for a few days in Scourge, and with everything at the lodge, they'd be set for weeks. They'd eventually need more, however, and no matter how much they collected now, it wouldn't be enough. During their first few weeks at the lodge, they'd have to make a lot of runs into the surrounding towns to get various supplies for everyday life. The essentials were already there, but they'd need things that would make life more comfortable. The one good thing about there being only eight of them now was that they needed fewer supplies. It was a terrible way to think, but it was true.

After thirty minutes, they had two garbage bags of medical supplies and one of random stuff. Throwing those into the back of Scourge, Tank started the rig.

"Where to?" Tank asked.

"Should we check out Flyin' Ryan's house?" James asked.

"Roger," Connor said.

"Who's that?" Tank asked.

"A bush pilot who sold guns," James said.

"Point me in the right direction."

A few minutes later, they pulled up to an old log house just outside town.

"We need to be careful," James said. "His place may be booby-trapped."

"Seriously?" Tank asked, and James nodded. "I like this guy."

"He was a badass," Connor said.

They all climbed out of Scourge, and Connor looked at the front door. There was no telling what this guy had rigged up. They'd need to think outside the box.

"We can't go in through any of the doors," James said, walking around the house.

"Way ahead of you," Tank said, throwing a large rock through one of the high windows. The glass shattered and he used a stick to clear it away from the bottom of the frame. "There."

"I guess I can squeeze through," James said, looking at the other two with their plate carriers.

"Get 'er done," Tank said. "We got your back."

"Check out that rug under the window," Connor said, noticing the oddly placed mat.

James walked over to it with a stick in hand and poked it. A large bear trap sprung under the rug, the large metal teeth snapping together with a loud *snap*.

"Good call," James said as he climbed up through the window.

"Damn, this guy's good," Tank said.

"I'm in," James said a few moments later. "It's a good thing we didn't come through the front door."

Connor just hoped Ryan wasn't planning to come back to his house. He probably wasn't and, in the end, it was him or them, and Connor would pick his family over anyone else out there.

"Jackpot!" James said from inside.

$$39$$

BLOOD BROTHERS

Post-outbreak day 25, late evening

Headlights illuminating the darkness, they pulled up to the hangar and James climbed out. That had been a very successful run. They'd gotten some medical supplies and two dozen guns. Ryan usually had double that number at his place, which meant he'd taken a bunch with him when he headed out. Hopefully that meant he wouldn't miss the ones they'd taken, and the broken window was high enough a zombie couldn't get in, so his house was still safe. They'd stopped at Three Bears and the Outpost on the way back to fill Scourge with more food, some ammunition, and sporting good items. Most of the stuff had already been taken, but it was amazing what could be found when one searched just a little harder. Now they'd be set for weeks.

They'd also made a quick pit stop at the gold store in town where he'd picked out a couple of wedding rings. It made the whole proposing thing feel much more real, and he'd taken a good ribbing from Tank and Connor about not telling them sooner—not that they hadn't known already, but they'd had to give him crap for it like good friends do. Now he just had to figure out how he wanted to propose. It had to be personal and special. Plans drifted through his mind as they drove back to the hangar, but he decided to figure it out later.

He walked into the office, passing Lucas sitting in a chair on the porch. Alexis was making a bed on the floor with one of their sleeping bags.

"How did you do?" she asked.

"It was a good run," James said, going over and sitting on the sleeping bag next to her. "How's Ana?"

"Stabilized. She should pull through although I don't know how happy she'll be about losing her right arm. Do you know if that was her dominant hand?"

"I'm not sure, honestly. She'll adapt though. She's tough."

"So, what happened to you out there? You look like crap."

James chuckled and told her a quick version of the story.

"Wow, God was really looking out for you."

"Yeah, he was," James said as she leaned against him.

It was good to be back together because being with her felt like home. His mind drifted back to the conversation he'd been having with Emmett before they'd been blown up. He hadn't changed his mind on that, and he almost asked her right then. Something held him back though. He wanted it to be special, even during this. Plus, he should wait until they were safe, or at least as safe as they'd ever be.

"Your dad wanted you to know that he loved you, at the end," James said. Moisture rose in her eyes. "He also made it clear when I was talking to him that you were what kept him going through the hard years. You meant the world to him, and I'm sorry I couldn't save him."

The tears slipped down her cheek. "I miss him, but I know by the way he lived that he loved me, and I'm glad I got at least one of you back. I wasn't sure if you'd make it..."

"I'm not going anywhere." James pulled her tight as the tears dried up.

"I love you, James Andderson," Alexis whispered.

"I love you, too, Alexis Wolfe." James kissed her on the forehead.

"Ugh, get a room," Tank said, walking in from outside.

"Excuse me?" James asked, looking pointedly at him.

"He does have a point," Chloe said, walking in after Tank.

"Whatever. Jamesy Boy, you're needed outside."

"For what?" He didn't really want to leave Alexis's side now that they'd been reunited.

"The Wolf Pack is relievin' Lucas on watch so everyone can get some sleep." Tank winked.

James didn't know why he was winking. His mind was too tired and sleep sounded good. Olive and Felix were already asleep in the small office just off the room they were in. Squeezer was also there in a small kennel. He'd laughed when they told him Olive had smuggled the snake along, though he should've guessed she wouldn't have left him.

Lucas walked in, yawning and it just made James all the more tired.

"Why does there need to be three of us?" James asked.

"For the love of all things holy!" Tank exclaimed. "We're gonna do some smokin' and drinkin'. Are ya comin' or not?"

"Why didn't you just say that?" James stood up.

"He enjoys being all secretive and such," Chloe said, lying down on her sleeping bag.

"I only have three cigars and didn't want anyone feelin' left out."

"Since when have you cared?" James asked, giving Alexis a quick kiss. "I'll be back later."

"Have fun," Alexis said.

"Fair point," Tank said. "The three of us are gonna have a little reunion party. The rest of ya can suck it."

Tank walked out the door and James chuckled, grabbing the tan Carhartt coat he'd taken from Ryan's house and throwing it on. Even though it was summer up there, the nights were still cool, which was a far sight better than in Montana. He'd liked living down there, but his true home had always been Alaska. That was no surprise since he'd been born and raised up there and had fallen in love with the mountains over the years. Soon they'd be at his favorite place in the world with the people he loved most.

Out on the airstrip—not far from the hangar—they built a campfire and dragged four logs out there to sit on. James settled on his as he stared into the fire. Connor also sat there doing the same and they enjoyed the crackle and warmth of it. It was a perfect night for this. Tank returned a few minutes later with a large bottle of amber-colored liquid and a little wooden box.

"Where did you get that?" James asked, looking at the booze and humidor.

"Bought this off Durt before we left," Tank said, sitting down on his log. "I was savin' it till we got out there, but I think tonight is as good as any."

"Hell yeah," Connor said.

"Great thinking," James said, taking the humidor, cigar cutter, and box of matches from his brother. Cutting off the head, he then lit the cigar and exhaled the smoke. It was smooth and one of the best-tasting cigars he'd ever had. "Damn, this is good."

"What?" Tank asked, "ya think I'd have anythin' less for my two brothers?"

"I never doubted you," Connor said.

"Good man," Tank said, lighting his and taking a puff. "You weren't kiddin'."

"See," James said.

Tank pulled out three shot glasses from a pocket and set them on the final log. Filling them with amber liquid, he passed James and Connor theirs and they all stood up next to the fire, shot glasses raised high.

"I'll do the first one tonight," Tank said, looking pointedly at James, "because I know there'll be plenty more to come."

James chuckled and shrugged. "What can I say?"

"To us, boys," Tank said. "The Wolf Pack has always been as important to me as my own family. Hell, ya are my family. I'm just glad we can all be together at the end. Let's kick tomorrow's ass and get ourselves out to that lodge!"

"Cheers," James said, and they clinked glasses. He threw back his shot and felt the familiar burn slide down his throat. It tasted like some kind of whiskey, and it was as smooth as the cigar.

Tank let out a sigh of satisfaction. "That hits the spot." He then poured them another round.

"I wouldn't want to be here with anyone else but my two brothers," Connor said, toasting.

"Amen," Tank said, and they threw back. He poured them a third round.

It was James's turn. "We've come far, and it's been a long road, but it's almost over. We've encountered hardships and lost many friends, but we didn't let it break us. We've made new friends and even found love. Here's to new beginnings and a job well done."

"Eloquently put," Tank said with a wink as they took the third shot, which James almost choked on as he chuckled. "That's enough for now. We don't want to get too *tanked* before our last day."

"Did you just pun yourself?" James asked, sitting down and taking a puff of his cigar.

"That I did," Tank said.

"Hey, that's my job," Connor said, smiling.

"You'd have to talk more to make puns."

"Touché."

James watched his cigar smoke rise into the night sky to join the twinkling stars high above. It was so peaceful out there. He could almost pretend that the world hadn't ended and everything was normal in the quiet of the night. That was, if it hadn't been for the images that were always in the back of his mind—the people they'd lost, the people he'd killed, the horrors he'd seen. He shook himself. Tonight was for celebrating, not dwelling on the past.

"I'm going to say something," James said. "I know you're going to want to make some smart-ass remark, *Allen*, but don't. Actually hear me and take it in. We've always been close because we're the freaking Wolf Pack."

"Oorah," Connor said.

"I mean it when I say this: I would *not* want to be here, in this exact moment, with anyone else. You are both my family and we've been through so much, even before all this. The fires have forged our brotherhood, not melted us down. I'm proud of you both for how you've grown and helped this group. You've each had your part to play, and you've played it well. I'm proud to call you my brothers."

Tank opened his mouth but stopped and instead took a hit of his cigar. "Thanks, brother," he said. "I'm proud of you, too. You were a big factor in gettin' these people here, so don't downplay that. I love ya, boys."

Connor stared at the ground, the cigar held in his fingers. It had gone out.

"Connor?" James asked. He didn't respond for several moments, and James was about to speak again.

"It's just so damned hard," Connor said, looking up. Something glistened on his cheek in the firelight. "I've tried so hard to move on, to bury my feelings somewhere deep, but they won't stay there. How am I supposed to deal with all this shit?"

"By sharin' it with the two people who've always had your back," Tank said.

Connor wiped his cheeks with his sleeve. "It hurts..." He hesitated.

"We're here for you, Connor," James said, his heart breaking for his brother.

"How do we know that we're the good guys? I've killed dozens of people. Some even had families. We've stolen, lied, and shot our way across thousands of miles. How do we know it was all *right*? And how do we live with it?"

No one responded right away. The point was valid; they'd committed some atrocities. He and Connor had killed defenseless, sleeping men while looking for their mother, and the killing had just continued from there—not only people, but all the zombies, too. They'd once been human. How did all that add up with their faith?

"Why d'ya kill 'em?" Tank finally asked.

"I want to say that I did it to protect others and save people, but there were times when I just *wanted* to kill them for no good reason. That's what scares me."

"Why?" Tank asked.

"Because how does that make me different from the people I'm killing?"

"Because you're having these doubts," James said. "That's what makes us different. We don't want to do it; we have to. Even when you think you *wanted* to kill them, I know that if they hadn't been threatening those you love, you wouldn't have done it. You never would've gone into a town and just started slaughtering people. The ones we've killed were evil people who didn't value life and just wanted to hurt others. We're not them, and they're not us. We *are* different, and you know that deep down. We're at war, brother, against the walking dead and evil incarnate. It's that simple."

"Yeah, but..."

"But what?" James asked. "There is no 'but.' We did what we had to, and not a day goes by that I don't see the faces of the people I've killed or the ones we've lost. Those faces will always be with me, but guess what? I'd do it all again, every single time, every single bullet. I'd do it all the same because it got us right where we are. God didn't cause all this, but He sure as hell can use it for good for those who love Him. I believe that with all my heart. I have to."

Connor took a deep breath and looked up at James. "Thanks," he said, and even his voice sounded lighter than before.

It made James's heart swell knowing his brother was able to deal with at least a part of the guilt he carried. They all had a lot more to deal with, but in time, and with a lot of prayer, they'd be able to get past it. These hard times wouldn't break them; it would only make them stronger.

"I need those matches again," Connor said, looking to Tank.

Tank tossed the small matchbox to him, and James noticed that now it seemed like something was wrong with *him*.

"What is it, Allen?" James asked.

"Nothin'," Tank said, and James knew something was definitely up because he didn't say anything about his real name being used.

"Bro," Connor said, "I just bared my heart and it sucked, but I did it. Your turn."

Tank took a puff of his cigar and then sighed. "I can't help but feel like a third wheel here."

"What?" James asked. "That's ridiculous. You're practically blood."

"But I'm not. You two are."

"And?" Connor asked.

"Blood is important. Blood is a bond, and we don't have that."

"Blood doesn't matter," Connor said. "It's about who we trust, and there's no one other than you two that I trust more."

"Allen, you've always been my brother, and you always will be," James said.

"Yeah, but I don't feel like it sometimes."

"You are," Connor said.

"Okay, I've got an idea," James said, a light in his eyes.

"And what's that?" Tank asked, looking up.

"We change that." James drew his knife. "We become blood brothers."

"That's a little weird," Tank said, but there was a smile tugging at his lips.

"I'm dead serious. I'd give my life for you, Allen, just as I would for Connor. Now, are we doin' this?"

"I'm in," Connor said, knife in hand.

"Hell, yeah," Tank said, pulling his knife.

"If we do," James said, "I don't want to hear any more crap about you not being blood. After tonight we'll all share blood and a bond that will never be broken, even with death."

"I can dig it," Tank said, his smile growing.

"Good." James brought the blade of his knife across the palm of his right hand.

40
SIMPLE MAN

Post-outbreak day 26, morning

Tank drove south on Highway 1 towards Glennallen, rocking out to *Been to Hell* by Hollywood Undead. Last night had been one of the best in his life. He'd spent it with his two brothers—now blood brothers—and they'd smoked the best cigars, drunk the best whiskey, and stayed up way too late into the night. Then, after hours of sitting by the fire with them, he'd gone back inside to Chloe. They'd gone to one of the far rooms and done what lovers do best. He'd spent the rest of the night talking with her about their future and everything it would entail. It just didn't get any better than that. Who needed sleep?

He glanced down at the tattoo on the back of his right hand and the bandage wrapped around his palm. It was another sign that the Wolf Pack's bond was unbreakable. They'd been friends for years, but after last night, something clicked in his mind. They were his *real* brothers, not just best friends, and he finally believed that.

Thanks, he said, glancing towards the sky. If there really was someone up there, he was definitely watching out for Tank.

Chloe was sitting in the passenger seat, and she reached over, resting a hand on his thigh. He looked at her and she smiled, dazzling him with her beauty.

"Damn, I'm lucky," Tank mumbled.

"Yes, you are," Chloe said, winking at him.

Tank burst out laughing. "Took a play outta my book, I see."

"I'm learnin'."

"That you are, baby."

"You guys see that?" Alexis asked from the middle seat where Ana lay, the IV hanging from a hook above the door. Ana had been recovering steadily after her surgery the night before. Where her right arm used to be was a stump just below the shoulder with a massive bandage wrapped around it.

"Yeah, I got him," Tank said, slowing Scourge.

On the side of the road up ahead was a man sitting in a lawn chair, playing a banjo. He had long blonde hair and was wearing a plaid shirt and blue jeans, and he had a ball cap on his head. Beside him rested a large backpack and a walking stick. Tank pulled Scourge to a stop next to him, and Connor did the same with the cop car. James rolled down his window and Tank could hear him yell at the man. Tank cracked his door open so he could make out the words.

"Hey," James said.

The music from the banjo drifted into the cab, and he was glad it wasn't the song from *Deliverance*. The guy was good. He'd never heard anyone play bluegrass so well before.

"Howdy," the man said, still strumming along. "You folks passin' through?"

"Yeah," James said. "You?"

"Just a traveller on this lonely road," the man said, looking between both vehicles.

Tank glanced around them to make sure this wasn't an ambush or trap. They were on the road somewhere between Tok and Mentasta Lake. There were trees lining both sides of the road and mountains rising all around them. The thing was, it didn't *feel* like an ambush.

"What's your name?" James asked.

"Timber Wolf," he said, still picking away.

"You're traveling pretty light and unarmed."

"My body's the only weapon I need."

"Oh," James said.

Tank was having a tough time not busting up laughing. This man was a real piece of work. He was just sitting there on the side of the road, playing his banjo without even a firearm as two vehicles of heavily armed people approached him, and he acted like it was the most common sight in the world.

"Do you need any supplies or anything?" James asked.

"I got all I need right here," Timber Wolf said.

He slowly set the banjo down and picked up a large jug from the ground. Tank would be willing to bet a million dollars that it was homemade moonshine. He took a large swig from the bottle, a little dribbling down his chin.

"Is that 'shine?" Tank asked, opening his door a little more.

"Yep," Timber Wolf said, wiping his mouth with the back of his sleeve.

"You have any for trade?" Tank asked.

"Yep," he said, pulling a much smaller bottle from his pack.

"What do you want for it?" James asked.

"My mama always said to be a simple man."

Tank waited for him to say more, but apparently that was his answer.

"Couple bottles of water and MREs?" Tank asked.

"That'll do."

"Felix, grab some off the top."

Felix rustled around in the back seat as the man set the small bottle of moonshine down in front of him and went back to playing his banjo. The kid handed Tank two MREs and bottles of water, and he climbed out of Scourge. James and Connor both had their guns out the window, but they were aimed non-threateningly towards the traveller. Tank walked over and picked up the bottle, setting the MREs and water down in its place, his eyes never leaving the man. Timber Wolf did nothing but smile at him as Tank began to walk backwards towards Scourge. His teeth were surprisingly all there and pearly white.

"Thank ya," Timber Wolf said as Tank made it back to the driver's seat.

"We'll be on our way now," James said, pulling his rifle in.

"Travel light, travel fast," Timber Wolf said. "This world is full of crazies."

"Thanks. You have yourself a good day," James said.

Tank pulled Scourge forward as he watched the man in the rearview mirror. He didn't make a move as he slowly faded from view. He just kept playing his banjo.

"Are you sure trading him those supplies for booze was a good call?" Alexis asked.

"Hell yeah," Tank said, taking the cork out of the bottle and giving it a whiff. It burned his nostrils. "If we need to, we can use this for rubbin' alcohol or even gasoline if we run out."

Chloe chuckled, grabbing the radio from the console. "Is everyone up here like that?" she asked into the radio.

"Eh, a few of 'em," James said with a chuckle.

"Makes sense you two are from here," Chloe said.

"Hey, I resemble that remark."

Tank chuckled. "Welcome to Alaska."

James watched the road ahead. They'd already passed Gakona, which meant they only had a few minutes to the airstrip north of Glennallen where their hangar was. It'd been a long few weeks, but they were finally almost there. He wasn't sure what he'd do with himself when they were actually safe at the lodge. Then again, they'd still have a lot of work to do in the first few months getting everything set up. They'd have to open camp, take stock of their supplies, and make a bunch of runs into town to get as much gas, propane, and other supplies as they could. Connor would also be teaching Tank and Felix how to fly because they definitely needed another pilot. If something happened to his brother, they'd be stuck out there and have to take a three-day hike to get out.

"What's it like out there?" Olive asked, sitting in the back seat with Lucas.

"It's beautiful," James said. "There's a big mountain right behind camp where you can see bears sometimes. The lake out front has some fish and is full of beaver and muskrats. The swans also land there, and moose come by from time to time. It's always peaceful and quiet, and the sunsets are amazing. It's the coolest place on earth."

"Wow," Olive said, "I can't wait to see it."

"You'll love it," Connor said, smiling back at her.

After last night, his brother had really been able to take a load off, which just showed that a little alcohol and some bro-time could solve anything. Plus, it didn't hurt that James had been praying for his brother for the past few weeks, and had been doing so heavily last night as well. God chose to work in mysterious ways sometimes.

"Are you sure this is the right choice?" Lucas asked.

"Yes," Connor said. "If you'd like to get a car and take some supplies, you're more than welcome to go."

"I might get lost."

"Hard to do that with only two turns," James said, "one at Tok and the other at Delta Junction."

"I think staying as a group is better," Lucas said.

"Good call," Connor said.

"You'll like it out there," James said. "Trust me."

"Will you, me, and Alexis have our own cabin?" Olive asked.

"Well," James said. "Just you and me at first..."

"But Alexis will be with us soon, right?" Olive asked, innocently batting her eyes.

"Yes, she'll be living with us soon," James said with a sigh. "But keep it a secret for now."

"I can wait to tell her," Olive said. "You still need to ask her, anyway."

James chuckled. "Exactly."

"Here we are," Connor said, turning onto the airport access road. "The Gulkana Airport."

41

HONEY BADGER

Post-outbreak day 26, late morning

Connor pulled to a stop next to the last building in the line of hangars. This was where they stored their bush plane in the off season. Their mechanic had just given it an annual checkup a month ago, so everything should be set. All the planes were missing from the airstrip except for the couple that weren't flight worthy, but that didn't matter as long as they had theirs, although they'd need a larger plane at some point because doing everything in a Super Cub would take way too long.

James picked up the radio. "We got some company."

Connor had noticed the few zombies scattered about. Most were lurking around the three other hangars they'd passed, but a few were out on the airstrip as well. They'd need to take care of all those because he wouldn't want to hit one during taking off or landing.

"Yeah," Chloe said into the radio. "Tank wants to know the plan."

As the two vehicles sat there idling, they were drawing the attention of the nearest zombies, and more were joining the ones already visible, coming out of the nearby trees. This place hadn't fared as well as Tok, it seemed. If only there was a way to draw them all out and take them down quickly.

"We need to lure 'em out," James said into the radio.

"That's just what I was thinking," Connor said.

"Why not do what we did at the lodge by that lake?" Chloe asked.

Connor remembered Tank telling them about using loud music to draw out the zombies.

"Great idea," James said.

"While you guys handle that," Connor said, "I'll take Felix and he can help me get the plane ready."

"I don't like splitting up," James said, "but it's a good idea. Felix, come over to us and we'll get in Scourge."

"He's on his way," Chloe said.

James climbed out of the front seat, grabbing his ACR. "See you in a bit."

"See ya, brother," Connor said, turning the car off.

James, Olive, and Lucas moved over to the LAPV while Felix stood outside. Connor joined him and then looked at their hangar. There should be no threats inside, but he wasn't going to let his guard down now.

"You know how to use that?" Connor asked.

"Yes, sir," Felix said, his Springfield XDM 9mm handgun pointed at the ground.

"Good," Connor said. "Watch my back. We're going to clear the hangar and then check on the plane."

Felix nodded and Connor started towards the hangar door. Scourge pulled out and headed over to the middle of the tarmac where the tie-downs were so the bodies would be out of the way for takeoff. Connor arrived at the door and picked up a small rock just around the corner of the building. Flipping it over, he pulled the spare key out of the inside and unlocked the door, then replaced it in the fake rock. He opened the door and they stepped in quickly, Felix closing the door behind them. The inside was open, with a single room to their left and a staircase going up to a loft above it. The downstairs room was a bathroom, and the upstairs was a small apartment. The rest of the hangar was a large, open room with toolboxes and benches.

Two bush planes were sitting side-by-side in the middle of the floor, and he let out a sigh of relief. They'd lucked out big time! The one plane was their business Super Cub—well, it was actually a PA-12 with PA-18 components, but it was close enough to a Cub that they called it that. The other plane was a Cessna 206, which was a tricycle gear—three wheels under the nose instead of the Cub's two large wheels up front and one on the tail. The 206 was a bigger plane, and he'd be able to haul a lot heavier loads. It was also easier to learn to pilot and would be a game changer in the long run.

Connor and Felix quickly cleared the building, which was empty of threats. He then went over and looked at the two planes again. His yellow-and-black Cub—the Honey Badger—could hold one passenger comfortably, with a total load weight of three hundred and fifty pounds. It had a hundred and fifty horsepower engine that could run on a mixture of Aviation and unleaded fuel, which made it very versatile, and it had a cruising speed of 80 MPH. While the Cessna 206 could haul up to five passengers with a total load of a thousand pounds and could cruise at 120 MPH, it needed at least a smooth thousand-foot runway to land and take off. That was the advantage of the Cub. It could land in a few hundred feet and the airstrip didn't have to be good. It could even be a rocky gravel bar.

They'd need to preflight both planes to make sure everything was kosher. Even though the Honey Badger was his baby, it'd make things a lot easier to get the 206 out there first. They might even be able to make it in just three trips.

"Okay," Connor said, smiling at Felix. "Time to get to work."

James donned his old tactical vest, now that his plate carrier was gone, and picked up his dependable AR-15. It had been fun using the ACR, but there was nothing quite like holding the rifle he'd had since the beginning of all this. He shut the back door of Scourge and walked around to where Tank and Lucas were standing by the front. Alexis was peeking her head out of the hatch on the roof, and Chloe was by the front with Tank's ACR. Olive and Ana were in the back seat, lying low. Tank held Frostmourne, while Lucas had an axe, and James had pulled out his trusty katana with his tomahawk on his belt as a backup. He wasn't sure how many more slashes the old sword had in her.

"Ready, boys?" Alexis asked from above them.

"Roger," James said.

"Time to get this party started," Tank said, hitting play on his iPod.

Last Man Standing by Pop Evil played through the open front doors and Tank cranked the volume. Scourge had a great stereo system, and he didn't doubt that every zombie within a half mile would be able to hear it.

Perfect, James thought. *We can get this place cleared quickly.*

"Here they come!" Lucas shouted over the music as zombies began to close in on them from all sides.

As the zombies started to arrive, the three of them began to efficiently take them down. First, it was just one here and one there, but then they began to group up more. James pulled his blade from the eye socket of a downed zombie as the closest one to him fell with a bullet hole in its head. He may have been able to recover in time to take it down, but he'd told the girls not to take any chances. They hadn't made it this far to fall to the dead now. Slashing at the next one, he smashed the blade into its neck, but the zombie's spine wasn't the only thing that broke. His blade was missing the front half. Jamming the broken katana into a zombie's eye, he drew his tomahawk and took down one that had gotten a little too close.

After several minutes, he stood there with blood splattered over his arms as it dripped from the head of his tomahawk. There were no more zombies on this side of Scourge, so he moved to the other side as *The Struggle* by Blacklite District played.

Huh, what a fitting song, he thought.

They'd had to struggle every step of the way to get to where they were, but they'd made it, and in a few short hours, they'd finally be safe at the lodge. The volume on the music decreased as Tank turned it down.

"Good over here?" James asked between breaths.

"Yeah," Tank said, breathlessly.

"I don't see or hear any," Lucas said, heaving harder than Tank.

"See anything up there?" James asked.

"Let me check," Alexis said, scanning all around them through the scope on her M4. "I got nothing."

"Good. Let's see what Connor found," James said as he started walking towards the hangar.

"I'll follow in Scourge," Chloe said.

Tank and Lucas followed James to the large building. They were all three covered in blood and other random fluids as well. They'd need to get cleaned up, so hopefully there was still some water in its system. As they drew near, the large garage-style door opened to reveal Connor and Felix standing on the other side.

"Just in time to help," Connor said, going back in.

James was shocked to see not only their plane but a 206 as well. "Jackpot! How do they look?"

"Both are good," Connor said, going to the strut of the larger plane. "We'll push it out and I'll get her started."

James grabbed the other strut and they pushed the plane out of the hangar and onto the tarmac. Chloe pulled Scourge up and stopped outside.

"Go ahead and pull that inside," James told her. "Then we'll get it unloaded."

Chloe pulled the LAPV past the plane and Connor climbed into the pilot's seat. A few minutes later, the engine roared to life. He let it idle and then shut it down.

"Everything's good," Connor said. "It's even full of gas."

"Perfect," James said. "We should get the loads divvied out. What're you thinking? Three of 'em?"

"Yeah, let's get the supplies out of Scourge and see what we've got."

$$42$$

FLYIN' HIGH

Post-outbreak day 26, early afternoon

"Are you sure this is the right call?" Chloe asked.

Tank pulled her back to look into her eyes. "Of course. You and Alexis will go first with Lucas to help out. Then the kids, Ana, and most of our gear, and then James and I will be right behind."

"What if..." Chloe began and then just hugged him tighter. They were still in the hangar while everyone else helped load the plane. She didn't like that they'd be separated, but it was how things needed to be.

"No 'what ifs,'" Tank said. "You're my first priority, and you need enough supplies to be safe. A storm could roll in and then you'd be stuck there. It's the smart play."

"I just don't want to be away from you for even a couple of hours."

"I know. I don't either, but I'll be there before ya know it." He wiped a tear from her cheek. "Be strong for me. You've been through so much, and this is just gonna be a couple of hours. You can handle that."

Chloe nodded, taking a deep breath. "I can."

"I know you can. Now, come here."

He pulled her into a kiss and lost himself in the feel of her lips pressed against his. The scent of her drove him crazy, and the press of her body on his made him feel like he could face anything. The end of the world and he'd found his other half. Who would have thunk it? After a few blissful minutes, he pulled away and smiled at her.

"Time to go, babe."

"You got everything?" James asked, looking in the back of the loaded Cessna.

"Yeah, we got it bro," Connor said, checking the strap on the dog kennel that held Squeezer. He was still shocked that Olive had smuggled him out, but he was happy she had. "No need to triple check."

"I know. It's just hard," James said.

"We'll be fine," Alexis said, coming up and giving him a hug.

"It's tough to let you go so soon."

He gave her a quick kiss.

"You said it should only be a forty-minute round trip, right?"

"Yeah, but—"

"No buts, I'll see you soon."

James let her go, and she bent down to Olive who stood by James. "I'll be seeing you, too, little Olive," she said.

"Of course," Olive said with a smile, giving her a big hug.

"We'll be there shortly, miss," Felix said.

"See ya, Felix," Alexis said, climbing into the plane. "You too, Tank."

Tank and Chloe were walking out of the hangar, and James noticed her wipe a tear from her eye. It was hard for them to be separated as well.

"See you soon, Alexis," Tank said. "Thanks for all the help gettin' us here."

"No, thank you for stepping up," Alexis said. "You did a great job."

"Thanks," Tank said, helping Chloe into the copilot seat. "I love ya, babe. Have a fun flight. The scenery should be killer."

"I will," Chloe said. "I love you too, Allen."

James saw him actually smile at the use of his real name. That was a new one.

"Allen?" Olive asked. "Is that your real name?"

"Nope," Tank said, giving her a wink.

"Not the winks again," Chloe said with a chuckle.

"Always, baby," Tank said, winking again.

"Time to fly," Connor said.

"See you soon," James said, shutting the back door. Then he turned to Alexis. "I love you."

"I love you, too." Alexis blew him a kiss.

"Take care of them," James said to Lucas, who was already in the other back seat.

"I will," Lucas said, nervously.

Apparently, he'd never flown before. Well, this would be a lot cooler than any commercial flight. James glanced up at the clear blue sky. Even though it was nice with the sun shining brightly, the weather could turn brutal in a matter of minutes up there.

Connor walked over and made sure the back door was closed properly. "I'll be back in an hour max, probably less."

"Tear up those skies, brother," James said, giving him a fist bump.

"See ya soon," Tank said, grasping his forearm.

"See you, brother." Connor grasped his as well.

Alexis waved at Ana, who sat on the cot they'd set up next to the gear for her to lie down on. She was off the IV, but Alexis made James promise to keep an eye on her. Ana actually waved back though the expression on her face didn't change. James wasn't sure if she was just tired, upset about her missing arm, or pissed off at them.

They stepped back as Connor climbed in and started the engine, checking all the gauges. Then he taxied out to the airstrip and faced the plane into the light breeze blowing down the runway. He revved the engine and the plane began to gain speed. Before James knew it, the wheels were off the ground and Connor was airborne.

"That's a beautiful sight right there," Tank said.

"I can't wait to fly," Olive said with a squeal.

"You will soon enough," James said, releasing a pent-up breath. "Compared to what we've been through, bush flying will be the least dangerous thing we've done in weeks."

Tank chuckled. "Remember when we went in guns blazin' on those Reclaimers?"

"That was awesome," James said, walking back to the hangar with his brother next to him and the kids following behind. They had to get the next load ready. "Remember when we went into the Reclaimers' hideout all decked out and there wasn't anyone there?"

"That was a huge disappointment. Oh, remember when we were drivin' the 'stang? That was a kickass ride."

"It was. What about when we fought our way out of the customs building and you got bit?"

"That was pretty badass. I'm glad it happened, too. Helped put things into perspective. What about before all this when we snuck into the school durin' summer and ate the teacher's puddin'?"

James burst out laughing. "I'd forgotten about that. Good times. Or when we went swimming in the lake at night?"

"Damn, we sure do have fun," Tank said, watching as Connor disappeared from view, heading south towards the Chugach Mountains and their lodge.

"Let's get the loads weighed out," James said, looking at their remaining gear.

It wasn't long after they were done getting the next two loads prepared that they heard the hum of a plane in the distance. James looked down at his watch. It'd only taken him forty minutes. They had both loads divvied out and sitting outside the hangar. Scourge was parked inside with a few supplies and a couple of firearms if someone got stuck out there. The keys to it were in a lockbox under the table with a combination. All they had to do was lock up the hangar and they'd be ready to roll. Connor didn't come straight in, and James could hear him circling to the south, but he couldn't see him yet.

"What's he doin'?" Tank asked.

"Not sure," James said. "Maybe he found something and is getting a better look."

"Could be trouble," Ana said. She was sitting on the ground, leaning against their gear since they'd taken her cot down.

"Maybe," James said.

"You'll be on the next trip, right?" Olive asked.

"Of course, my little munchkin," James said, kissing her on the top of the head.

"Good," Olive said, holding his hand.

With her little hand in his, he could feel his heart swelling with love. So this is what it felt like to be a dad. He could get used to this.

Connor must've finished whatever he was doing because the hum was getting closer again, and soon he could make out the white plane in the sky.

"There he is," James said.

"That was less than an hour," Felix said.

"By the time he lands and taxis over, it'll be just over forty-five minutes," James said.

"Damn good," Tank said. "We'll be there before we know it."

Connor landed on the strip flawlessly and taxied over, but he did it a little faster than normal.

"Something's up," James said, running over as soon as Connor pulled the plane to a stop by their gear.

Connor shut the engine off and jumped out. "There's a horde coming from the south."

43

INTO THE HORDE

Tank cursed. "How far?"

"Probably an hour out," Connor said, opening the back door.

"We have time then," James said as they started to quickly load the gear.

"I'll make it a quick turnaround," Connor said, grabbing a duffle bag. "We'll have time."

"You made it round trip in forty-five minutes," James said.

"Good. Get Ana and the kids loaded. Tank and I got this."

"Come on, guys," James said, moving over to help Ana into the plane.

"I got it," she said, but James insisted.

"If Alexis finds out I let you walk to the plane alone, I'll get my ass chewed."

"Fine," she said as he helped her stand and then get into the back seat of the plane.

He helped Felix into the copilot seat, buckled him in, and then lifted Olive into the back so she could go to the other back seat.

"Promise you'll be next?" Olive asked, a tear in her eye as James buckled her in.

"Of course, sweetheart," James said, holding her face. "I promise."

He kissed her on the forehead.

"I love you, James," Olive said. "I'm so glad you're my dad."

James smiled. "I love you too, little munchkin. See you soon."

He shut the door and went around as Connor was locking the loading door.

"Safe flyin', brother," James said.

"Thanks. See ya."

"We'll be here, waitin' on a woman," Tank said.

Connor chuckled, climbing in. "I'll be back."

He didn't waste any time. The engine started, and he pulled out onto the airstrip and took off. The plane slowly gained altitude in the warm summer air, and then he was out of sight.

"So, we got about forty-five minutes," James said. "Let's get the hangar all buttoned up and give it a good once-over to check for anything useful."

James and Tank went back into the hangar, pulling the cop car in with the LAPV and the Honey Badger. Then they boarded up the two windows and closed the big door. Next, they went through the hangar, collecting a few miscellaneous items and a good toolbox for the plane. They locked the small door and took the tools over by the rest of their gear, which they moved farther from the hangar so Connor could pull right up to it.

"How long?" Tank asked.

"We have another twenty minutes or so," James said.

"Damn. I hate sittin' here."

"We could check these hangars for anything useful. We still have fifty pounds we can add to this load."

"Better than doin' nothin'."

James picked up his AR from next to the pile and hooked it onto the sling looped around his torso. Tank grabbed his SAW and they quickly walked over to the closest hangar. They posted up at the door and James went in first, with Tank right behind him. The place was clear, and they started searching.

"How do you know that the Big Man upstairs is real?" Tank asked.

"What?" James turned from the box he was looking through.

"Ya know, God. How do you know He's real?" Tank threw a roll of rope into a trash bag.

"I just do. I've felt His presence before, but I just *know* it."

"Ya ever doubt?"

"Oh yeah, that's part of being human, but it always comes back to trusting that He's real. That's why it's called faith."

"Huh."

"Where's this coming from?"

"Just been doin' a lotta soul searchin' lately."

"And?"

"I'm not sure yet. I've always believed there's a god. Just not sure on the details."

"You know the spiel. Jesus died for our sins to save us and all that."

"Oh, I remember all those times in youth group and the winter retreats."

"Yeah, those were fun... and awkward. All you have to do is make the choice to follow Jesus and make him your savior. Nothing fancy."

"Yep, I remember the prayer. It always sounded lame and rehearsed."

James chuckled as they moved back to the door. "That's because it is. You could just say, 'Hey dude, take my life, use me, and forgive my sins, yo.'"

Tank chuckled. "That sounds *way* better."

"You know what I mean."

"I do, but we have another buildin' to check."

"I can tell you more—"

"Nope, that answers my question."

"But—"

"James, let it go."

"Sure."

James moved on to the next hangar in line, glancing at his watch. They still had fifteen minutes. Stacking up at the door they cleared it and then moved on to the last hangar. James was ready to nod to Tank to go inside when he heard the plane.

"He's back already?" James asked, looking at his watch. "He's early. Let's go."

James and Tank ran back to the pile of gear as Connor came straight in with the plane. He kept it just off the runway until he was halfway, cutting down on the taxi time. He pulled over to the pile of gear and James had to jump to the side as he practically ran them over. Connor glanced back to make sure the door was next to the gear. His face was white as a sheet.

Tank cursed when he saw him.

"Get the plane loaded," James said, opening the door before the engine was fully off.

"The horde is almost here!" Connor shouted, jumping out. "And I'm almost out of gas!"

James cursed. "I should've thought of that."

Connor threw out two red gas cans he must've picked up from the airstrip at the lodge. "The aviation fuel is down past the last hangar," he said. "These two will be enough to get us back."

"I know where it is," James said, swinging the AR to his back and picking up the cans. "I'll fill 'em. You guys load the plane."

"Be careful," Connor shouted as James sprinted away.

He should've thought to get gas. They even had two empty jugs stashed in their hangar. Instead, they'd gone and looked through all the hangars for random stuff they didn't need. It had been a stupid mistake. James came around the last building and could see the first zombies in the horde coming up Highway 1. There were hundreds of them, with the nearest less than fifty yards out. They were in deep shit. Setting the jugs down, he drew his handgun and shot the lock on the fence surrounding the fuel tanks, making sure to not aim anywhere near them.

Pulling the chain off, he picked up the jugs and went to the tank labeled Aviation fuel. He began to fill them up, watching the zombies close in. They must've been drawn to the sound of the plane taking off and landing. Something would need to be done about that in the future. Maybe they could build a fence around the airstrip and their hangar. He remembered Emmett mentioning that. He glanced down at the jug. It was only half full and the zombies were closing the distance. Why did it take so long to fill a damn jug?

Finally, it was full, but the zombies were only twenty yards away now.

They didn't move very quickly, but when he was just standing there waiting for the jugs to fill, it made them seem fast in comparison. The nearest two zombies reached the other side of the fence, and they pressed against it, trying to reach him. Another dozen were close behind, with a hundred or more still coming. He was so busy watching them close in that he wasn't paying attention to the gas, and it came pouring out of the jug. Some splashed onto the bandage over his fresh cut from the night before, and it burned like hell.

He cursed, letting off the lever, and dropped it while tearing off the soaking bandage. Wasn't the lever supposed to click off before that happened? Dumping a little out, he screwed the cap on, noticing his boots were covered in avgas. Turning for the gate, he saw that a few zombies had wandered between him and the nearest hangar, coming his way. Cursing again, he pushed one of the gates opened and started to run with the two full jugs in hand. Something jerked him back and he spun, falling towards the ground. He tried to stop himself, but his hands were full, and he couldn't let go in time to catch himself. His face collided with the hard asphalt and he saw stars, his nose crunching as pain shot up his face.

Pushing himself off the ground, he glanced around frantically as blood poured from his nose. Something was seriously wrong. He couldn't see. Everything was blurred. Reaching up to feel at his face, he realized his glasses were gone. Blurry silhouettes closed in on him from all sides. The ones he could make out that were for sure zombies were only fifteen feet away and closing. The rest were just fuzzy shapes moving on a canvas of vague lines and colors.

Searching for half a second, he came up empty. His glasses were either gone or broken, and he didn't have time to find them. Grabbing the two containers, he tried to stand up, but something still had ahold of him. Terror gripped him like none he'd felt before. A zombie had him by his shirt! He looked back with wide eyes, but it wasn't a zombie. His AR had gotten caught in the fence somehow. Standing, he grabbed the rifle and tried to pull it free, but it wouldn't budge.

He was running out of time.

Drawing his knife, he slashed out at the sling. It cut cleanly and he wasted no time drawing his handgun and turning. Three zombies were within five feet, but he could barely make out the sights on the end of his gun. Without aiming, he pointed and began to fire, trying to keep his hands from shaking. The first one went down in three shots, and then the next in two. By the time he took those down, the third was practically at the end of his barrel. Its face exploded out the back of its skull as James shot it pointblank.

The rest of the zombies were too far away for him to make out, but they were closing in. Picking up the jugs, he took off towards the plane. Coming around the corner of the closest hangar, he almost ran right into a group of zombies. He was able to stop at the last second and swung the jug into the face of the nearest one. It knocked the thing to the ground but didn't kill it. He turned and ran more out onto the taxiway to get away from the group, only to notice there were more out there as well. The plane was a vague shape in the distance; at least he thought that was the plane, but he wasn't sure. He sprinted towards it anyway, going right by the group he'd almost run into. He couldn't tell how many there were, but there seemed to be dozens of vague shapes moving around the hangars between him and the plane. He began to change direction and head straight out onto the mostly open taxiway, but then he was falling to the ground again, his foot hooked on something. This time he was able to turn a little and not smash his face, but his head still smacked into the asphalt and he blacked out.

The horde was there.

Connor blasted the few undead that were closing in on the plane as Tank watched James run towards them, blood gushing from his nose. What the hell had happened?

"Keep them off the plane!" Tank yelled. "I got James!"

He took off running. He wished he could thin out the undead between James and him, but there was a risk of hitting his brother as well. All of a sudden, James pitched forward and landed hard on the asphalt. Tank watched his head connect with the ground and his body go limp, the jugs tipping over next to him.

He'd just knocked himself out.

Tank didn't stop running as his mind worked a million miles an hour. James was out cold. They needed the gas jugs to get out of there, and there were at least three dozen undead between them, as well as fifty more closing in from behind James's prone form. Tank shouldered his SAW and opened fire, careful not to aim too low and hit his fallen brother. A handful of undead went down, others lost limbs, and others just shrugged off the bullets in a spray of blood. He wouldn't be able to take them all down before James was overrun. There were too many, and they were too close.

His dream came back to him with vivid clarity. It all made sense now. This was the moment he'd known was coming deep down in his heart. He'd made that promise to Tom not knowing what it meant at the time, but now it was all crystal clear. Peace settled on him, and he smiled despite the situation. This was his crescendo. Swinging the SAW to his back, he charged forward into the horde.

44

DAYLIGHT DIES

Post-outbreak day 26, afternoon

Tank shouldered his way through the group of undead, ignoring their scraping nails and biting teeth. Pain shot through his shoulder as one bit into his flesh. He punched the damn thing in the face, dropping it. Another dragged its nails across Tank's bare forearm, but he pressed on. Shoulder-checking one to the ground, he broke out into the small clearing around James. He'd made it just in time. Without stopping, he scooped James up and threw him over his shoulder. Then he bent down and grabbed both gas cans. He noticed a loop of metal stuck into the ground that was used to tie down the planes. That must've been what had tripped James.

Determination blazing in his eyes, peace in his heart, and a snarl on his face, he ran back the way he'd come into the waiting arms of the undead.

Before he'd taken his second step, something tore at the back of his leg and he jerked it away. Flesh ripped from his calf and he screamed, almost going down to a knee. He shrugged off the pain and used the jugs to keep the undead off his right side where James was slung over his shoulder. Pain exploded across his exposed left side as he smashed an undead in front of him in its face with a jug, keeping it from getting near his brother.

The undead before him began to drop as bullets smashed into their heads, and Tank surged forward, ignoring the pain on the left side of his body as teeth and nails tore through his clothes and skin. Then he broke free and stumbled without the resistance of decaying bodies. Connor was there, grabbing the gas jugs. Tank continued the hundred yards to the plane at a full run. His left leg was wrecked, and as he arrived at the plane, he stumbled to a knee, careful to keep James from falling. He set his brother lightly on the ground, and James groaned.

Looking down at his body, he confirmed what he knew to be true. He'd been bitten and scratched in a dozen places. With that out of the way, he checked James and didn't find a single scratch on him besides the massive bump on the side of his head and his broken nose.

Thank God.

Tank stood up quickly and opened the back door on the plane, pulling out Frostmourne from the top of their gear. He shut the door and checked his plate carrier pouch, pulling out two fragmentation grenades. They were being saved for something epic, and this was just that moment.

His mind conjured images of Chloe, and a tear slipped from his eye. That was his biggest regret, but there was nothing more he could've done. He was just glad he'd decided to truly live and be himself with her. But the sorrow of leaving her couldn't contend with the peace he felt, and soon it was swept away.

Connor went over to the other wing and climbed onto the wheel, sticking the gas jug's spout in the wing tank. One hand on the gas, one hand holding his ACR—which rested on the wing—he opened fire at the horde. Tank glanced at the undead; they were still eighty yards away.

"Tank?" James asked, squinting his eyes as he held his head.

"Yo," Tank said. "Ya lose your glasses?"

"Yeah." James stood shakily as he leaned on the plane.

"Here." Tank handed James his own glasses case from his side pocket. "Had those in case my contacts were damaged."

"Thanks." James put them on and blinked a few times. "They aren't quite strong enough but—" James cut off abruptly and Tank looked at him, thinking he was in trouble. But James was staring at Tank with a look of pain on his face and tears gathering in his eyes. "What the hell! What happened?"

"We don't have much time," Tank said with a sad smile.

"Did you come to save me?" James choked back a sob.

"I did what I was meant to." Tank pulled his iPod out of his pocket and stuck an earbud in one ear. Then he pulled out an envelope from his other pocket and looked at it funny. "Well, hell. I guess it's a good thing I wrote these."

"What...?" James asked as Tank handed him the envelope. Tank could tell he was trying hard not to break down.

"I have been thinkin' a lot lately about if I didn't make it." Tank turned to the horde so James couldn't see the tears in his eyes. "Tell Chloe I love her somethin' fierce, and I'm sorry to do this to her."

"Tank..." James wasn't trying not to cry now. The tears were flowing freely.

Allen Hook turned to his brother as Connor finished with the second gas jug, tossing it aside. He walked over to them, moisture in his eyes as well.

"I came into this world as Allen," Allen said, "and that's how I'll go out, but remember Tank as my legacy because without me you'll have some massive treads to fill."

James chuckled through the tears and embraced him, Connor doing the same.

"I don't know how we'll do this without you, brother," James said.

"You will," Allen said, pulling back and glancing at the horde only twenty yards away.

"We won't forget this," Connor said, a tear streaking down his cheek.

"Good, now go!" Tank said, looking both of them in the eyes.

Connor moved first, pulling James over to the open plane door. Tank turned to the horde that was almost upon them and reached into his pocket, hitting the play button. *Daylight Dies* by Killswitch Engage began to play and he smiled. This was a hell of a song to go out on.

Thanks Big Man, Tank said. *I'll be there shortly.*

Then he prayed that rehearsed prayer he'd heard in church, but it didn't sound rehearsed as he prayed. It felt real in his heart. Turning back quickly, he caught Connor's eye before he closed the door.

"I'll see you boys up there!" Tank yelled as the brothers looked back one last time.

Connor nodded and started the engine as Tank put his other earbud in. Swinging the SAW from his back, he held Frostmourne by the sheath in one hand and rested the front of the machine gun on his forearm. He opened fire at the undead that were heading for the plane. They were mowed down in a spray of blood and brains as Connor got the plane onto the runway. The wheels lifted off the ground, and the plane was airborne.

His brothers were safe.

Brass rained down on the asphalt as he turned his attention to the undead only feet away. They dropped like bloody snowflakes, and it gave him some breathing room. The SAW ran dry and he unclipped the sling, letting the gun fall to the ground. He drew his handgun, slowly backing up as he fired. His bitten leg gave out and he went down to one knee, emptying the rest of his magazine. Slapping another in, he opened fire.

A few moments later, Tank knelt there, dozens of fallen undead before him, his SAW and handgun discarded next to him with magazines and brass strewn about, mixed with blood and gore. He could hear Connor circling the plane above him, but he didn't look at them. They'd already said their goodbyes. The song grew to a crescendo with the line about the cost of one life, and he smiled despite the pain all over his body and the infection quickly spreading in his veins. He wasn't dying in vain. There'd been a purpose to his life all along, even when he hadn't known it. It'd taken the apocalypse to make him realize that he had an important role to play. This was the culmination of everything he'd done before, and he knew he should've been terrified of death, but he wasn't. The peace from before hadn't left him. He knew where he was going now. His place at the table was set, and he'd be with the Wolf Pack again. Their bond wasn't one that was easily broken, not even by death.

"What're ya waitin' for?" Tank yelled at the undead almost upon him. "Come get a piece of me!"

Connor watched out the window as he banked the plane. Tank suddenly stood up, drawing Frostmourne from its sheath like a badass knight. Then he raised the sword above his head, shouted something, and charged. Where he got the strength, Connor didn't know, but he smashed into the horde like a tsunami, taking them down with sweeps of his massive sword. The power he showed as he cleaved through the heads of three zombies in one stroke was unreal. It was literally not possible, but neither was glowing with a dim, golden light. The sun must've been reflecting off the metal hangar or something because he swore that Tank was actually *glowing*. He didn't slow down, and it seemed like he didn't tire as he cleaved a path through the horde. There was something else at work here, there had to be.

I Am, said an unfathomable voice in his head.

Connor flinched, jerking the yoke at the voice. That hadn't been his voice or the others that frequented his mind, but he *knew* that voice, even though he hadn't heard it before. Something broke in him, and the tears he was desperately trying to hold back came pouring out. A deep sob wracked his frame and his brother glanced over at him. Without being asked, James grabbed the second yoke in front of him and helped Connor steer the plane as they made another circle.

Tank was in the middle of the horde now, and his strokes became less and less frequent. A cloud had passed in front of the sun and the glow was gone, but in that moment, Connor knew God was still with him. Something had changed in Tank in the last few days, and Connor knew he believed—their prayers had been answered. Tank had finally found his faith, and in the process, he'd saved James's life and broken the darkness that had a firm grip around Connor's heart.

In the end, Tank had saved them both.

Just when it seemed like he was going to be overrun, he stabbed Frostmourne into a crack in the asphalt that Connor wasn't sure had been there before. He pulled two grenades from a pouch and gripped them in one hand as he pulled the pins with the other. Then he looked up past them, with a freaking *smile*.

Allen Hook closed his eyes, his face to the sky with a look of pure peace.

The ensuing explosion was greater than what two grenades should've produced, and as the debris settled, not a single undead was left standing.

45

SEE YOU AGAIN

Post-outbreak day 26, afternoon

James sat in the copilot seat of the Cessna 206 in a daze as *Into the Fire* by Asking Alexandria played through the headset. He didn't even hear it. What'd just happened was unexplainable, and his mind was having trouble comprehending it. Yet in his heart, he didn't doubt for one second. He, too, had heard that voice again, and with it had come memories from the dreams he'd forgotten—talking to his parents in the barn and then his father on the shore of the lake. It all came back to him, and a peace settled on his heart. That peace was fading now, but it was still there, and that shocked him. He'd just watched his best friend—no, his brother—go down in a blaze of glory because he'd rescued James at the cost of his own life.

The set of Tank's face after he'd gotten James safely to the plane was not one of regret because he'd thought he could get out unscathed; it was the look of someone who knew exactly what he'd done and the cost of that action. He'd shown the ultimate expression of love and sacrificed himself to save another. There was nothing more selfless than that. Tears leaked from his eyes, yet he didn't break down like he thought he would. They still had a job ahead of them. The rest of their group was missing supplies and the knowledge of how to survive in the wilderness. He knew they'd be able to figure it out eventually, but for now they'd need the Andderson brothers.

James took a deep breath, wiping the tears from his cheeks. Guilt tried to work its way into his mind as he began to pull himself together. Pushing it aside, he looked out the window as the mountains grew closer before them. It was a very familiar flight and one James had taken every year since he was born. He was finally going home.

Too bad Tank won't get to see that home, said a voice in his head. *It's because of you he's dead.*

No, James said to the voice.

Tank had gone into that horde to rescue him, yes, but it wasn't James's fault. It couldn't be his fault, because if he let that thought settle into his mind, the guilt would destroy him. That would then render Tank's sacrifice useless, and he wouldn't do that to himself or the memory of his brother. James would do everything he could to honor and remember him, but he would *not* live with the guilt of his death. *See You Again* by Wiz Khalifa played through the headset, and it was like a dagger to his heart. He hadn't even known Connor had that song on this playlist.

The tears began to flow again, and James looked over to see his brother shaking with sobs. James kept one hand on the yoke and rested the other on his brother's shoulder. Connor looked over at him with tears streaming down his face. Never before had James seen him this broken, but there was a vulnerability in his eyes. This wasn't the kind of broken that would destroy someone; this was the good kind of broken—the kind that was necessary to heal wounds and move forward. Even more tears came from James's eyes, and he was surprised he had more in him.

Thank you, James thought, both to God and to Allen.

James had been worried about Connor since this had all begun. Finally, this had been the thing that allowed him to break. Now he could begin to heal and grow into the man he needed to be. James could see it in Connor's eyes.

"Why?" Connor asked in a whisper, the microphone on his headset barely picking up his voice.

James shrugged, taking his hand off his brother's shoulder to wipe his eyes for the hundredth time. "I don't know."

"Why did he have to die? Why did things have to go down like this? If only we'd done something different. We could've... could've..." The words wouldn't come out as he began to sob again.

"I don't know. But we can't think about what could've been done differently. The past is the past, and we have to move on—for Tank, for Emmett, for our parents and everyone else we lost along the way. We have to keep going without looking back. In order to honor them and their sacrifices, we must live on."

Nothing else was said for the remainder of the trip as they each dealt with the heavy loss in their own way. All too soon, they'd have to tell the rest what'd happened, and for their sakes, James and Connor would need to be strong. Glancing out the window, James saw the green metal roof of the lodge glinting in the sunlight up ahead. Connor had stopped crying, and James relinquished the steering of the plane to him. They passed over their camp, and he saw it with new eyes. This could be their home for the remainder of their lives.

Camp sat between the base of a mountain that rose behind it and a lake out front. The mouth of the valley opened to the north, the direction they'd come, and the rest of the valley spilled to the south and split. The lodge sat at one end of camp, and the rest of the cabins stretched to the south in a sort of double-file line, with the main road—if it could be called that—between them. A hundred yards from the southernmost cabins was the tack shed and corral, and just past that was the airstrip.

Connor brought the plane around and in for the approach. They passed over their small group standing on the side of the gravel airstrip, and James's heart broke for what was about to happen. His brother landed them flawlessly, and they were stopped at the midway point where everyone was waiting. Alexis stood with Olive by her side, and they waved with large smiles on their faces. Ana was propped up on one of the cots they'd sent, a small grimace on her face. James saw her glance down at her stub of a right arm. Felix sat on the pile of gear, gun in hand as he scanned their surroundings. Lucas stood, leaning against a shovel. It seemed that Connor had already put him to work fixing the airstrip. Chloe looked anxiously at the plane as Connor brought it to a stop next to them and turned off the engine.

He didn't immediately open the door as the brothers shared a look and then nodded. Connor got out first, and James climbed over his seat as they came around the front of the plane together. Everyone's smiles were slowly fading, and Chloe started to shake her head.

James took a deep breath as tears started down Chloe's cheeks.

"Allen didn't make it," James said. Chloe fell to her knees, bursting into tears. "He sacrificed himself to save me. There was a horde—"

He choked and was unable to continue. Alexis went over to Chloe and leaned down with her, holding her tightly as she sobbed. James looked at the few people left of their group. They all looked devastated, even Ana.

They were finally here after had what felt like a lifetime on the road. They'd made it to their destination, but had the cost been worth it?

46

IN MEMORIAM

Post-outbreak day 26, evening

T he setting sun painted the sky in golden hues. Connor had seen some beautiful sunrises and sunsets out there over the years, but the one that night was unlike any he'd ever seen. The slightly overcast sky was lit up, and there didn't seem to be a single cloud that wasn't bathed in a peaceful shade of gold. Not only was it the best sunset he'd ever seen, but it had started a few minutes ago, and it showed no sign of fading anytime soon. God was giving his own sign that He was blessing the service.

Off the trail between the main camp and the airstrip there sat a clearing. There hadn't been a path leading to it, but Connor and his brother had stumbled onto it in their youth. It had always been a special place for them as in it grew a myriad of wildflowers—fuchsia fireweed mixed with violet lupine and monkshood, Indian paint brush ranging from gold to scarlet, azure forget-me-nots and blue bells, and white and yellow daisies. There was now a narrow path leading to the clearing, and it was there that their group was gathered.

A collection of small wooden crosses was spread out amidst the wildflowers, each with a name carved into it and a large cross that simply read: *To all who helped along the way.* Connor read the names on the smaller ones—*Allen "Tank" Hook, Emmett & Jane Wolfe, Saul Miller, Troy, Greg, Neil & Beverly, Mila, Mike, Peter, Felicia,* and others. He stopped at one and let the tears flow freely as he read the names of his parents—*Jack & Diana Andderson*. These weren't grave markers as they had no bodies to place in them. They were memorials to all those who'd passed on this journey, to all the people who had either by choice or inadvertently helped them on their way. They'd all paid a price.

Chloe stood straight, a look of pride on her face even as tears gathered in her eyes. Just earlier, they'd told her the full story of Tank's sacrifice and his last words to her, and to them. She was dealing with this surprisingly well, and Connor knew she would get through it. There was an inner strength in her that would not be broken. Next to her, with an arm around her shoulder, was Alexis. The woman his brother loved was strong as well and would be a good person for him to settle down with. Connor could see her father in her, and a piece of Emmett would always live on in her and their kids. Alexis was holding Olive's hand, and the little girl looked up at her. That one had been through so much, and yet even now she had a smile on her face as she cared for those around her. Felix stood protectively next to Olive, his eyes down in respect. He would grow into a strong man—hell, he already was. Lucas was next to him, tears flowing down his face. He'd helped them engrave some of the crosses for the friends and family he'd lost. Even just today, Connor had seen a change in him; this place would become his home as much as it was theirs.

Next to Connor was Ana, standing despite protests from Alexis, and he knew she'd lost a part of herself along with her arm. Her eyes were not as hard as when he'd seen her again a few days ago. There was still a dangerous light there, but it was subdued now. She swayed on her feet a little, still weak from blood loss. Connor took hold of her arm to help steady her, and she looked up at him. Yes, there was still danger in those eyes, but there was something else as well. A small smile spread on Ana's lips, and she leaned into him to keep from falling. Something stirred in his heart. It wasn't much—just a whisper of something long forgotten—but it stirred, nonetheless.

James stood before them on the other side of the memorials, the setting sun at his back. A tear slipped down Connor's cheek as he looked at him. He'd always looked up to the man standing before him, but in the last few weeks, that respect had increased. He'd seen his brother step up and make decisions that Connor didn't even know if he could've made himself. His faith had stayed strong, and in the last few days, nothing had shaken him, not even all the times he'd faced death. Tank's sacrifice could've been something that crippled James with guilt, yet Connor saw him rising above it. James had grown into a strong man, and Connor was proud of him. He was a true leader, someone Connor would follow until his last breath.

James nodded to him and Connor walked over to a small table by the entrance to the clearing. His iPod was hooked up to a speaker on it. Some thought it odd how much they loved music, but what they didn't understand was that these songs were more than just melodies; they were expressions of emotions when they couldn't express any themselves. Music had helped them through some hard times, even before the apocalypse. It wasn't just about the tunes or even the lyrics, but rather what they represented. It was a celebration of what made them human.

Clicking the play button, *Carry Me Down* by Demon Hunter could be heard from the small speaker. It was the perfect song for the occasion. He and Tank had talked many times about how they wanted this played at their funeral. And even though this wasn't exactly a funeral, it was still a way to honor and remember those who had passed. He walked back to the rest of the group as his brother cleared his throat. James hadn't prepared any notes. He hadn't rehearsed what he was going to say, and he said he'd tried not to think about it. He was going to let the words flow and let someone greater than him do the talking.

"This journey has been hard," James began, the sky a golden collage behind him, "as we all knew it would be from the beginning. We had to live through events that no one ever should, yet here we stand. The destination is here, and the journey is over. We've made it, but not because of our own strength or cunning. It was with God's help that we were able to survive this—not only by His strength, but by the sacrifices of many others. We have made it here, but there are many—too many—who did not.

"Tonight, we honor them, for each one paid the ultimate price. We are here now because of their sacrifices—from my parents to Peter, and Allen to Emmett, but it is not just about remembering them tonight. We must remember them each and every day because *they* made this dream a reality. For the first time in almost a month, we are finally safe because of them. And on the strength of their sacrifices, we will build a better future, a new future, one full of hope."

By the time James was through speaking, not a single eye was dry. Connor could see the faces of the people they'd lost—from the strangers in Miles, Montana, to the people from Burns, Wyoming, to Allen Hook, his brother and best friend. Some of them had gone on to a better place, and some he didn't know where they were, but he prayed they'd made the right choices in the end. And even though his faith had been waning lately with all they'd been through, Allen had changed that, and he would never forget. For Allen, he would not doubt again because he knew his brother waited for him in heaven and he would see him someday in the place that was their final destination.

47

THE FINAL CHAPTER

Post-outbreak day 40, afternoon

Two weeks had passed since their arrival, and they finally had the place set up to its full capacity. There was still a lot of work ahead to get everything ready for winter, but they were safe and more comfortable than they'd been in weeks. James had been going through a list of all they'd need to do before the winter hit when the music started and his attention snapped to the present, bringing him to an awareness of why he'd been so into his thoughts. He was nervous even though only three people sat in the "crowd."

Today was the day.

James was getting married.

They stood in front of the lodge with the lake before them and the mountains rising behind. He couldn't imagine being married anywhere else or to anyone else. Lucas stood off to his side, and even though he had no experience doing this, he'd be officiating. Felix sat on one of the benches they'd taken from the campfire, running the iPod. They didn't have a traditional wedding song, so they played *Die for You* by Otherwise instead. Ana sat on another bench, smiling warmly. She'd made a full recovery and was coping well with her missing limb. And, unless James was mistaken, something might even be budding between her and his brother. Olive came from around the edge of the lodge and started down the small aisle between the benches. She threw fresh wildflower petals on the ground, making a multicolored mosaic.

Then Connor and Chloe came around the side of the lodge and walked down the aisle. His brother was trying not to smile because—well, he was Connor—while on the other hand Chloe was smiling ear-to-ear. James felt a pang of guilt at seeing her, thinking about the sacrifice his brother had made. It still stung bitterly, but they were making the most of that selfless act. Chloe split from Connor as he went over to stand a few feet in front of James. His brother gave him a fist bump, their tattoos showing—just another reminder that they'd lost a part of their family. Cerberus had three heads, yet they only had two living members of the Wolf Pack left. But he didn't allow himself to entertain those grim thoughts for long—not today. Tank was in heaven now, and the Pack would be back together again.

James glanced behind him past where his brother stood. Sticking out of the soft dirt was a massive sword with a horned skull on the hilt. They'd recovered Frostmourne and the SAW, which somehow hadn't been damaged in the blast. The sword had suffered some blackening on the blade and the leather wrap was burnt off, but overall it had survived well. It was a sign that Tank was still with them, even though his physical body had been destroyed. The music changed and his attention went back to the aisle for a few seconds.

Then *she* walked around the corner.

James's heart skipped about a hundred beats, and he almost passed out. Alexis was beyond beautiful—the smile on her face lighting up the afternoon sky more than the sun itself. Her eyes locked onto his and his heart skipped again as butterflies rose in his stomach. Her hazel eyes danced in the light, and he couldn't help the massive grin that grew on his face. This was perfect. She had pink fireweed flowers woven into her hair and even wore a wedding dress that Connor and Chloe had been able to scavenge from a house in Tok.

Alexis stopped before him and he took her hand in his.

"Damn, you're beautiful," James mumbled.

She smiled even wider, if that was possible. "You're not so bad-looking yourself."

The rest of the ceremony was a blur of laughter, warm feelings, words of love spoken from the heart, and those hazel eyes.

"By the power vested in me by absolutely no one, I now pronounce you husband and wife. You may kiss the bride."

James did just that.

The warmth started in his lips and quickly spread to his insides, like he was in a giant microwave. When he reluctantly pulled back, those eyes of hers bore into his soul, and he let them. They were finally together, and nothing short of death would tear them apart.

James walked down the dirt path to the airstrip, stopping partway to turn off onto a narrow trail that opened into a clearing. There was a wooden sign at the end of the path with the words *In Memoriam* painted on it. A bench now faced the wooden crosses with names engraved on them, and he sat down. In the front row was a cross with the name *Allen "Tank" Hook*, the man who'd saved his life.

A tear slipped down his cheek. Not a day had gone by that he hadn't come down there to pay respects to his blood brother. They hadn't always been brothers. Once, they'd just been friends, then best friends, but at the end they'd been nothing short of family. He would never forget the sacrifice Tank had made to save him.

"You're early," Connor said, walking into the clearing.

"I found a moment and got away," James said, standing. "You bring it?"

"Roger." Connor held up a bottle of clear liquid and three shot glasses.

"Perfect."

Connor set the shot glasses down on the bench and poured. The moonshine smelled extremely potent, and considering some crazy dude had distilled it during the apocalypse, it probably was. There was a white label on the bottle that read *Alaskan Dew*. James chuckled. His brother handed him two shot glasses and they walked over to Tank's memorial.

"It's your night," Connor said.

"To the best friend and brother anyone could ask for." A couple of tears pooled in his eyes. "You gave your life so I could live, and that'll never be forgotten. To Tank and the Wolf Pack. We'll see you again, brother."

James poured one of the shots onto the ground and then tipped his back. The stuff burned all the way down his throat and into his stomach where it continued to sting.

Connor cursed, looking at his glass.

"That's nasty," James said, coughing.

"Yeah, I don't even think Tank would've liked it."

They both shared a laugh as they put the cork back into the bottle. They were saving the rest for the anniversary of his sacrifice, although they did consider just dumping the whole bottle by his memorial and getting something better. But Tank had stopped and gotten this 'shine, so they'd drink it with him every year till it was gone. Then they'd find the most expensive bottle of whiskey they could and continue the tradition.

The brothers shared in the silence of the wilderness as they sat there, the night closing in on them as stars began to glimmer in the sky.

"You'd better get back," Connor said finally, standing as the sky darkened. "You have a honeymoon to get to."

"That I do." James stood. "I'll be there in a second."

"Don't take too long." Connor gave him a pat on the back. "Alexis is waiting."

James smiled as he listened to his brother's footsteps fading in the distance. Looking at the memorial, he sighed deeply and pulled a folded piece of paper from his pocket. Opening it, he looked down at Tank's handwriting. It was the letter he'd given James right before they'd taken off. James had delivered Chloe's and Connor's, but he hadn't read his yet. He'd been saving it for this moment.

James,

We haven't always seen eye-to-eye, but you've always been there for me. Even in times when I didn't deserve it, you were a true friend. I hope that in the last few years you've seen a change as I've been tryin', but life just kept knockin' me down. Then all this happened, and I know I shouldn't have been, but I was excited for the fresh start it offered. It shouldn't have taken the apocalypse to get me out of my funk, but it did. Now here we are.

We're so close to Alaska—only a day and we'll be there. I hope you're doing okay. It would blow to get all this way and have you croak, but I have this feelin' deep down that you'll make it. I've been havin' a lot of those gut feelin's lately; maybe it has somethin' to do with the leadership role. And you'll be happy to know that I've been prayin' a bit, too. I almost didn't write that because it makes it seem real, and that terrifies me. You know how the other few times I've started to believe, bad things always happened, like ma dying, but this time is gonna be different. I need it to be different because I can't shake the feelin' that I don't have much time left. I hope I'm wrong and you never have to read this. But just in case...

I want you to know I'm proud of ya. I've seen you grow from that little annoying shit in middle school to the great leader you are now. If somethin' does happen to me, I know the rest will be safe if they have you. Just do somethin' for me. If I die, make sure to take care of them, especially Chloe. She'll take this hard, but she's strong. Be there for her and help her if she needs it. I expect you to be the man she may need at times.

That's all I got.
We ride together,
We die together,
Badass Brothers for life.
Allen Hook

"Thank you," James whispered, tears in his eyes. "I'll take care of them, I promise."

Glancing down at his right hand, he was pleased to see that the cut was still visible from their pact on that night that seemed like a lifetime ago. The scar was a constant reminder he'd carry with him for the rest of his life. He'd do right by Tank and make this place a sanctuary in his honor. Tank had made a promise, after all, and James would do his best to fulfill it.

He turned and exited the clearing, heading back towards the lodge and the cabin he'd share with Alexis behind it. After a few steps, the sorrow subsided to a dull ache that he was growing accustomed to. This place wasn't the same without Tank and never would be, but he'd make the most of it and live for him, every single day.

He stopped at the large wooden sign that hung between two rough-hewn logs sitting just off the main track before entering their camp. It was impossible not to admire the sign as it filled him with a sense of home. Once, it had held the name of his family's outfitting company. Now a different sign proved that even in the apocalypse life was still possible, and hope was never far away. Filled with conflicting but ultimately peaceful emotions, he walked away, his silhouette fading as he turned a corner towards the lights of the lodge.

Behind him, the wooden sign swayed slightly in a gentle breeze, and the two words painted on it said it all: *Last Hope*.

EPILOGUE

Two months later

"What about salt?" James asked Olive as they sat at the large dining room table with lists of all their supplies scattered before them.

"Seven hundred pounds," Olive said, looking at their inventory.

James checked salt off on the list. "Sugar?"

"Five hundred and ten pounds."

They'd be able to have plenty of baked goods for a while. That was a good thing about living in Alaska. In the bush and more rural areas, people needed to have a lot of goods on hand. That meant when they usually found a cache it contained all kinds of nonperishable foodstuffs. They continued like that for the whole morning, going down the list of supplies they would need for the approaching winter.

When they were done, James leaned back and Olive mimicked him. They were set. Everything they needed for the winter was in their storehouses. There was always more work to be done, like getting a few more trees for firewood, but after that, all the crucial preparations would be taken care of. He smiled, things were coming together perfectly. They hadn't even seen a zombie within a hundred miles of this place as it was almost impossible for anyone to get out here on foot. They still kept guns on hand and always went around with at least a knife and they'd built a watch tower behind the lodge that allowed them to see for a good long ways. All that was precautionary though, they were truly safe.

"Can I hold Squeezer?" Olive asked, standing up.

"Sure you little munchkin," James said as she took off for the glass cage sitting by the large wood stove.

Things really were coming along. Lucas had worked for a contractor back in Burns and he knew quite a bit about building and had a knack for it. He'd put together a hangar down at the airstrip for the planes and they'd been working on building a better and bigger shop. Chloe was doing very well and had taken to flying, of all things. She was now their second pilot and they'd been able to get both the 206 and the Cub out here. Felix had been stepping up to help out Lucas with building, but the kid was also turning into a mighty fine pilot. Alexis was getting better at cooking and actually enjoyed it now, which was a huge step for her. She'd gone from burning noodles to making some hella good lasagna. Olive was helping her out a ton and loved to cook, she was also spending a lot of time with James, which he didn't mind in the least. James had been going on runs with his brother and figuring out all of their logistics. He'd just gotten back from a big hunt where they'd been able to bag two cow moose. Getting the meat packed out of the field was tough, but it was hanging in the meat shed now where they'd leave it to age before they cured it.

Connor was flying on runs almost every day with Ana accompanying him for all but the most dangerous. He said that he picked her because without her arm she weighed less than anyone else, but James could see the budding romance there. Ana for her part had changed drastically from whom she'd been when she'd killed Jezz. That part of her was still there, but it seemed as though she'd learned to channel it and, even with missing an arm, she was still one of the hardest workers they had.

They were one large mismatched family although there was one downfall. They hadn't grown and they weren't turning into a community like he'd hoped. They hadn't seen a lot of survivors on their runs and the ones they did weren't the kind to invite back. It was a problem he didn't know how to fix and Connor didn't want to. So he let it go, but at night lying next to his amazing wife with Olive sleeping in the loft above them, he couldn't help but think about it. How did they go about building this into a beacon of hope for humanity?

"You dreaming again?" Alexis said, coming out of the kitchen with a dirty apron and sliding next to him on the bench.

James chuckled. "How d'ya know?"

"You had that look in your eyes." Alexis kissed him and his hand immediately went to her stomach. "You won't feel anything yet silly. It's only been two months."

"I know, but still."

In seven months, they'd have two new little members of their community. Maybe it would take them generations to build something there.

"You think of any names yet?" Alexis asked.

"If it's a boy? Allen."

"I love it."

"How's Chloe?"

"The morning sickness has been worse for her but she'll be okay."

"Has she been thinking of a name?"

"Carter."

"Ah," James said, a smile coming to his face. "Allen's grandpa. That'll be perfect."

They sat there on the bench in the sunlight streaming in from the large window facing their cabin on a hill. After a while, Olive came over holding Squeezer and nestled in between them. They were a happy little family and they were growing.

Static broke over their ham radio and then a voice could be heard. James jumped to his feet, rushing over to turn the volume up.

"Is anyone out there?" said the voice again.

"We hear you," James said, holding the button down on the handheld.

"Oh, thank God."

"Where are you?"

"In Glennallen. Where are you?"

"At a lodge in the bush."

"Is it safe?"

"Yes."

"We've been on the road for so long; I never thought I'd hear that."

"Where did you come from?"

"A small town in Texas."

"Why did you come all the way up here?"

"We—"

The voice cut off and James waited but nothing else came through. "Hello?" he asked.

"Who are you and why should we trust you?" asked a gruff new voice.

"My name is James Andderson, the leader of Last Hope and you can trust us, but I don't blame you if you don't."

"Last Hope? Is that a town?"

"It's a community that we are building in the wilderness. Who am I talking to?"

"Drake Gibson, I speak for this group."

"Gibson?" Alexis asked, her brow scrunched. "That name sounds familiar. Where at in Texas are they from?"

James relayed the question through the radio. It was met with silence.

The voice on the other side sighed. "I guess it doesn't matter now. We're from Hill City."

"That's it!" Alexis exclaimed, grabbing the handset for the radio. "Is this *Sheriff* Gibson?"

"How d'ya know that?"

"My name is Alexis Wolfe, I used to live there."

"You're Emmett's daughter," Sheriff Gibson said, sounding astonished. "Your father is the whole reason we came up here. Is he with you?"

Alexis's face fell a little. "He didn't make it."

"I'm sorry to hear that, but if you're truly his daughter, then I'll stick my neck out. Your father was a good man. Is your group truly safe?"

"Yes. There's only a handful of us, but it is safe out here. This is the real deal, Sheriff."

There was silence for a few moments.

"How do we get there?" Gibson asked.

"Are you sure about this?" James asked Alexis. "Do you trust him?"

"My dad always had a great opinion of him and he's not the kind of man that would break from this."

"Okay," James said, holding out his hand and she handed the radio over. He spoke into it. "My brother and I will be out in the plane to check you out. If it seems like you are what you say you are, we'll help you in. How many do you have?"

"Sixteen," Gibson said. "We used to have more."

"We did too."

"It should be said, we have twenty head of horses as well that we brought up."

God bless Texans, James thought.

"That would be a game changer, Sheriff," James said smiling. This was an answer to prayer. "Hold tight and we'll be out in an hour."

"Thank you, Mr. Andderson."

"No thank you, this is just what we were looking for." James hugged and kissed Alexis, spinning her around. "This is it, honey!"

"I know," she said with a wide smile as he set her down.

"We're getting more people?" Olive asked, beaming.

"If they check out and we can trust them," James said, bending down and kissing her on the head.

With sixteen more people they would need more supplies and another cabin or two, but that should be no problem with that many hands to help. They still had most of a month until the hard winter hit. They would have time and with the growth they'd need to cement the role of leadership and have a police force and laws and maybe even a court. But if their leader was a sheriff, then he could help with all that too. This was finally going to be what he'd dreamed, a true settlement. He thought of one last question and picked up the radio.

"You still there, Sheriff?" James asked.

"Yes, sir," Gibson responded.

"How the hell did you end up here?"
"That, my friend, is a story for another time."

Acknowledgements

I couldn't have finished this book without the help of numerous people. Huge thanks to:

Jesus, it was awesome writing this final book with You.

My wife, you motivate me like no one else!

My family, for the nonstop support.

My Bata Readers, you've made this whole series better!

Guildies in the KARG & ARG, you gave me a bunch of awesome ideas that made it into this book!

My awesome editor, you're the one who polishes a *very* rough draft and makes it readable!

My cover artist, you outdid yourself on this one!

And last, but certainly not least, to ALL my awesome readers. You guys took what was going to be a standalone book and turned it into an award-winning and best-selling series. I literally couldn't have done this without you!

About the Author

Joshua is a Jesus Freak and adventurous nerd, who loves the outdoors. He's the award-winning and best-selling author of the zombie apocalypse series, *The Brother's Creed*. When he's not escaping into the mountains, he can be observed living in Northern Wisconsin with his wife, two sons, guns and katanas. He has a love for all things imaginary and finds inspiration in the wilderness, away from the distractions of life. He's currently pursuing a career as an indie author and writing coach. Some of his other passions include hunting, shooting, board & video games, hard rock, reading, and anything fantasy & sci-fi.

Learn more at:

joshuacchadd.com

Also by Joshua C. Chadd

The Brother's Creed Series
Outbreak
Battleborn
Wolf Pack
Bad Company
Last Hope

To see more, scan below or visit:

joshuacchadd.com/books

MORE FROM PUBLISHER

Be sure to check out our other great science fiction and fantasy stories at:

bladeoftruthpublishing.com/books